Love On The
SIDELINES

MO FLAMES

FLAMES
ENTERTAINMENT

TABLE OF CONTENTS

AUTHOR'S NOTE

Dear Beloved Readers,

Thank you for purchasing and/or downloading this book.

While this story can be enjoyed as a standalone, for a richer experience and better understanding of the interconnected characters and plotlines, it's highly recommended to read *The Enough Series*. The events of this tale unfold and run parallel to the timeline in those books.

Troy and Mia Harris are one of the most unforgettable and controversial couples from ***The Enough Series***. In a scandal that shattered their marriage, now estranged from a pregnant Mia, Troy faces the gamble of his life in Sin City. With temptations around every corner and the stakes higher than ever, he must play his cards right to earn a shot at redemption.

As he navigates a path from gridiron glory to rock bottom, Troy bets everything on becoming the man his family deserves, knowing that in this game, one wrong move could cost him it all.

Keep in mind that this is a fictional story, so things you might find unrealistic or unrelatable, may be real and relatable to someone else.

TRIGGER WARNINGS

This novel contains strong language, detailed sexually explicit scenes, and certain topics involving abandonment, adult-minor relationships, infidelity, incest, child abuse, emotional abuse, domestic abuse and violence that might be sensitive to some readers. ***Please be mindful of these and other possible triggers.***

This novel is for mature audiences only.

PLAYLIST

While in the writing lab, there's always music playing. There are some dope tracks that kept me inspired throughout penning this story. You can check out the vibe for this book on Apple Music and/or Spotify, under the same title, ***Love on the Sidelines***.

Apple
https://apple.co/3NFoFYV

Spotify
https://spoti.fi/3CbNngU

1. *I'm N Luv (Wit A Stripper) - Remix*, T-Pain
2. *Love the Way You Lie*, Eminem, Rihanna
3. *03' Bonnie & Clyde*, JAY-Z, Beyoncé
4. *Issues*, Julia Michaels
5. *Flawless - Remix*, Beyoncé, Nicki Minaj
6. *Unstoppable*, YFN Lucci
7. *Sideline Ho*, Monica
8. *Rumors*, Daisy Gray
9. *Brenda's Got A Baby*, 2Pac
10. *Finding Peace*, Summer Walker

CHAPTER 1

Four years ago . . .

"There ain't nothing she can do for me 'cept sit on the sidelines and be a sneaky link," Troy Harris declared before taking a sip from the lowball glass.

He peered over its rim, watching the woman he'd been chatting with moments earlier, put an extra swing to her curvy hips as she sashayed away with her friends. They giggled like teenage girls, her laughter mixed seamlessly into the ambient buzz of conversations filling the room. Troy smirked in amusement. The woman halted in her tracks and glanced back at him, batting her eyelashes and flashing a charming smile. Troy returned her gesture with a flirty wink, and then shifted his gaze toward the two men standing off to the side, offering them a sly grin.

"Yeah. She can definitely get it."

"Was *she* a sponsor?"

Troy's childhood best friend, Derrik Carter asked the question, but he didn't wait to hear the answer. Instead, Derrik rolled his eyes and addressed Troy's other friend, Shawn "Speedy" Adams. The sarcasm in Derrik's tone was not lost on Troy.

"Speedy, why did we pay for these high-ass tickets if this is what he was planning to do? He could've done all this at another party. For free. And I thought this was supposed to be about the kids. Did shawty over there say anything about lil' Dashawn or Shaniqua? I know I didn't hear shit about no foundation. Did you?"

A low chuckle came from Shawn as he shook his head. "Nah, D. I ain't hear her say shit 'bout no bad ass BeBe kids. And he ain't lying, T, them tickets wasn't cheap, bruh. Now if you want her friend thickums to work for a foundation, she can take up the position as ball handler at *Speedy Connections*. I'll be more than happy to introduce my kids to the back of her throat."

Derrik's expression remained blank as he stared at Shawn. Shawn raised his palms and shrugged. Troy waved his hand, dismissing their foolishness.

"Man, fuck both of y'all. Stop acting like y'all clowns can't afford it. And I am here for the kids. I done checked out a couple of these so-called sponsors. I was just checking out the other scenery," Troy muttered, bringing the tumbler up to his mouth. He took another swig and pointed out, "But what I do know is, I ain't see neither one of you muthafuckas leave when they came over. Y'all was kekeing up in their faces too. Was you tryna be a sponsor, D?"

"Fuck outta here," Derrik scoffed in response, clicking his tongue against the roof of his mouth.

Shawn went back to talking about the girl from earlier and confessed, "Ay, I ain't gon' front, T. I ain't hear nothing after thickums claimed to do all that strange shit. Then she twirled both of them cherry stems 'round her tongue and made that purty lil' bow."

"Word! I peeped when shawty did that. I was like Day Day—I ain't never had that shit happened to me before. I'm tryna see what else she can do. Know what I'm saying?"

Troy pretended to speak in gibberish and held out his hand to Shawn, who eagerly smacked it with a series of low-five claps before pulling each other in for a quick embrace. The sound of their boisterous laughter filled the grand ballroom, resonating through the crowded space and drawing disapproving glances from nearby guests. Derrik, always the level-headed one and voice of reason in their group, went into damage control mode, apologizing for their disruptive behavior. While Derrik made a conscious effort to maintain a more reserved and professional image, Troy and Shawn were carefree and having a good time. Troy didn't concern himself with their opinions of him. Amidst a crowd of ostentatious and wealthy individuals, Troy was aware that their sole purpose was to finance his foundation and enhance his public image as a successful athlete giving back to the community. Troy let Derrik handle that while he listened to Shawn continue to reminisce about the girl.

"Yeah, man. Shawty was talking real slick with that mouth. I'm tryna see what she talmbout doing sumn strange for a piece of change though. Think she really up at Magic?"

"Only one way to find out." Troy declared, knocking back the remainder of his Hennessy. At the same time, one of the wait staff appeared next to him. Troy placed the lowball tumbler on the shiny, silver platter.

After giving the young man his empty glass, Derrik grumbled. "I know y'all not talking about going back to Magic City tonight. Y'all not tired of spending all your money on titties and ass?"

"Hell no!" Troy and Shawn answered in unison.

Shawn bobbed his shoulder up and down as he did the finger snap dance, enthusiastically rapping Twista's verse in "I'm N Luv (Wit A Stripper)," adding his own spin. Instead of using T-Pain's name, he replaced it with Trouble T-Roy, a nickname he'd given Troy back in their college days. Shawn winked at Derrik while declaring, "My boy invited me to the A and said we gon' turn up. We going er'day I'm here. So get them bands ready, D. 'Cause we gon' make it thundastorm tuhnight!"

"Yo! Who the fuck is that?" Troy tapped Derrik on the shoulder.

Derrik scrunched up his face in a frown. "Who?"

"*Her.*" Troy tipped his head in the direction of the grand ballroom double doors that'd been opened. "Thick, light skinned shawty on the left that just walked in."

Derrik's eyebrows shot up, his eyes widening as he blurted, "Damn! She looks just like—"

"I know. But shawty over there different. She got class. Sophistication." Troy interrupted, without taking his gaze off the vision of beauty.

Shawn rocked his head back and forth, disagreeing. "Nah, T, your ass definitely got a type. D ain't lying. Top to bottom—they could be twins, just different complexions. I'mma holla at her friend. Unless you want her, D."

"Nah. You good, Speedy. And T, that's the senator's daughter. I've seen them before at a few events. But I can't think of her name."

Troy gave a slight nod of acknowledgement, but his complete focus was on the gorgeous woman. As if time itself had slowed, she sauntered into the room, and everything else faded away. Her waist-length, jet-black hair framed her round face perfectly. He couldn't help but wonder how it smelled and what shampoo she used. When her glossed lips curved into a gorgeous smile, Troy felt like he was gazing upon an angel in human form. Troy was hypnotized. He couldn't look away. Her eyes slanted upwards, and her light makeup only enhanced her striking features. While Troy didn't have a specific preference for the ethnicity of women he dated, Black women would always be at the top of his list. But this goddess in front of him was a perfect fusion of African American and Asian roots, making her even more alluring to him. She moved gracefully while the media vultures swarmed around, vying for her attention. In that moment, Troy decided that before the night ended, he too would find out everything there was to know about the mystery woman.

"Don't even think about it, T." Derrik's voice yanked Troy out of his musings.

He spun around to face his best friend. A smirk tugged at the corner of his mouth. "Fuck you think is on my mind, D?"

"I know what's not on it—going home to Desi."

"Or cutting Kim's crazy ass off. Fuck around and have double the trouble," Shawn added with a deep chuckle.

Troy studied his friends for a second as they looked at him expectantly, waiting for his next move. He stole another glance at the light-skinned bombshell now calling out to him like a siren's song. Temptation, desire, and risk all flashed through Troy's mind as he debated whether or not to give in to his curiosity. He knew this woman was dangerous, but he couldn't shake the pull she already had on him, and they hadn't even met. Not yet. Like him, she exuded poise, confidence, and charisma. They both commanded the room with ease. And then she surprised him by doing something unexpected. She gave a fake smile for the cameras, but as soon as they turned away, she rolled her eyes, something he himself had done countless times. A satisfying grin spread across Troy's face as he pondered their possible shared traits. Could she be his twin flame? This woman intrigued him even more now. He dragged a hand across his bald dome and peered back at his friends, shrugging.

"Man, listen. That one right there might shut all that shit down. I'on know what it is. But she walked in, and I just got this weird feeling in my gut about her. I ain't never felt no shit like this before, D. I need to meet her."

Troy watched his friends exchange disbelieving expressions. Shawn lifted his shoulders, but Derrik shook his head. His best friend pointed a stiff finger at him and issued a stern warning.

"Nah, T, leave her alone. I swear you're like a fucking tornado. And that's one girl you don't wanna get sucked into your bullshit." Derrik stepped closer. He leaned in, whispering. "Senator Wynters is from the southside. And you know that brotha didn't get in his position doing everything legally. From what I heard he got enough goons to start a fucking war without the government if he wanted. Just saying, T, she's not the one you wanna fuck over. Don't forget what you got at home, bruh. Desi's good people."

Troy met Derrik's gaze, the words sinking in. His best friend was right. He did have a girl at home, but things were far from good between them. After almost a year together, everything changed when he signed with the NFL. Desiree used to bring him peace, but now she just seemed to nag him. All. The. Fucking. Time. And during this crucial point in his rookie season, stress was the last thing he needed. Desiree's constant fussing and nagging drove him to do something he never wanted to do—cheat on her. But Troy was unable to resist the temptation of women throwing themselves at him and offering a break from the pressure. He thought Desiree would be enough, but perhaps they had rushed into things too quickly. Once more, Troy's attention was drawn to the mysterious woman as she and her friend began making their way to the bar.

Her white gown had been tailored to fit her curvaceous body like a second skin, but the satin material did little to conceal the perfect shaped globes poking out below her waist. Troy had to keep his mouth from hitting the floor. Curved in all the right places, she'd been blessed with the natural shape of a soda bottle.

Damn! She's thicker than a snicker. Troy paused, tucking his bottom lip into his mouth and stroking his hairy chin as he shifted his gaze back to Derrik and spoke. "See. That's where you're wrong, D. Tornados do more pushing shit outta the way in their wake. And if I'm guessing right, she's a spit fire and can erupt just like a volcano. We're the perfect match, bruh. And I wanna know her name. No. I gotta know her name. I'm finna go holla at Miss Anonymous."

Derrik scrunched up his face. "The fuck. You been listening to Desi's R&B playlist again? I know your ass didn't just quote Bobby Valentino?"

"He shol' did. You know this fool thinks he's the sports edition of Chris Brown."

Shawn jokingly whacked Derrik's chest with the back of his hand, and both friends doubled over in hysterical laughter. Troy cut his eyes, giving them both the middle finger. Derrik calmed down as Troy began walking away. Trailing behind, he called out after him.

"Please don't go over there with your corny ass pick up lines. A girl of her caliber not trying to hear the fuck shit, T."

Troy spun around and shot a playful glare back at Derrik. "Oh, so *you* doubting my game, D? Who always ends up with the pussy? We know my charm works like magic."

"Charm? More like delusion," Derrik retorted, rocking his head from side to side in mock disapproval.

Troy flipped Derrik the bird once more before refocusing on the task at hand. "Y'all just jealous 'cause you ain't got game like me. Watch and learn, fellas. I'll have her eating outta the palm of my hand in no time."

Shawn nudged Derrik, both quickening their pace to keep up with Troy. "This is gonna be good. We gotta see how this plays out."

Undeterred, Troy shrugged off their teasing and continued his confident stride toward the beautiful vixen. When he settled onto the bar stool beside her, Troy exchanged amused glances with his boys who stood on the opposite side of him, knowing exactly how this interaction would end. He twisted his head in the bombshell's direction, momentarily stunned by her beauty. Troy composed himself, straightened his back, and cleared his throat, preparing to unleash his smoothest line yet.

Present day...

"Get yo' punk ass up!"

Troy remained motionless, his muscles tense and his body rigid. For the past ten minutes, he'd strained to listen in on their conversation, desperate for any clues about his current location and the situation he was in. Noticing he wasn't restrained, Troy began moving, inadvertently alerting them to his consciousness. He held his breath, hoping the men would ignore him and go back to what they were doing.

"Nigga, we know yo' ass heard us," one of them spat in a heavy southern accent.

"And I know you don't want us to *help* you get the fuck up."

The menacing tone of the second man's voice had Troy doing as he was told. Opening his eyes, he sprang upright. Troy held his throbbing head, wincing at the searing pain in his temple. The room was too bright. He shielded his eyes from the blinding light, and after a minute, he lowered his hand to survey the unfamiliar surroundings. From where he sat, Troy could see they were in an open concept living room with high-end furnishings. His gaze traveled around the spacious area, where he noticed the two figures seated before him. The larger of the two occupied a plush sofa, while the smaller man perched on a sleek accent chair. Troy recognized them right away—*Roscoe and DaeDae!*

The brothers were Mia's cousins, but they also worked for her dad, Maxwell Wynters, Sr., as his goons, for his shady operations that had nothing to do with politics. Troy had seen firsthand how Roscoe and DaeDae handled business on the senator's behalf. He miscalculated, believing he had nothing to worry about after the negative publicity surrounding his marriage had died down. What he hadn't considered was Maxwell taking matters into his own hands to address the abuse he'd inflicted on his daughter. Roscoe and DaeDae handed him the beat down of his life on Maxwell's orders.

Troy didn't know how long he'd been unconscious, but wherever they were, it was daytime. He noted the amount of sunlight coming in through the window blinds, then he winced again as he scooted back and leaned against the front of the couch. He felt stiff and sore. Pain radiated throughout his body as though a semi-truck hit him. Troy stretched his jaw and cradled his chin. "Wh-wh-where the fuck am I?"

"Nah, you don't get to ask us no questions." DaeDae's lip curled.

Sneering, Roscoe added, "We gon' tell you whatchu need to know."

"Tell me what I need to know then." Troy cocked his head and flexed.

DaeDae got up so fast Troy didn't have a chance to brace himself for the bum-rush. He seized Troy by the neck lifting him from the floor. Troy fought to breathe, clawing at DaeDae's hands to get them from around his neck.

Roscoe hopped to his feet. "Man, nigga, put him down. Unc said we 'pose to give him the instructions and dassit. He ain't say to make him disappear, now did he?"

In addition to outweighing him by a hundred pounds, DaeDae towered over Troy at seven-feet-tall. His dark skin almost blended in with the all-black suit he wore from head to toe. At six-foot-three and weighing around two hundred, thirty pounds, Roscoe was almost the same height and build as Troy. Troy could feel his eyes popping out of the sockets as he sought Roscoe for reprieve. DaeDae exchanged challenging stares with Roscoe before returning his attention to Troy, who continued writhing and pounding on his arms while fighting for oxygen. After giving him a look of disgust, DaeDae threw Troy on the couch. Troy coughed and gasped as he looked on, holding his neck in disbelief while both men gave him menacing glares.

"Hurry up and tell him before I cave his fuckin' face in," DaeDae snarled before walking over to the large island and taking a seat.

Roscoe took up his place in the accent chair that faced Troy. He shot him a devious grin and leaned forward resting his elbows on his knees. "Ay, man, my uncle saved you from what we really wanted to do. I think you should count yo'self as lucky. Yo' punk ass wouldn't even be sittin' right thurr if he let us do what we wanted."

Whatever! Y'all wouldn't be so tough without each other. Troy bit back the words. He didn't need DaeDae running up on him again. It would've been easy for him to hold his own if they hadn't jumped him. Troy thought to himself if DaeDae's black ass tried him on another day, he would've put up a helluva fight. He wasn't no punk. Holding his head confidently, Troy pushed his chin out and puffed up his chest.

"You need to go 'head and finish this shit up, 'Sco. I'on like the way he lookin' at us."

Roscoe twisted his head to DaeDae and jabbed his thumb in Troy's direction. "Aww bruh, maybe he tryna show us he got a lil' heart."

"He gon' fuck around and end up missing fuh real." DaeDae folded his massive arms across his chest and shot Troy the dirtiest look.

Roscoe glanced at Troy and cautioned, "You can sit thurr acting like you can take us, but this ain't whatchu want."

Troy's attention went to Roscoe's hand where he gripped the handle of the gun in his pants. He would bring a gun to a fist fight. Who was the punk ass? Instead of making contact, Troy lowered his eyes.

"Now, my uncle wanted me to relay some thangs. Yo' ass better do er'thang I'm telling you," Roscoe continued, his hand dropping from his side.

DaeDae hit his fist into his palm. "Or else."

Troy's gaze went to that side of the room, but he didn't dare look at DaeDae. As much as he wanted to say, *or else what,* Troy knew for his own safety he needed to remain silent. For now, they had the upper hand.

Roscoe sent a knowing glance to DaeDae and shook his head. He then returned his attention to Troy and issued the warning. "Unc said or else we gon' come see 'bout you. Heh, so, yeah, it's in yo' best interest to do as he say. Yuh feel me?"

He stared back at Roscoe without flinching.

"Nigga, I said *yuh* feel me? That wasn't no statement, it was a question."

After exchanging unblinking stares with Roscoe, Troy finally nodded. Roscoe clenched his jaw and blew air out of his nostrils. Without breaking eye contact with Troy, he rose from the chair. Then with an eyeroll, he made his way to the side of the sofa. He picked up a duffel bag, then headed back over to stand directly in front of Troy. Roscoe dropped the bag at Troy's feet.

Once he sat down, Roscoe pointed at it. "In that bag is yo' future, 'cause Atlanta is now a part of yo' past. You ain't welcomed thurr no mo.' So, don't bring yo' ass thurr unless y'all playing the Falcons. And last time I checked they ain't on the schedule this season. They expecting you to be thurr on Monday. Don't be late. And this hurr is yo' new spot, so get used to being in hurr. They gon' ship yo' cars and truck hurr in a week. Until then, thurr's a rental out front, a red Camaro. Keys in the duffel. And you hafta check in with yo' shrink next Wednesday."

"A shrink? The fuck? I ain't going to no shrink." Troy scrunched up his face.

DaeDae rose from his seat and began walking toward the sofa, but Roscoe stopped him with a raised hand. Reluctantly, DaeDae returned to the kitchen island, shooting an angry glare at Troy. The two stared each other down for a few moments until Troy finally turned his attention to Roscoe, who then continued speaking.

"Nigga, yo' ass gonna see this fucking shrink. It's non-nefuckingotiable. In order for yo' ass to even play, you gotta talk to this nigga. And since yo' ass wanna hit women. This shrink gon' figure out why. Tell you this much: if you ever wanna see MiMi again and yo' baby, you better let this shrink fix yo' punk ass."

Troy's eyes widened. His voice was barely above a whisper. "Baby?"

Roscoe threw a fist up to his mouth. With a maniacal laugh, he blurted out. "Ohhh shit, nigga you ain't know MiMi was pregnant? Damn, my bad. She was prolly gon' tell you last night. I guess we fucked that up. Well, Unc said until yo' ass proves you can handle yo' anger without putting yo' hands on his daughter, you won't have nothing to do with them." Roscoe paused long enough to unzip the duffel bag. He pointed inside. "In thurr is yo new phone. So everything looks copacetic between y'all, Unc said he won't make you unfollow her on IG or TikTok. But don't contact her, T. If you do, we'll know. Thurr's a laptop, and some papers in thurr. It's yo' new contract. Get with Mark, and he'll bring you up to speed with er'thing else . . ."

Roscoe continued, but Troy didn't hear anything else he said. The realization that he was going to be a dad occupied his thoughts. Troy's focus shifted from the bag to Roscoe's mean mug. Did he hear him correctly? He had to ask.

"Sy—I mean, Mia's pregnant?"

Roscoe tilted his head in DaeDae's direction. "Is he serious?" DaeDae gave him a headshake in reply. Roscoe looked back at Troy frowning. "Nigga is you deaf or slow? Ain't that what I just said?"

"I'm . . . I'm umm, wow. She's pregnant. I'm gonna be a dad." Ignoring the pain, Troy's face split into a wide grin.

"Nigga, what you happy fuh? What the fuck I just say? You and MiMi ain't gon' have no contact. Nope, ain't happening right now. Unc said until the shrink says yo' ass is reha . . . rehuh . . . re-umm, fuck it. You gotta show yo' ass ain't gon' hit on women no mo.' If this shrink says you good, then Unc will consider if he'll let you talk to MiMi. Now, if yo' ass ain't changed for the better. Kiss ever seeing our cousin and yo' baby bye-bye."

"What you mean no contact? That's my baby, and I have a right to—"

"Nigga, you ain't got no rights. And 'no contact' means you don't call, text, hell you can't even send her no fucking smoke signal." Roscoe gestured in the air for emphasis.

Troy refused to sit there and let them dictate his fate. They couldn't do this to him. He raised his palms in protest while he tried to reason with them. "Come on 'Sco. Y'all act like we ain't fought before. And you of all people know how it was between me and Mia."

"I ain't loyal to you. The fuck you thought. Yo' ass shouldn't've touched our baby cousin even if she did hit you first. Words of wisdom: walk away next time." Roscoe tilted his head and shrugged his shoulders.

DaeDae pounded a fist into his hand. "Fuck this! I swear if you even think about calling her, I'm gon' smash yo' fucking face in."

Troy didn't bother acknowledging him or the empty threat. Instead, he kept his eyes trained on Roscoe who glowered back at him. He couldn't believe they weren't going to allow him to speak to Mia even though she was carrying his child. It started sinking in how serious Maxwell was about protecting his daughter. He then realized that, undoubtedly, he would act the same if he and Mia had a daughter of their own. She'd already expressed a desire for him to see somebody who could help him deal with his past traumas and learn nonviolent ways to express himself. He couldn't lose Mia and he was not about to miss out on being a part of his baby's life. Troy would do what he had to in order to get her back.

"Okay," he mumbled.

Roscoe lifted an eyebrow. "Okay, what?"

"I won't contact her, and I'll see the shrink 'cause I wanna be a part of their lives."

"You actually thought you had a choice? Ha!" Roscoe responded with a mirthless chuckle. His nostrils flared. He leaned forward with an elbow on one knee and a stiff index finger pointed. "Nigga, I didn't ask nor need yo' fucking agreement. You was gon' do all of this anyway. What you failing to understand is, thurr ain't no options hurr."

Roscoe reached in the duffel bag, pulled out a manilla envelope, and threw it Troy's way. Before it could strike him in the face, Troy caught it. He looked down at his name scribbled on the front.

"Go 'head. Open it. Gotta make sure you read the first page." Roscoe relaxed back in the chair.

Troy ripped the top open and retrieved the stack of papers. He scanned over the first page that laid out some of what Roscoe had already shared with him. There was the statement in bold where he was not to contact Mia under no circumstances. If he did, there would be consequences which included him forfeiting his endorsements as well as his position with the Raiders. Maxwell's words came rushing to the forefront of his mind.

"Consider this a parting gift because you're not going back to Atlanta. You have a one-way ticket to Vegas where you will keep your punk ass until I say you can leave. Don't worry, you'll still get to play ball. I made a call. The Raiders are expecting you to suit up in a week."

Troy frowned. He looked up at Roscoe and pointed to the paper. "How is any of this legal?"

DaeDae snarled, "Didn't we tell yo' ass you don't get to ask no questions?"

Once again, Troy didn't bother looking in that direction. He kept his eyes trained on Roscoe, who gave DaeDae a look and smirked. Roscoe shrugged as he turned to face Troy. "You heard what he said."

It was as though someone applied heat to Troy's ears. The muscle in his jaw twitched. DaeDae's so-called tough guy act was getting old. As much as he wanted to ball the papers up and throw them in Roscoe's face, Troy kept his cool. He cut his eyes from Roscoe to the document and continued reading.

"Man, I ain't sitting here while his slow ass reads that shit. Nigga done agitated me so much now I'm hungry."

Your big, black, crusty ass is always hungry, Troy thought to himself. He hid the smirk on his face, keeping his eyes glued to the paper.

"I'm out," DaeDae announced as he got up.

Roscoe rose from his seat and began following DaeDae out, but he stopped mid-stride. In a matter-of-fact tone, he stated, "Doesn't matter whether it's legal or not when Uncle Max is the one pulling all the strings. Just make sure yo' ass stick to the fucking script."

When Troy heard the door slam shut, he flung the packet on the floor. "Fuck!"

CHAPTER 2

Four years ago . . .

"I see they've allowed the riffraff in tonight. This should be rather interesting."

"Miss Wynters, you can go in."

"I know. But before I step foot in that room, I need to see who's in there."

Exhibiting an air of arrogance, Mia Wynters tossed her flowing locks over her shoulder and shooed away the unwelcome presence of the hostess with an impatient flutter of her fingers. With an eyeroll, she returned her attention to the cracked door scanning the crowded venue once more. After glancing at her Cartier watch, she shifted her gaze to her best friend, Angela Washington standing off to the side.

No need in dragging this out any longer. The thought entered Mia's mind before a small sigh escaped her lips. "I guess I better go make my rounds."

"Looking that good? Goddamn, you better."

Mia took a step back and turned to Angela with a smirk. "I should have them play *Flawless* when I walk in."

"And you better be ready for the simps to holla." Angela teased while straightening out the lace train of her sequin dress.

"That right there is exactly the reason I detest coming to these events. I don't even know why I let him talk me into coming."

"You know as well as I do. Max requires you and MJ to attend at least two of these a quarter. You can't be the senator's daughter and not show you also care about these kinds of things. And you do care about these kids don't you, Mia?"

Mia remained silent, seemingly occupied with examining her freshly done French manicure. When she tried to lift her other hand, Angela playfully swatted at it.

"Mia!"

"What? I don't know them. I'm not their mama. Fuck them kids."

"Girl don't play. Your daddy will kick your ass if you don't go in there and schmooze on his behalf," Angela chastised, wagging a finger at the doors that led into the grand ballroom.

Letting out a grumble, Mia muttered under her breath but conceded. "Ugh, you know I'm gonna support my daddy 'cause I always wanna see him—no, *us* win. I just don't wanna get caught up in any of this political nonsense. It cramps my style."

"At least you know how to curve the media hacks."

"You're right about that. Well, come on. Let's go and get this over with. We can still make it to SkyLounge before last call."

Mia adjusted her cinched waist, running her palms down the sides. The off-white, strapless satin evening gown hugged her hourglass figure and flowed elegantly to the floor with a daring thigh-high split. She gathered up some of the fabric in front to avoid snagging on her stiletto heels before confidently striding through the ornate double doors. As she made her way into the opulent great hall, the energy in the atmosphere changed almost instantly. She knew why. It was no surprise to Mia that all eyes were on her.

Although there were plenty of attractive, successful women filling the spacious room of the Ritz-Carlton, Mia's presence brought everyone to her within seconds. As the daughter of the esteemed Georgia senator, she commanded an air of reverence. Guests flocked to bask in her glow, to grovel at her feet. Doing her best to keep a poker face, she forced a smize for every photographer who requested she smile for their camera. Questions came from every angle. She answered them as politely as her patience would allow. But then there were the pesky reporters hoping she'd spill information about her father's campaign.

"Mia, how does Senator Wynters feel about the President's proposed policy to improve the economy?"

That came from a man who must not have received the memo this was a black-tie affair. She fought the urge to frown at the unflattering brown suit that clung to him like a rumpled potato sack. Before she could muster a response, a grating voice pierced the air, its owner dressed in a God-awful garish pink gown that assaulted the eyes. Mia struggled to focus on her query, but the Pepto-Bismol hue clashed with the woman's complexion, doing her no favors. At this point, Mia had a question of her own brewing in her mind:

Who in the hell dressed these people?

"Excuse me, Mia, does Senator Wynters think it was a fair decision to ask Americans in the upper-class bracket to pay more on their taxes?"

Does it look like I would know any of this shit? Mia looked to Angela with an expression of annoyance. Forcing her mouth in an upward curve, Mia turned to the reporter and quipped, "Umm, when did I become a member of my daddy's staff? I think you all know what I majored in at Spelman. Now, if you need help with, let's say, your outfit for the next gala or custom designing a luxurious space, I got you."

The group erupted into laughter. Mia caught a glimpse of someone raising their hand to ask another question, but without acknowledging them, she lifted her dress to avoid tripping over it. "If you all would excuse me, I did just get here and need to grab something for my parched pipes before answering anything else." Mia gestured to Angela, and they made a beeline for the bar on the other side of the room.

"I'm glad you nipped that right in the bud before they went crazy. Remember the last time they got you?"

Mia gave a subtle nod to the bartender, who made eye contact with her. She then replied to Angela. "That's why I had to shut them down. I wasn't going through that crap again and somebody writes up a story that I said something on my daddy's behalf."

"What can I get for you beautiful young ladies tonight?"

Angela and Mia swiveled their heads in unison toward a sophisticated older man with neatly-styled silver hair and a deep-blue vest and matching bow tie adorning his chest. While Angela ordered her usual glass of Cabernet Sauvignon, Mia went for something different and requested a French 75 with vodka instead of gin. As they waited for their drinks, they scrolled through Instagram and took pictures to share on each other's pages. When their beverages arrived, Mia captured a boomerang of them toasting and posted it to her *stories*. Just as she took a sip of her crisp cocktail, she was hit with the scent of an alluring cologne from a man who had taken the seat next to her. It wasn't overpowering, but it was enough to make her breathe it in deeply. And then he spoke, his smooth voice filling her ears.

"Ummm, excuse me, but I think you dropped something."

Mia twisted the barstool to her left and struggled to maintain her composure when she saw him. His intense gaze, strong jawline, full lips outlined by a perfectly groomed goatee, and straight teeth that framed one of the most stunning smiles she'd ever seen, almost took her breath away.

"I'm sorry what?" Mia frowned.

He pointed to his face. "My jaw!"

Now how could a man this fine have such a cheesy pickup line?

Angela let out a stifled giggle. Mia was quick to give her an elbow. Before Mia could respond to dismiss him, he hit her with another lame pick up line.

"Other than being sexy, whatchu do for a living?"

Mia burst into a fit of laughter but stopped abruptly. Locking eyes with the incredibly handsome, bald man, she stated, "No."

"Whatchu mean, no? I'm tryna figure out if that was you on the cover of Vogue."

Without another word, Mia spun away from him and quickly grabbed her flute and clutch. She tapped Angela's shoulder and motioned for her to follow. Mia tossed her long, jet-black tresses over her shoulder and sauntered off. When they were several feet away, Angela stopped to face her.

"Okay, *who* was that?"

"Don't know. And don't care." Mia shrugged, taking a sip from her glass.

"Are we in the same room? Did you see what I just saw? Did you smell what I just smelt? Mia, he is fine as fuck! No. How about all three of them are drop dead fine! And they all smell like money. Not simps. Ballers! Oh my god, he's looking over here. They all are. Mia, you should—"

"I should nothing. If you and your horny pussy don't calm the fuck down. Ang, you know we've seen fine men at these galas before."

"Nah uhn. We ain't never seen any that look like them. Mia they're huge. Like over six feet, maybe six-three or four. Where in all the galas we've been, have we seen any men taller than Kevin Hart?"

Mia had taken another swig of her drink and covered her mouth to hold back a laugh. "Ang! You almost made me spit this champagne out!"

"But am I lying?"

"Okay. No. If anything we've seen a bunch of short, rich mofos."

"Exactly! Always with their big rides and boats to overcompensate for their angry inch." Angela quipped before doubling over in laughter.

Mia couldn't help joining in, but eventually composed herself to respond. "Don't get me started on these guys at the bar tonight. That wasn't even money you smelt. It was fuckboy. I could smell it from a mile away, Ang'. And it's written all over them. Trust me, they ain't shit."

Right then, Mia's attention was drawn to someone on the other side of the room, and she grinned with mischief. "Oooh, there's Camilla DeVine. I see she decided to make an appearance tonight after all. I'm sure she knows where the real ballers are at. Come on."

With a confident sway of her hips, she led Angela to the opposite side of the room. By the time they made it over to her acquaintance, an indescribable feeling washed over Mia that she was being watched. She angled her head slightly to the right and peered over her shoulder. There *he* was. Truthfully, the tall, fair-skinned stranger that smelled divine had left an impression on her. Not only was he fine as hell, but he was rather funny with the way he tried to run game. His smoldering brown gaze burned a hole right through her from across the expansive space.

Fuck! He is so fine! Mia quickly turned away feeling her heart skip a beat. She steered Angela far away from him. But it was pointless. She felt it. She could feel him. For the next hour, it was like that. Regardless of who Mia conversed with, the towering and handsome stranger would make an appearance, standing nearby and watching her.

Angela found an opportunity when the second bar opened up and they could get seating for another drink before the evening's presentations got underway. Mia relayed her order, but her senses were overwhelmed when she caught a whiff of his panty-soaking fragrance. He approached the granite bar countertop, standing just inches away from her and emanating intense warmth. The bartender gave a nod once he ordered a shot of Hennessy. Mia glanced to catch him angling his body in her direction. He propped his elbow on the counter and tucked his bottom lip in his mouth, giving her a once over. Her core clenched, leaving her insides feeling gooey. Fixing her posture, Mia squeezed her thighs in hopes it would quell the sudden throbbing in her pussy. She cleared her throat.

"Okay. Are you really here for the cause? Or do you come to these types of events just to stalk the women?"

He lifted a brow. "Of course, I'm here for the kids. And I think it's obvious I'on have to stalk nobody." Twisting his head, the man's gaze drifted out to the crowd behind them. When he brought his dark brown eyes to meet hers again, he lowered them with a sly smirk dancing on his thick lips. "There's enough of them in here already stalking *me*."

"Ooh, aren't we cocky."

"Nah, just calling it how I see it. And it's no cap when I say this: I ain't a photographer, but I can picture us together."

Mia snorted. "You can't be serious. Where do you come up with these cheesy-ass lines?"

"No lines. I'm being serious, girl. You're beautiful as fuck. I like what I see. And I can see us together." He flashed Mia a dazzling smile that practically melted her panties off as he extended his hand. "I'm Troy Harris. What's your name?"

Present day . . .

Mia rummaged through Troy's laundry hamper, pulled out one of his jerseys, and trudged from the walk-in closet back into their master bedroom. She hugged it close to her body while climbing onto the unmade bed, where some of his other clothes were. Inhaling deeply, Mia could still detect the familiar scent of Creed cologne imbedded in the fibers. As she curled up amidst the scattered clothing bearing his smell, an ache swelled within her chest, threatening to overwhelm her. Mia held on tighter to the shirt in her hands, blinking back tears, trying in vain to hold on to this precious link to him.

It'd been a week since she'd returned from New Jersey. Seven whole days since MJ blindsided her, and their dad and cousins assaulted Troy. As she'd done every morning, noon, and night, she checked her phone, praying Troy would finally respond to her frenzied messages. But her device remained cruelly silent. Before Angela called, she'd dialed Troy's number compulsively, listening to his voicemail that seemed to mock her as it picked up again and again.

"Mia, did you hear me?"

Mia knew Angela was probably talking about coming home in a few weeks. After the tragic death of her brother, Angela turned to alcohol and prescription drugs and almost overdosed. Thankfully, Jamal, Angela's surgeon boyfriend, saved her in time, but she had experienced a complete mental breakdown. After a brief stay in the hospital's psych ward, she was transferred to an inpatient facility dedicated to helping people with addictions, and it was working. She was getting better, thanks to being away from her vices. Mia should've been listening, but her mind was elsewhere. With a heavy sigh, she offered an apology.

"I'm sorry, Ang. No, I didn't. What did you say?"

"I was asking if you could be on standby. One of Jamal's colleagues asked him to come help out on this groundbreaking research. That means he'll be in D.C. for a few weeks. Then he has this medical conference in Florida. I'm not sure if he'll be able to come pick me up. But do you think, well, would you be able to come and get me?"

Once more, Mia tuned Angela out. She couldn't help it. Her thoughts went back to that night. Her dad stood over Troy while DaeDae and Roscoe held him up. Before MJ closed the door, she could see they'd already busted Troy's lip. Knowing her dad and cousins, the beat down was hardly over. They were ruthless. There was no telling how bad they hurt her husband. MJ stood guard at the door until their dad came. Even though she begged to know where Troy was, neither of them would talk to her. Her dad told her to get dressed and left. MJ waited until she followed their dad's instructions, then they met up with him at Teterboro airport. Maxwell had chartered a private plane to take them all home. Despite crying and pleading with them the entire flight, they wouldn't tell her anything.

"Mia!"

"I'm sorry, Ang. My mind is elsewhere." She could hear the cracking in her own voice.

"Hey, are you okay?"

Mia rolled onto her side and grunted. "No, I'm not okay."

"What's wrong? Did Troy hurt you?"

"No. But Troy's been hurt, and I don't know where he is." Mia began to cry.

"Goodness, I hate that I'm here, and I can't come to you. Please, calm down. Can you tell me what happened?"

It took a few minutes for Mia to pull herself together. When she was able to stop sobbing, she took her time to explain everything. "I don't know where they took him, Ang. MJ brought me back here, but he still wouldn't tell me anything. He said they were doing what's best for me. I should've known. They've been plotting against us for weeks. I don't know what to do."

"What can you do? Max thinks this is best, and maybe he's right. Mia, you and Troy—"

She sprang up in the bed. "No! Don't you dare agree with him, Ang."

"I'm not taking Max's side. That's not what I meant. What I'm saying is that after everything you've been through with Troy, you have to believe Max is looking out for you."

"Looking out for me, how? By beating my husband up, huh? I can't believe you think my daddy was right in this. I don't care what I did or what anybody thinks! Troy's *my* husband! This is *our* marriage! Everyone needs to just mind their own fucking business and leave us alone!"

"Look, I'm sorry. I don't mean to upset you."

Out of nowhere Mia began to feel lightheaded. Her mouth watered. "Ang, I gotta go. I'm not feeling so hot."

Mia ended the call and bolted for the bathroom. She knelt in front of the toilet as her stomach churned. Gripping the sides of the commode, she purged everything she'd eaten that morning. When she finished vomiting, Mia flushed the toilet and sat still, hoping her stomach would settle. The nausea lingered. She went through a few more bouts of dry heaving before pushing herself up from the floor. Mia stood over the sink and rinsed her mouth. It hit her when she looked in the mirror. The month was coming to an end. Her cycle was like clockwork—always on time. But not this time. *"I'm two weeks late!"*

Mia bent down and yanked the wooden cabinet door open. She rummaged through the basket until she found the box. She opened it quickly, pulled out the foil packet, and ripped it open. Squatting over the test stick, Mia relieved her bladder. She placed the test stick on the counter. After closing the lid of the toilet, she washed her hands and sat down. Her heart thumped wildly as she waited. A few minutes passed before she stood up. Looking heavenwards, Mia said a silent prayer. She looked down. She covered her mouth in disbelief as she focused on the two lines.

With trembling hands, she picked up the stick. Tears stained her cheeks as she cried out. "I'm pregnant. Oh my god, I'm pregnant!"

Her joy and excitement were quickly overshadowed by the realization that her husband wasn't there to celebrate with her. Sadness washed over Mia as she left the bathroom. She sat on the edge of the bed for a moment. From the corner of her eye, she saw the shirt she'd pulled from the hamper. Mia laid the test stick on top of it, grabbed her phone, and snapped a couple of pics. She was about to send Troy the text when an IG notification banner caught her attention. When Mia opened the app, she couldn't believe her eyes. *Troy!*

As she read the caption underneath his picture, her anger boiled to the surface. She could hardly contain it. Not wasting another minute, Mia got up and threw some clothes on. She didn't bother calling. This had to be done face-to-face. As soon as she got into her Mercedes G-Wagon and started driving, Mia dialed the number of the one person who could calm her down. After a couple of rings Mai Wynters' face popped up on the device's screen. Mia saw her parents' kitchen behind her, the magazine-worthy design on display. A spacious island with waterfall quartz countertop stood out, surrounded by gleaming stainless-steel appliances. Natural light poured in through large windows, illuminating custom cabinetry, soft-close drawers, and under-cabinet lighting for a polished look. The chic subway tile backsplash tied it all together with a modern flair, reflecting the Wynters' refined taste.

"MiMi, I called you earlier. Why no answer? You okay?"

Mia glanced away from the road for a moment to see her mom bustling about. Ever since she was a child, her mom had always called her by that nickname, except when she was in trouble, and only then would her full name be used. She shook her head before looking back at the moving traffic.

"No, Mama. I'm not okay. Where's Daddy?"

"He not here. Him and Nigel went to do important business. You try calling him?"

"No! 'Cause I don't wanna talk to him right now. I can't believe they would do this! After I told MJ to mind his fucking business. They just had to go and make matters worse! Troy could've played for New York, Mama but I know Daddy messed that up. Now, well now he's in Vegas and, and it's all their fault!" Mia banged her hand against the steering wheel.

The clatter of silverware hitting the countertop reverberated through the speakers. Mai's voice rose as she slammed her palm down on the surface.

"Guhl, the hell you yelling for? Nah uhn, you better decrease your volume when talking to me, MiMi. Back forward and reverse what you said, 'cause I don't even know what you talking 'bout!"

Mia couldn't help but let out a small laugh, even though she didn't mean to. English wasn't Mai's first language, so sometimes her emotions would cause her to speak in a broken dialect.

"Not funny, MiMi. You call me yelling 'bout Max and MJ. I no like that shit!"

"I'm sorry, Mama but you had to hear it from my end. That shit was funny."

Mai kissed her teeth and moved closer to the screen. "Was not. Now tell me. What's going on?"

"Mama, what did Daddy tell you happened in Jersey?"

"Nothing. Why, something happen?"

"Mama! I just don't get why they couldn't leave well enough alone! Daddy, MJ and those idiot nephews of his, Beavis and Butthead, beat Troy up!"

"What?" Mai leaned in more.

"Yes, Mama! And I know he got Uncle Jeff to help him 'cause why is my husband in Vegas? But I can't reach him. He hasn't called me in a week, Mama! A week!"

"MiMi, your father say nothing to me. He been with MJ and Nigel. I see him maybe three times since y'all got back. You know he a busy man. But lemme call him."

"No, Mama. I'm going to MJ's house. 'Cause I need to know where Troy is."

"Lemme call Max. Talk to him, mkay? Goodness. All worked up. You need to pull over and relax yourself."

Mia sighed, waving her off. "Mama, I'm fine. I'm almost at MJ's house. He's gonna tell me where Troy's at and I'm going to Vegas to see my husband. I'm good now. I'll call you back okay?"

"MiMi—"

"No, Mama. I'll call you back."

Without giving her mom a chance to protest, Mia hung up the phone feeling more determined than angry. Her brother would tell her where her husband was. As she sat at a red light, she scrolled through some songs on her playlist and settled on, *Feeling Myself* by Nikki Minaj. In less than thirty minutes, Mia arrived at her brother MJ's house. Roscoe and DaeDae were standing guard outside and attempted to block her, but Mia ignored them and made her way inside.

"Move, you fucking morons! MJ! Daddy!"

"Sorry, Unc. We tried to stop her." Roscoe announced from behind before Mia began her rant.

"You always get Roscoe and DaeDae to do your dirty work, but this time y'all went too far! Vegas! How could you, Daddy? He had a chance with the Giants. Did you get Uncle Jeff to help you do this?"

MJ held his hands out, pleading. "Mia, you need to relax."

"Shut up, MJ. You're such a kiss ass! I know they couldn't pull this off without your hands in it."

MJ folded his arms across his chest. "No, I won't shut up. And if being a kiss ass is me protecting my family, then so be it. What you're failing to realize is, we did this for you and the baby's safety."

"You told him?"

When Mia first announced her pregnancy to MJ and Tanya a month ago at Pentagon, it was to get him off her back about Troy and leave them alone. As much as she wished it were true, it wasn't—at least not then. With a few weeks left until she could confirm, Mia did everything in her power to make her lie become reality. Now it was. But she never expected her brother to tell anyone else. As MJ admitted to telling their dad, Mia's face morphed from surprise to anger.

"Of course, I did. You weren't going to say anything, trying to protect his punk ass. I wasn't about to let him hurt you or this baby."

"He wasn't going to hurt me anymore or our baby! I told you I had everything handled, but you just had to run your mouth. You let him drag Beavis and Butthead into this. They beat him up while you stood by and did nothing. Nothing, MJ!" Mia's gaze shifted away from MJ and landed on the woman standing at his side. She jabbed a rigid index finger in her direction with venom in her tone. "And you!"

Mia had warned Tanya Ryan, her talent acquisition agent, not to get involved with her brother MJ. She knew Tanya had a crush on him, but Mia also knew he was a player who couldn't be loyal to anyone. Despite this warning, Tanya now stood in MJ's house wearing one of his fraternity t-shirts. Furious, Mia narrowed her eyes and continued to unleash her rage.

"I told you he was a ho. Heh, you need to ask him who was in that shirt last. I guess now that you're fucking him you've found a way to make yourself useful in more ways than one. I told you if you crossed me for him you were done. You're fired!"

"Enough, Mia!" Maxwell bellowed.

Mia didn't flinch. She balled her fists at her sides and scrunched up her face. "No! Because none of you had the right to interfere in *my* marriage. I don't give a damn about the reputation of *your* last name! Did you forget that my last name is Harris? Troy's *my* husband. I'm going to be with him, and you can't stop me. If you want to see me or your grandbaby, I suggest all of you fall in line or stay the fuck out of our lives for good!"

She didn't give either of them a chance to respond. Mia stormed out of MJ's living room and a moment later, slammed his front door shut.

CHAPTER 3

Troy's mind was in turmoil as he fidgeted with his wedding band. He longed for Mia and resented the circumstances that caused their separation. She should've been with him. If things had gone differently, he would be in New Jersey right now, preparing to play with the Giants. He'd given it his all, proving that he would've been a great addition to their team. However, Mark delivered the blow that the general manager rescinded the offer for Troy to join their roster. Mark claimed the decision had been influenced by the drama happening off the field in Troy's marriage. Initially, it pissed Troy off. Mia was the one who made the public aware of the domestic abuse.

No! Troy shook his head. There was no one else to blame but himself. He couldn't keep his hands to himself, and that wasn't Mia's fault. He'd treated her cruelly and cheated on her. Mia did what she felt was necessary. Interestingly, after Mark announced the decision and Troy reacted, Mia continued to show her love and support. She reassured him of his skills and gave him hope for the future. She practically made him forget about the rejection.

A smile crept on his face as he remembered the tryst they had in the back of the limousine on the way to the hotel. When they got to the hotel room, he was ready to continue with their lovemaking session, but he had to have ice with his Hennessy. Looking back, Troy wished he hadn't bothered and had stayed in the room with Mia. He'd planned to spend the rest of the night deep inside of her. Troy's smile turned upside down.

Before he could make it to the ice machine, one of them, likely DaeDae, snuck him with a punch to the back of the head. When he turned around, Roscoe landed another one that sent him careening backward into Maxwell, who tried to hold him, but Troy wriggled free. He tried to swing wild on any of them, but DaeDae was successful in landing an unsuspecting blow that sent him to his knees. They gave him a merciless beating unlike any he'd experienced before. Troy was familiar with the ruthless individuals on Maxwell's payroll. They could've done much worse. More of Maxwell's words from that night rang loud in Troy's mind like an alarm: *I spared you from them cutting your fucking hands off.*

The blazing afternoon sun beat down on him as he now stood outside the Raiders football facility, squinting against its rays. "This is some bullshit," Troy grumbled under his breath.

"Hey, it might be some bullshit, but are you ready?" Even under the unforgiving Nevada heat, Mark remained poised with his usual air of finesse and discipline. It'd been a week since everything had transpired. Once Roscoe and DaeDae left, and he calmed down, Troy didn't bother going through the rest of the documents alone. He called Mark, who'd been waiting to hear from him after MJ contacted his office. Troy begged Mark to fix it so he could get out of playing for a team he had no plans of ever playing for. Mark explained the Wynters had gone to great lengths to secure Troy's position with the Las Vegas franchise. It was an iron clad deal. Troy would be on the Raiders roster for the next three years.

"Do I have a choice?"

"No. You don't."

"Then I'm 'bout as ready as I'll ever be."

"That's all I needed to hear," Mark gave him a firm pat on the back.

Troy's shoulders sagged. He let out an exasperated breath. "Man Mark, I feel shitty. How can I do this knowing what I know? If he would just let me . . ." his voice faltered. Feeling the stinging behind his eyes, he looked away.

He'd spent the past few days moping around the condo. As the news of Mia's pregnancy settled in, so did his anxieties. The thought of not being able to experience any part of it gnawed at him. The hopelessness that crowded his thoughts became overwhelming. Troy needed to see her. He'd asked Mark to try reasoning with Maxwell, but it'd been pointless. Her dad stood on his decision that Troy and Mia would have no contact.

Mark gripped Troy's shoulders. With a firm squeeze, he spoke in a sympathetic tone. "Look buddy, I know this is going to be difficult, but remember the goal. This is your chance to prove yourself, not just to Max, but to everyone who's doubted you. The sooner you focus on that, the better. You'll get to see her again. And guess what? You've got your boys here to help you get through this."

As if on cue, two men with bulging biceps and rippling muscles rounded the corner of the sports building, laughter bubbling between them. The first man was a couple of inches shorter than the other, with a copper complexion and a mischievous glint in his eyes. His companion sported short, wavy hair and a dazzling smile that could sway a soul in an instant.

Mark chuckled. "Speak of the devils. How are you, Rome?" He shook the hand of the taller man once he approached him.

"Good. Ain't no complaints this way." He then turned with a big smile and offered Troy a more relaxed fist to bump. "'Sup, T?"

"Ain't nothing pretty boy, Rome." Troy grinned, exchanging the bump along with a quick hug.

Romeo Vanzant was the epitome of ruggedly handsome, with his chiseled features and confident demeanor. His hair fell in perfect waves, his jawline was sharp, and his brown eyes were nothing short of captivating. He was fully aware of the power his charm and good looks held, especially among the ladies who swooned over him as the star quarterback of the Raiders. Troy had met Romeo a few years before at a party. They'd crossed paths several times throughout the season when Romeo visited Atlanta with his teammate, who also happened to be Troy's former college team-mate and close friend.

"Ay, it's Marky Mark from the funky bunch and Trouble T-Roy!" He gave Mark a fast handshake before turning to smack Troy on the back, nearly knocking the wind out of him.

"Damn, Speedy what the hell? 'Sup, you fool?"

Shawn let out a belly laugh, his voice loud. "Same ol' shit, different day! I would ask how you been but like always, I see yo' ass in some damn trouble." Troy's face twisted into a frown prepared to argue, but Shawn pulled him into a tight embrace. "But I'm sure as hell glad to see you, T."

Shawn let go, and they did their secret handshake. He and Troy had both played football for and graduated from Boston College. While Troy's journey to the NFL had included playing in the Canadian and XFL leagues, Shawn's path began right after he finished college. After a brief stint in Chicago, he was traded to Tennessee and eventually found his home in Las Vegas, where he had been living for a couple of years.

"I'm happy to see you too, man." Troy gave a cursory glance at Mark, then shrugged, "Yeah, you right. I been in trouble, but I'm here to get my shit together."

Shawn snorted. "In Sin City? The fuck you bring him out here for, Marky Mark? You know he gon' be surrounded by nothing but ass. You tryna set my boy up to fail?"

"Absolutely not. Troy knows exactly what he needs to focus on, Speedy." Mark gave Troy a side-eye. "Ass should be the furthest thing from his mind. No matter the temptation."

Before Troy could respond Shawn bellowed out, "Ha! That just means more fuh me."

"You get enough on the regular at Bleu Saffire. This fool spends half his check up in there. You don't need no more," Romeo quipped.

Troy chuckled, rocking his head from side to side. "Why am I not surprised? He stayed in Magic City."

"What can I say? I'm in love with 'em. I know 2 Chainz wrote that song for me." Shawn threw up his hands with a shrug.

The guys cracked up when Shawn started reciting the lyrics and chorus to "I Luv Dem Strippers."

As the laughter subsided, Mark got Troy's attention. "Alright buddy, like I said, you're in good hands. I'm heading up to the front office for a few meetings. I'll check in with you later."

"Come on, T." Shawn gestured in the direction of the building. "We'll introduce you to the rest of the guys."

Troy followed them into the massive sports facility. As they walked, Romeo entertained them with a hilarious story about an unfortunate incident involving a hot tub and a rival player. His exaggerated gestures and animated expressions had them in stitches. Temporarily, the stress Troy felt faded away and he fully immersed himself in the present moment.

Shawn slung an arm around his shoulder. "Hey, T how 'bout *we* hit up Saffire after practice?"

Troy thought about what Mark said. He pulled away from Shawn, shaking his head. "Uhh, I don't—"

"Hell no! He just got here," Romeo responded before Troy could.

A playful smirk danced across Shawn's lips. "Shit, I just thought it might be good for his spirits. My boy looks tight as fuck right now."

"Nigga, fuck you." Troy flipped him off.

"Just saying, I know how to cheer you up. Get one of them thick asses in your face. Trust me, it'll make everything you worried 'bout disappear."

Romeo's eyebrows shot up as he exchanged a look with Troy, who shook his head. They stepped onto the practice field, and Troy immediately felt the energy and excitement as his friends introduced him to the rest of the team. The sight of more familiar faces put him at ease. He'd played against some of these guys the last few years. By the time the remaining staff and coaches arrived to discuss drills, weightlifting sessions, nightly meetings, and game plans, Troy felt right at home with his new team.

Several hours later, the sun dipped low in the sky, casting a warm, golden glow over the football facility. Troy, Shawn, and Romeo lounged on a bench away from the rest of the team, nursing their sports drinks after the low-impact practice. Troy appreciated how they welcomed him without asking any questions or prying into his personal life. It made him realize how important it was for Shawn and Romeo to understand his desire for success while he was here. He couldn't afford to make any mistakes. Troy needed to talk to them about his current situation.

"Umm, Speedy, Rome ..." Troy began hesitantly, rubbing the back of his neck and looking down at his cleats. He lifted his gaze and checked around them before speaking. "There's something I wanna talk to y'all 'bout."

The air around them seemed to thicken, charged with anticipation. Shawn and Romeo looked at each other before giving their undivided attention to Troy. Shawn nodded.

"So, umm, for starters I'm pretty sure y'all know this wasn't no trade Vegas wanted." Troy's voice was barely above a whisper. "I had a chance with the Giants. I know I did. But I think my father-in-law, Max, got involved and messed that up. Anyway, after they passed on me, Mark said we would catch up the next day 'cause a couple other teams seen the high-lights and wanted to talk. So, I went back to the hotel with Mia. I left the room to get some ice. Why Max and his punk ass nephews jumped my ass. He told me I couldn't go back home. And I was expected here in Vegas. He said because of—well y'all already heard about the shit that went down with me and Mia. He don't want me near her and said I can't see her unless I do this therapy for my anger. But we was already gonna do some counseling before they got involved. Thing is, I found out she carrying my seed. They won't even let me talk to her. Man, I'm missing her like crazy. I'on know what to do."

"Damn. I'm sorry, T. It ain't cool not letting you talk to her," Romeo finally said, his eyes filled with empathy.

Shawn agreed. "Yeah, that's fucked up." With his hands spread open, he asked in a gentle manner, "Has she tried to reach out?"

Troy shook his head back and forth before dropping it into his hands. The men sat quietly. There was nothing that could be said.

Shawn spoke up, breaking the silence. "You know what? You need to clear your head from all this stress. What if I said we can get away and you could forget your troubles for a little while?"

Troy looked up warily. "How?"

"Jamaica, that's how. We can go there for a few days to relax. We'll be back just in time for practice."

"Man, that sounds amazing. Hells yeah! I'm down," Romeo chimed in.

Troy hesitated, torn between the temptation of escape and his reasons for being there. "I'on know, man. I'm 'pose to see that shrink."

Shawn nudged him on the shoulder. "Come on, T." A gentle smile graced his lips, his voice coaxing and filled with encouragement as he went on. "You can ditch therapy for a week. Take this lil' getaway to clear your head before you let somebody get in your head. Come back refreshed and ready to take on whatever gon' be thrown at you. 'Cause trust that a lot is gonna be coming your way."

Troy thought about it for a moment. *What could it hurt?* He could begin his sessions with the therapist once he got back. Nodding, Troy squashed any lingering doubt. "Aight. Why not? Let's do this." He held up a hand. "But first I gotta link up with Mark. I know he gonna be looking for me. I can't bounce without letting him know something."

Shawn hopped to his feet. "Aight, let's hit this locker room so you can gimme your address." He slapped Troy on the back and shouted, "Time to pack, Trouble T-Roy. We're going to MoBay, baby!"

CHAPTER 4

"I just want to know where he is." Mia said as she paced back and forth across the hardwood floor. "I was there for two days. He never showed up. They posted it on the team page. He was supposed to be there."

Her designer red bottom heels click-clacked on the surface. The walls of their home seemed to taunt her with memories, closing in on her. Troy's absence weighed heavily on her heart. Frustration and anger boiled to the surface thinking back to her initial attempt to find him. She'd flown to Las Vegas, only to discover he wasn't there. No one at the Raiders facility knew where he was and no one had seen him. That'd been over three weeks ago. To Mia, it felt more like a lifetime.

Angela was sympathetic as she tried to reassure her. "He was there. You just missed him."

Mia wished she hadn't. Her heart ached for Troy's presence. With Angela trailing close behind her, Mia entered the workspace that was meant to be her creative sanctuary. Natural light flooded in through the floor-to-ceiling windows, illuminating the serene and uplifting green and yellow hues adorning the walls. This room was meant to be a place of creativity and refuge, but lately, Mia had lost all inspiration and motivation. She stepped behind the sizable executive desk, running a hand through her long, thick hair in frustration.

"Have you tried calling back up there?" Angela asked.

"When I spoke to the girl in the front office, she told me most of the team was away before they were due to start their preseason games."

Angela plopped down on the chaise lounge and concluded, "Okay, then that's it. He probably went out of town with his teammates. Relax, Mia. He's going to show up. And he's going to reach out to you."

"I'm trying, Ang. And he's not going to reach out to me. Daddy and MJ made sure of that. I sent him messages on IG. All of them have been read, but I think they have someone else running his page."

"So, you really think Max and MJ are behind this?"

Mia let out a heavy sigh as she sank into the luxurious office chair, her frustration morphing into hurt as she remembered everything that night at the hotel. "I know they are! I still can't believe they did that to him."

"Damn, Mia. Your family really don't play around, do they?"

"They take this loyalty shit too far. I can't help but feel like it's my fault. MJ said I shouldn't have exposed what Troy was doing. Maybe he's right. All of this is just . . ." Her voice trailed as the emotions threatened to overwhelm her.

"Don't you dare think that any of this is your fault, Mia. I can't believe, you of all people, would start second guessing your actions."

"How can I not, Ang? Everything is torn apart. If I'd just—"

"No! You listen to me, Mia. Do not blame yourself for anything that's happening right now. None of this is your fault. Do you hear me? None. Of. This." Angela's tone was firm.

Mia heard her best friend, but the guilt weighed heavily on her heart. Her family's actions put Troy further away from her when she needed him the most. Mia rubbed her flat abdomen. Out of nowhere, the familiar sensation of nausea settled in. The relentless bouts of morning sickness had consumed her days and nights as of late, leaving little mental space for anything else but her turbulent emotions.

"Angela, you don't understand. I-I just . . ." Mia paused, trying to find the right words, but her stomach started a violent churn. With uncontrollable heaves, she raced to the closest wastebasket. Angela was at her side holding her hair while she expelled all she'd eaten the night before.

"It's not getting any better, huh?"

"Ugh . . ." Mia moaned, using the back of her hand to wipe her mouth. The bitter, acidic taste lingered on her tongue. After another bout of nausea, she was able to respond. "Ang, girl this morning sickness is kicking my ass. Yuck. Let me go brush my teeth."

"Okay and I'll get this cleaned up." Angela offered, already moving to discard of the wastebasket's contents of Mia's bile.

"Thank goodness for having a best friend who's a nurse. This type of shit wouldn't be easy for everybody to deal with."

"You know I got your back, girl."

"Thanks, Ang. I appreciate you being here."

"I'm glad I can be here. Now go. Get yourself together. I know food isn't on your mind, but you need to stay hydrated, Mommy. I'll go get you something to drink."

Mia was relieved to see her best friend, Angela, improving in terms of her mental health after the sudden and heartbreaking death of her brother. Accepting the loss of a loved one was always difficult, and it had caused Angela to spiral into a dark place. Mia feared losing Angela to drugs and alcohol as she tried to cope with the loss. Without Angela by her side to help her through this difficult time, Mia wasn't sure how she would handle it all. While she gargled and rinsed her mouth, Mia caught a glimpse of herself in the mirror above the bathroom sink. Her once glowing complexion, with its warm yellow-brown hue, was now dull and marked with dark circles under her exhausted eyes. The sight only intensified her longing for Troy. She wished he could be there to help her manage everything better.

Several minutes later, Mia emerged from the bathroom. She walked up on Angela while she was on the phone with her boyfriend, Jamal. It took everything for Mia not to say something rude. Because Angela was so happy to be home, Mia would hold her tongue. But it wasn't only the nausea that had her stomach roiling. Mia's gut instincts told her that there was something shady about Angela's man. She wished her friend could see through his charming facade and realize he wasn't good for her. However, Mia couldn't say much considering she was also trying to keep her own marriage together.

The doorbell rang startling Mia from her thoughts. She checked the surveillance camera from her cell. *What the hell does he want?* At the same time, she overheard Angela ending her call.

"I'll see you when you get off tomorrow then. Love you. Bye." Angela slid the phone in her pocket and turned to acknowledge Mia. "Hey, I got a call while I was heading to the kitchen. I heard the doorbell."

"Yeah. You won't believe who it is."

"Who?"

"My asshole brother MJ."

"Oh damn. Y'all still not talking?"

Mia glanced down at her device and grumbled. "No. Not after he decided to go rogue on me with daddy."

"I know you're happy it happened this month." Angela grabbed her arm and with a gentle tug. "Could you imagine MJ and your dad did all of this, and you weren't even pregnant?"

Mia instinctively placed a hand on her midsection as she pondered over Angela's question. A small smile played at the corners of her mouth as she replied, "No, Ang, I can't imagine because my plans almost always work. Whether this month or the next, I was going to get pregnant. I just didn't anticipate on my brother running his mouth to our dad and cousins about it like a kiss ass."

"Well, I'm here if you want me to stay. I'll go hang out in the office until he's gone. I need to call my mom anyway."

Mia wanted to talk to Angela about her phone call with Jamal anyway, so she nodded in agreement. "Yeah, hang out in there. Hopefully he won't be staying long."

While Angela headed in the other direction, Mia made her way to the front of the house. After unlocking the door, Mia opened it wide. Her brother stood in the entryway, his muscular physique commanding the space, his face etched with concern.

"Damn, big sis. You look like hell," MJ remarked rather bluntly, but not unkindly.

"Thanks for the observation, Sherlock Assholms." Mia retorted, rolling her eyes. She moved to the side and gestured for him to enter. Once MJ had passed, she wrapped her arms around her body, as if to shield her fragile state from further scrutiny.

"Hey, I'm sorry. Didn't mean to be a dick." MJ held up a medium-sized, brown paper bag. "Ma sent me over with a care package. She has that monthly meeting with the women from the HOA. It's her turn to run it. But she'll stop by later."

"What's in there?"

He set the bag down on the console table against the wall and rummaged through it. "Let's see. Ginger candies, saltines, applesauce, and lemon wedges. Oh, and she said to make you this ginger tea."

"Tea sounds nice." Mia admitted. The idea of food had her stomach roiling.

"Coming right up."

MJ headed to the kitchen, leaving Mia to follow. She admired her brother's willingness to step in and help, despite the discord between them. They still hadn't addressed what transpired at his house. If it weren't for their mom knowing about her struggles with morning sickness, MJ wouldn't've been there.

While MJ busied himself preparing the tea, Mia leaned against the counter. She averted her gaze and focused on her phone, grateful for the distraction it provided. All she wanted and hoped for was a message from Troy. Nothing. Scrolling through social media and emails brought no excitement or intrigue. The silence stretched on in the room, weighing heavily and creating an oppressive atmosphere for what felt like endless minutes.

Finally speaking, MJ glanced over and made a comment. "You know, big sis, you don't have to do this alone."

"Except I am left alone to do it, aren't I?" Mia looked up and replied bitterly, "Thanks to y'all getting rid of my husband."

MJ came over and rested his hands on her shoulders, his grip firm yet gentle. "Listen to me, Mia. Troy doesn't deserve you. And he sure as hell doesn't deserve this baby."

"How dare you!" Mia snapped, knocking his hands away. "Who made you the judge and jury over my life, MJ? How about you just make the damn tea? And then leave."

"Fine," MJ gritted out, returning to the stove. A minute later, he poured the steaming water into a mug with the ginger tea and added the lemon wedges. "Ma said it should help settle your stomach some. Here."

"Thanks," Mia murmured, taking the mug from him.

Carefully, she sipped the piping hot liquid. The warmth spread throughout her entire being, soothing the inner discomfort she'd been feeling.

"Anytime, big sis. I'll always be here for you. Whenever you need me." MJ's expression softened with genuine concern.

Mia appreciated his good intentions, but his words only served as a painful reminder of Troy's absence. As she sipped, Mia wondered if and when she would ever see Troy again. Did he and their father play a role in keeping them apart during her recent trip to Las Vegas? Her grip tightened on the mug, her knuckles turning white from the pressure. She couldn't hold it in any longer.

"MJ, you know what Daddy and those idiots did to Troy—it was brutal and senseless."

"Of course, I know." MJ replied, appearing unfazed. He leaned against the kitchen counter, with his arms crossed over his chest in a defiant manner. "He deserved more than that."

She set the cup down to prevent spilling the hot liquid. Despite the nauseating churning in her stomach, Mia lashed out in anger. "Nobody deserves that! What if they'd gone too far and actually killed him?"

"Maybe that would've been for the best." MJ's words were cold and calculated. His light brown eyes darkened as he revealed his true feelings. "You don't think I wanted to do worse to him myself? If it were up to me, he wouldn't even be walking this earth right now."

Mia's chest heaved, and her heart thudded against her ribcage. She felt as though she couldn't catch her breath. In a hushed tone, trying to keep her emotions in check, she pleaded with him, "Please, MJ. I can't believe you're saying this. You're my brother, and I love you, but what they did to Troy was so wrong."

MJ snorted. "Wrong? He's brought this on himself, Mia. You should be thanking us for handling him for you."

"Thanking you? For nearly killing the father of my child? For putting me through this hell and making me worry about whether or not he'll even come home to me? No, MJ, I will never thank you for that." Mia shook her head, unable to comprehend her brother's twisted logic.

MJ's jaw tightened, and then he huffed. "That's fine by me, big sis. I just hope you didn't expect us to sit back and watch him destroy you. We're your family, and we'll always protect you, no matter what."

She recognized that a choice had been made and it was irreversible. Mia drew in a deep breath, trying to steady the swirling emotions within. She stood her ground as she leveled a determined gaze at MJ. "I don't want you here right now. Get out."

MJ's face contorted into a fuming grimace as his eyebrows furrowed and his nostrils flared. His eyes blazed with fury. He looked like a volcano on the verge of erupting. But he didn't protest. MJ pivoted sharply on his heel and stormed toward the door.

"Before you go, I want you to know something, baby brother. Once I'm feeling better, I will find my husband." Mia paused, letting the words sink in, before continuing. "And no one. Not you or Daddy, not even his precious team of hounds are gonna stop me."

MJ froze. His hands were clenched into fists at his sides. He turned around and stared at her for a moment. Mia could feel his anger in the stillness of the room. But beneath the rage, there was something else in his eyes—a glimmer of understanding.

In a voice that was both subdued and tense, he finally spoke, "I hope you know what you're doing, Mia. We were only trying to protect you from him."

Mia scoffed. "Protect me? Heh, by hurting the man that I love? The father of my child? No, what you're doing is keeping us apart." She shook her head. "That's not protection, MJ. That's control. Something you and

Daddy have an unhealthy fetish with. Does Tanya even know who she's really dealing with?"

MJ hesitated, as if searching for the right words to say, but ultimately, he remained silent. After a final intense glare at Mia, he stormed out of the house, slamming the door behind him with enough force to rattle the windows.

Mia stood alone in the kitchen, her hand instinctively resting on her belly. She knew that she was risking a lot by defying her family, but there was no other choice.

She made a silent vow. *I'll find you, Troy. Whatever it takes. And we'll deal with all of this together. Like we always do.*

CHAPTER 5

What the fuck am I doing here? Troy thought to himself, running a hand over his clean-shaven head. He fumbled with the hem of his shirt and bounced his knee. His time in Jamaica hadn't relaxed him enough for what he needed to do today. The thought of being vulnerable made him uncomfortable, and he had doubts about whether therapy would help him overcome his problems. He cast a quick glance around Dr. Warren's vacant reception area. The walls were a cold, sterile white, devoid of any character or warmth. Shelves lined the room, adorned with an array of decorative objects, ranging from African sculptures to vintage photographs. A few indoor plants were scattered throughout, their green leaves offering a touch of life to the otherwise stark space.

"Mr. Harris?" The receptionist called his name, interrupting his musings.

Troy stood up. Out of nowhere the feeling of being exposed washed over him despite being fully clothed in a short-sleeved shirt and jeans. "Uhh, that's me. I'm right here."

"Dr. Warren will see you now."

Troy followed her down a short hallway lined with closed doors. The air had a lingering, calming scent of citrus and lavender. They stopped in front of the last door on the right. She knocked before slowly pushing it open. The hinges let out a loud creak, announcing her entrance into the room. The man sitting behind the large wooden desk was middle-aged with warm brown skin. His salt-and-pepper hair was neatly combed back, and his well-trimmed beard added an air of sophistication to his appearance. He was dressed in a crisp white shirt, sleeves rolled up to his elbows that displayed a sleeve tattoo on his left forearm. Dr. Warren looked up from his computer screen. His piercing green eyes met Troy's.

"Why hello. Come on in and make yourself comfortable." He gestured with an open palm as he stood and then came from behind the desk.

Troy paused as he stood in the doorway, examining the details of the office. It was similar to his waiting room, but here the white walls were decorated with framed diplomas and licenses. The shelves were lined with books on psychology and sports medicine. A large window behind Dr. Warren's desk let the vibrant Las Vegas sun pour in, filling the room with a golden radiance.

"I'm Dr. Isaac Warren." He proffered his hand.

Troy shook it firmly. "Hey, umm, I'm Troy. Nice to meet you."

"Have a seat," Dr. Warren motioned to the deluxe, leather chair facing his desk while he returned to take his place on the opposite side.

Troy stepped into his office and glanced around, as if searching for an escape route, before finally sinking into the chair with an audible sigh. He squirmed in his seat, feeling uneasy and vulnerable. It was like being a sheep led to the slaughter; he just hoped it wouldn't be his emotional well-being on the chopping block. The main reason for hesitation was Maxwell's insistence on him being here. And he'd heard the stories about therapists who were judgmental or incompetent, making things worse instead of helping. He didn't trust any of it. And he would let it be known.

"Look, Doc, I'on know 'bout this whole therapy thing working." Troy paused for a beat and spoke again, his unsure tone conveying his doubts. "I ain't never been one for talking 'bout my feelings or whatever."

Dr. Warren leaned back in his own chair, studying him for a moment. "Believe me, Troy, I understand where you're coming from. And I'm not here to judge you or tell you how to feel." He brought his chair upright and clasped his hands together. "But you're here because you want to turn your life around, right? And I specialize in helping athletes like you overcome past traumas. I'm here to help you work through your issues in a safe and supportive environment. Is that okay?"

Troy's lips formed a thin line. His features contorted into a scowl as he pondered Dr. Warren's words. He finally responded, "Yeah, but I'on see how talking 'bout my problems is gonna make 'em go away."

"They won't. But think about it this way: as an athlete, you know that you can't just ignore an injury and hope it goes away. You have to address it, rehab it, and take care of yourself in order to perform at your best. The same goes for your mental health. You have to take care of yourself in order to be the best person you can be."

Troy nodded. "Okay, I see your point. But what if I'on wanna talk 'bout certain things?"

"Then we won't talk about them. Therapy is a collaborative process. We'll work together to figure out what's best for you and your goals."

"Aight then. Fine. I guess we can give it a shot."

"Good. Let's start by talking about why you're here," Dr. Warren suggested, with his pen poised above the notepad in front of him.

"I'm here 'cause Max wants me here."

Dr. Warren hiked up a brow. "So, you're not here for yourself?"

Troy knew he needed to work on his anger if he wanted to see Mia again. But was he there for himself? Yes. It was time for a change.

"Well, yeah, of course I'm here for myself, but if it wasn't for my father-in-law minding our business, I wouldn't be here in Vegas, with you. I'd be home, in Atlanta with Sym. And we'd be handling this on our own."

"I see." Dr. Warren set his pen down and clasped his hands together. His tone was gentle, curt. "But you're here. And you just said you'd give it a shot. Let's do that. I think you'll find that therapy can be a powerful tool for personal growth and healing."

Troy wasn't completely convinced but bobbed his head in agreement. Once their session was underway, Troy noticed Dr. Warren had a way of speaking that made him feel at ease. It was as though he was talking to one of the older heads on the block from back home. Dr. Warren shared stories from his own life and talked about the ways therapy had helped him overcome his own struggles with past traumas. He encouraged black men, in particular, to seek out a professional for mental health support and reassured Troy there was nothing shameful about seeing a therapist. He then opened the floor for Troy to speak about his fears and anxieties.

"I know it ain't right. I ain't 'posed to treat her—my wife—like this." Troy ran a hand over his bald dome, exhaling sharply. His voice was barely above a whisper. "I know I can't keep being like this and expect her to stay. My marriage almost ended 'cause of the stuff I did. Doc, I'on wanna lose Sym. She means everything to me."

Dr. Warren gave him a nod, his eyes full of understanding. "We'll work together to help you identify why you've made certain choices and work on how to change those patterns in the future."

Troy's mind raced with thoughts of Mia. His heart yearned to get lost in the depths of her dark eyes, to run his fingers through her hair, and to kiss those full, luscious lips. Every time she popped into his head, he wished he could hear her contagious laughter again. She meant the world to him, but he'd let his reckless behavior mess things up. His forehead creased with the weight of regret as he reflected on the mistakes which led to their current estrangement. Troy blurted out, "She's pregnant."

"That's wonderful news, Troy. Wait. From that look on your face you don't seem happy about it."

"No, I'm really happy, Doc. It's just . . . I, well, something happened. I swear I wouldn't've never touched her if I knew she was pregnant." Troy let his head drop. He fought against the stinging behind his eyes, but it was pointless. The remorse for his actions still tore at his conscience. A single tear slid down his cheek, tracing a wet path when he lifted his head. "Nobody else knows this 'cept me and her, but I-I caused the dea—I caused her to lose our first baby. She lost it 'cause I-I hurt her, Doc. And now I'm thinking 'bout how Brenda treated me. I'on wanna be like that. I know I won't 'cause I want my baby, but I'm scared I'm gonna be just like her if I'on get help."

"Who is Brenda?"

"My mama. And before you ask, lemme explain. She said she was too young to be somebody's mama. It cramped her style and messed things up for her meeting guys if they knew she had kids. I know it's weird. But me and my brother, Mikey, could never call her anything else. So, that's what it's always been."

"I see." Dr. Warren scribbled on his notepad and looked up. "And your father, was he in the picture?"

"Yeah, of course. My dad, Mike . . . I love that dude. But Brenda made it hard for him after my brother Mikey was taken away and Nana passed." Troy swallowed the boulder threatening to expand in his throat. "We all used to live together, my dad, Brenda, Mikey, and Nana. But it came out that Mikey wasn't my dad's. All they did was argue. When Nana died, my dad took it hard. He couldn't handle it and shut down. Him and Brenda broke up. I ended up going to live with Brenda in this nasty building. She wouldn't let me go back with my dad when he got better. Not until he convinced her to let me live with Uncle Vic so I could get more exposure to play ball." Troy stopped. He didn't like Dr. Warren's observant gaze on him. "Ay, can we talk about something else?"

"Yes, of course. How about we discuss your anger. It's clear that it has been a driving force behind some of your destructive behaviors, like infidelity."

Troy admitted with a strained voice, "Man Doc, anger is all I've ever known. There was always somebody mad and arguing. At first, it was my dad and Brenda. When they broke up, it was Brenda's boyfriends, and them nig—I mean, those guys would just beat her up. Sometimes they'd do the same to me if I jumped in. And after they left, Brenda would turn on me. I just learned to do the same when somebody pissed me off."

Dr. Warren jotted some notes down and looked up at him. "Indeed, the origins of your anger can be traced back to your past traumas involving the relationships with your parents. By recognizing that, we can work on breaking down this destructive pattern."

Images of his past flashed through Troy's mind—the bruises and broken bones, the sound of Brenda's sobs echoing through their small Orchid Gardens apartment. He'd spent his entire life trying to control the chaos around him, wielding his anger like a weapon to protect himself from further harm.

"Your anger became a means of survival, Troy. But it also kept you trapped in a cycle of pain, unable to break free and truly live. You owe this to yourself." Dr. Warren's gentle voice broke him out of his mental battle.

"Doc, I wanna do whatever it takes to save my marriage. If you got 'em, I'll go to support meetings. You want me to read some books, I'll do that. And I'll even do some meditation if it helps me to be better for Mia and our kid," Troy declared.

"Good. But I need you to keep one thing in mind. All of this is a process. It will take some time. Change won't happen overnight. However, with dedication and patience, you can break free from the patterns that have caused you to behave the way you have. Well, our time is almost up, but I think we have a good starting point."

Troy watched in silence while he wrote a few more notes before closing the notebook.

Dr. Warren peeked up and smiled. "See? Therapy isn't so bad. Ready to schedule our next session?"

"Maybe. But don't get too excited, Doc. I'm still not a hunnid percent sure this is gonna work."

"That's fair. Think about it and get back to me. I don't want you to feel forced into coming here. And I can let Max know the same thing."

Troy thought about it and rose, stretching his muscles. "Nah, no need. I wanna schedule the next one and see what you got for me."

"Great. Remember, change is a process, Troy. Don't forget to be patient with yourself and those around you. Before you leave, I want you to repeat this affirmation: *I am worthy of love and forgiveness. I will do better.*"

"I am worthy of love and forgiveness. And I will do better." Troy repeated the words aloud twice, and again silently, feeling them resonate in his chest. "Thanks, Doc. I 'preciate it."

Leaving the office and stepping into the blinding Las Vegas sun, Troy knew he had a challenging journey ahead of him. But for the first time in a long while, he felt like maybe, just maybe, he had a chance to turn his life around.

CHAPTER 6

"Go away," Mia groaned, turning over. She didn't feel like it. The relentless bouts of morning sickness were taking a toll on her. It didn't matter what time of day it was; she couldn't hold down any food. The constant nausea left her feeling exhausted and drained of energy.

The doorbell sounded off again. This time it was a succession of tones —a clear indication that MJ had held down the button.

Asshole! Her meddling brother wasn't going to leave. Not when he'd been sent by their mom. Although she tried to assure her that everything was fine during their daily check-in call, Mia should've known that Mai Wynters was not easily convinced.

"I just wanted to lay here in peace. Is that too much to ask for?" she grumbled as she dragged herself from underneath the comfort of the fluffy blanket.

Once more, the doorbell chimed. If Angela didn't have a therapy session, Mia would've had her go downstairs in her place. The truth was, after their last encounter Mia had nothing to say to MJ unless it was to tell her where Troy was.

Mia reached for her cellphone, muttering to herself while she opened up the security app. "Goodness, why is he so damn impatient?" She pressed the icon for the speaker and huffed, "Okay, I'll be down. Gimme a minute."

Without waiting for a response, she closed out of the app and got up from the bed. Mia made her way into the master bathroom as slow as a tortoise. After taking care of her hygiene, she trudged downstairs to open the front door. To her surprise, MJ wasn't alone. Standing next to him was Tanya—her former agent and now her brother's girlfriend. Mia didn't hide her disapproval. With an irritated sigh, she tossed her hair and spun on her heel, leaving them standing at the doorway.

"I guess y'all can come in." She said over her shoulder while walking away.

MJ entered the grand foyer and shut the door behind them. He then proceeded to greet Mia with a hint of sarcasm in his voice. "Hello to you too, big sis. Oh yeah, I'm good. Thanks for asking. Tan, baby, you good?"

"Your mom asked us to come by and check on her. Not for you to come and pick a fight." Tanya spoke in a hushed tone as she chided MJ.

It wasn't low enough. Mia whirled around so fast, she almost felt dizzy. She steadied herself and spat vehemently, "Check up on me? Really? I don't need nobody, especially y'all, to do a damn thing. So go 'head, turn around, and get the fuck out."

Instead of responding to her, Mia watched as MJ spoke to Tanya. "See what I mean? She can be a petty snob, but I think the baby's got her acting out more. My sister's never been like this."

"Ugh, will you just go!"

Narrowing his eyes, MJ angled his head and spoke in a stern voice, "No, 'cause Ma asked me to check on you, and that's what I intend to do. You can be nasty and throw a tantrum all you want, but we know you're going through it. She's kept us in the loop, Mia. You do need somebody, so cut this shit out!"

The two of them exchanged heated glares. He didn't understand. None of them could truly comprehend what she was going through. Every day, she struggled against an illness that drained her strength. And the one person she longed to have by her side was not there. This added even more stress to her pregnancy. *I want my husband!* Mia wanted to stomp and scream, but she contained it balling up her fists. Her trembling lips betrayed her emotions and tears formed in her eyes. Before she could stop them, they cascaded down her cheeks.

"Dammit, MiMi. I'm sorry for yelling." MJ held his arms out, moving toward her.

Mia shook her head. She didn't want to hear it. He only used her childhood nickname when he wanted something or had upset her. She waved a hand between them right as the loud sob came out. "No!"

Ignoring her protest, MJ gathered her in his arms. Mia bawled for several minutes while MJ did his best to comfort her, rubbing circles along her lower back. "Shhh. Please try and relax, MiMi."

Mia sniffled. She struggled to speak, but her words came out stuttered and broken, "H-how? I-I-I'm all-all alone!"

"Stop saying that. 'Cause you're not. I'm here."

"I-I don't w-w-want you! I-I want Troy!" she wailed.

"Well, I'm here. Now come on." He guided Mia down the hallway into the spacious living room. Once he helped her to the plush, white sofa, he reached for the tissues Tanya offered. Carefully, he dabbed at Mia's tear-stained cheeks. MJ then took her hands into his. "I really can't stand to see you like this."

What do you expect? Mia had to bite her tongue to keep the sarcastic response from escaping. He, along with their dad, were the root cause of her emotional exhaustion. It felt as if they'd ripped her heart out of her chest in their so-called efforts to "help" her. Mia yanked her hands away. She snatched the tissues from him and blew her nose. Daggers could've shot from her eyes when she glared at MJ. As the words spilled out, they had a bitter taste to match their sour tone.

"It's your fault. Y'all took him from me."

MJ parted his lips but must've thought better of responding and closed them. The room fell into an awkward silence that seemed to stretch on for hours. The only sounds were Mia's occasional sniffles and the gentle hum of the air conditioning system. Tanya sat down in the accent chair closest to MJ. Mia took note of when his gaze shifted to

Tanya, and she in turn gave him a subtle nod. MJ then faced Mia with an expression she hadn't seen on her brother's face in a long time—regret.

"MiMi, you know I love you. You're my big sister, my only sister for Christ's sake. You should've known I wasn't about to let this shit fly. Seeing you cry over what he did. I don't know what you thought, but I wasn't gonna sit by and watch you keep going through that. Let alone doing dumb shit thinking that's how to get your lick back. You could've done far more by doing much less." MJ paused for a split second. He rocked his head from side to side and let out a mirthless chuckle. "And you coming for me and dad about what we do up at Club Infinity. Big sis, do you got an embarrassment kink you wanna talk about?"

"What!" Her nostrils flared. Mia opened her mouth, but MJ put a hand up.

"What, nothing." MJ said, reminding Mia that she was the one behind the video of Troy's abuse being played during his NFL comeback party, and she also gave a copy of another video exposing his infidelity in their marriage to the gossip show Baller Bizness. While the confrontation at the domestic abuse awareness event may have been Troy's fault, having the cameras from the reality show present only escalated the situation. Mia trying to retaliate by ruining Troy's reputation had only brought more unwanted attention to their relationship.

"Your ass been reckless for months. This whole thing started with a video *you* leaked. And you ignored me when I told you not to do anything else. You pretty much gave me the finger when I said dad was gonna get involved. You know his one rule: keep the media out of it. But no, not you. Got everybody, everywhere running their mouths about the senator's daughter and her bad boy, athlete husband. Crazy thing is there's always been rumors about you and Troy's toxic ass relationship. We all knew, but minded our business until we found out he was putting his hands on you."

"Okay then! Miss me with all this, MJ. Beyonce told people how this shit works. When you got a billion dollars on a fucking elevator, trust that some shit gon' pop off! And what is Daddy talking about, the internet trolls? He should stop worrying about broke muthafuckas that need to get their dirty mattresses off the floor!"

As MJ's eyebrows knitted together and his expression contorted into a frown, Mia knew he wouldn't be able to refute her words. The signs of the physical fights were impossible to ignore. Everybody knew about the tumultuous relationship between her and Troy. Just as MJ had shared, their family kept to themselves, never asking or getting involved even when they knew what was going on. That was the one thing that infuriated Mia more than anything else. *Why couldn't they mind the business that paid them?*

"I just wished y'all would've let me handle it. We were getting help." Seething with anger, Mia leaned back and crossed her arms tight against her chest.

MJ squeezed the bridge of his nose and let out a sharp breath, releasing a puff of air from his cheeks. "As much as I wanted to believe you, I couldn't. And you had Nigel's daughter, Keeva training you on self-defense tactics. That's what his family is for. Did you somehow forget that? She's supposed to protect you for Christ's sake! Doesn't even matter 'cause all you've been doing is embarrassing yourself and this family! You don't have to share our last name legally anymore, but you're still a fucking Wynters. Don't you ever forget that, MiMi! Every move we make is carefully scrutinized and always judged simply by who we're related to."

Fuck them! They don't know us. She didn't care about what those people thought of her. Mia rolled her eyes and kissed her teeth in annoyance.

MJ pointed a serious finger while he continued his lecture. "And if you don't like it, too bad. You can't change it regardless of who you're married to. Remember who the fuck you are. Respect our family, our legacy, and stand on what it means to carry the Wynters name, MiMi. Like I said, if anybody, you knew I wasn't gonna stay quiet for long. I'm gonna do whatever it takes to protect *my* family. *Our* family."

Following his training in various forms of martial arts with their dad's best friend, Nigel and his sons and daughter, MJ emerged from Mia's shadow as her "baby brother" and became one of her protectors. Mia would never forget that night during her senior year of college. MJ proved his fierce devotion to safeguard and defend those close to his heart.

While she finished her studies at Spelman, MJ was a second-year student enrolled at the University of Georgia. He would visit her campus to hang out with his fraternity brothers from Omega Psi Phi to hang out and, of course, pursue the numerous Spelmanites who went crazy over the Que dogs. It was the weekend of their annual end-of-year college party. Mia and Barron, her boyfriend at the time, went to the highly anticipated event together. The evening began without any issues. But as the hours passed and more drinks were consumed, there was a noticeable shift in the dynamic between Mia and Barron.

Barron wasn't known to be a heavy drinker, but that night he'd definitely gone overboard. It was clear he'd had too much to drink when he caused a commotion after one of the frats from Morehouse started hitting on Mia. Even though she rejected the guy's advances and he moved on to another woman, Barron couldn't let it go. He kept arguing with Mia, criticizing the outfit she wore, and accusing her of flirting with other guys. When Mia tried to walk away from their heated exchange, Barron escalated things by becoming more aggressive. It all unfolded in the blink of an eye. In an instant, Barron had her arm in a tight hold and was yelling at her, not allowing her to leave. And then, before she could even process what was happening, MJ lunged into action and was on top of him. MJ's fraternity brothers stepped in and yanked him off Barron, but not before he'd already thrown a flurry of punches and kicks, leaving Barron with a visibly battered face. Later, it was discovered that MJ had also broken Barron's arm during the altercation.

"Oh my god, MJ! I can't believe you did that!" Mia glanced back at her boyfriend on the ground writhing in pain. She steered MJ away from the crowd that had gathered, biding their time until campus security came. She continued to scold MJ in a hushed tone, ensuring no one else could hear. "Daddy's gonna be so pissed! You better hope you don't go to jail. No, you better hope this doesn't end up on the news."

"It won't," MJ replied without betraying any emotion on his face. He turned to look at Barron and then shrugged his shoulders. "Trust me, dad won't be when he finds out what happened. And what do you think the Morettis are for? Vince and his dad will make sure I don't see a day in jail."

"Of course, you have the dream team on your side. What was I thinking?" Mia cut her eyes.

MJ shot her a grin of satisfaction while he retrieved his phone. "In light of all this, I'm talking to dad and Nigel about having Keeva add a few more self-defense techniques to your lessons. Ain't no way his punk ass should've been able to put his hands on you, big sis."

While MJ typed out a text message, likely informing their dad of the situation, Mia stole another look at Barron and shook her head. "He never drinks like this. And when has his fine ass ever been insecure?"

"Don't matter." MJ slipped his phone in his pocket and looked at Mia. "He shouldn't've had my sister yoked up like that if he didn't wanna see 'bout me. His arm for yours."

Mia leaned in and whispered, "Seriously, MJ that could've gone left."

"What you mean?"

"If your frat brothers didn't pull you off of him, there's no telling what would've happened." Mia pointed to his hands. "I don't understand why you don't have them registered as lethal weapons. You can go to jail behind them."

"Pfft, there's no such thing. That was a joke about Chuck Norris from the 80's and somebody ran with it."

Just as she was about to respond, campus security and the police approached them to get their statements. By the time Mia finished providing a detailed account of what went down moments earlier, their dad and his attorney, Vincent Moretti, Sr. had arrived. They took over the task of communicating with the authorities. There were no charges filed against MJ. While he lay on a stretcher, Barron's face twisted in agony. He emitted low groans to convey his discomfort. Barron reached out for her.

"Mia, sweetheart. Please, look at me. I'm sorry, okay?"

"Nah, you can keep that sorry-ass apology. You ain't Ruben and this ain't 2004, my dude." MJ intervened, placing his hand under Mia's elbow and guiding her away in the opposite direction. "Dad agrees with me that you're not talking to Barron anymore. It's obvious he can't handle his liquor, and when he's drunk, he likes to touch. Not my sister, not on my watch."

She stopped walking and turned to face him. "Thank you, baby brother. I'm glad you were here."

"Me too, big sis. M & M, always." MJ extended his pinky finger.

Mia wrapped her own smaller one around it. "And forever, M & M."

The memory hit Mia hard, causing her throat to tighten and tears to well up in her eyes. Mia was aware of the lengths her dad and brother had gone to in order to keep Barron from getting close to her again. It would be no different with Troy. Her shoulders slumped. She lowered her head, and the waterworks started once more.

"MiMi, stop this please. I'm begging you. I know this can't be good for the baby. Don't you want to be in the best health possible for him or her?" MJ draped his muscular arm around her shoulder, drawing her closer.

Mia wanted to relax. She longed for peace of mind, but the thought of navigating her pregnancy without her husband filled her with angst. The future she'd envisioned for her and Troy's family was being jeopardized by her own relatives. "MJ pleeease, I-I can't do this. I-I-I need Troy!" Mia buried her face into his chest.

MJ embraced Mia, holding her while she wept. She cried until her sobs turned into quiet sniffles. As she listened to the steady rhythm of his heartbeat, Mia felt herself calming down.

After taking several deep breaths, MJ squeezed her tight and whispered, "Okay."

"Okay what?" Mia raised her head and met his cautious eyes.

MJ released Mia from his arms. He leaned forward, balancing his elbows on his knees and intertwining his fingers together. An audible sigh of frustration escaped his lips. His eyes flicked from Mia to Tanya, who gave him a slight head bob. He then turned back to meet Mia's quizzical expression head-on.

"I'll talk to dad." MJ then warned with a wag of his finger. "But don't get your hopes up. I'm not making any guarantees. You know him."

Mia used the back of her hands to wipe her face, then grasped his forearms. She exclaimed with gratitude, "Oh MJ, thank you so much! Thank you, thank you! I can't thank you enough."

"Don't. 'Cause you're not welcome. But it's killing me to see you like this. I want my big sis back, and my niece or nephew coming out healthy."

For the first time in weeks Mia felt like smiling. She had every reason to. If anybody could convince their dad to change his mind in her favor, it would be MJ. She was about to continue expressing her appreciation, but the grumbling in her stomach cut her off.

"Uh huh, see my niece or nephew is hungry. Ma told me to make sure you eat."

"Nah uhn, I can't, MJ. All it's gonna do is come back up," Mia whined with her lips poked out.

"It can come back up. I'll hold your hair. But you're eating something before we leave. I'll make you some ginger tea and put on some soup." MJ patted her on the knee, then rose to his feet.

Before exiting the living room, MJ stopped next to Tanya. Mia watched as he gently lifted her chin and leaned in, placing a chaste kiss on her lips. Tanya's eyelashes fluttered and she blushed when he pulled away.

Ugh, please. Mia restrained herself. She was tempted to show her disgust, but her baby brother appeared happy with her former agent. Mia's mom told her that MJ had brought Tanya over to meet them. It came as a shock to Mia, considering he'd only brought a girl home once before, his high school sweetheart who broke his heart when he left for college. Mia blamed that girl for MJ's whorish ways. When they split up, her brother transformed into a heartless and indifferent person, constantly switching out women as easily as he changed his underwear. Kudos to Tanya if she was the woman to tame the charming, gorgeous, smooth-talking lothario.

"So, umm are we ever going to call a truce between us?" Tanya asked, breaking the awkward silence that had settled in the room once MJ left.

Should we, traitor? Mia gave Tanya the side-eye and pressed her lips together. Initially, Tanya tried to downplay her interactions with MJ as purely professional when Mia confronted her about the noticeable shift in her demeanor around him. But the sparks between them were impossible to miss for anyone in their presence. It was bound to happen that Tanya would fall for MJ. Mia just didn't want Tanya to get hurt if her brother's motives were only to add another conquest to his list. But Mia's issue with Tanya had nothing to do with her feelings for MJ. She felt betrayed by Tanya's involvement in the plan to send Troy off to Las Vegas. For that, Mia wasn't ready to wave a flag, but rather give Tanya the middle finger.

"Hmph, I don't know. Should we? You lied about fucking my brother, and then you were in cahoots with him and my dad to get rid of my husband."

Tanya twisted her hands together and looked down, avoiding her penetrative gaze. After taking a deep breath, Tanya lifted her head to meet Mia's eyes. "I apologize, okay?" Tanya extended her palms up in a gesture of sincerity. "I didn't lie to you. But I should've resigned from my position once I knew MJ and I were moving forward with our relationship. And I wasn't in collusion with them on what happened with Troy. By the time they came to me for assistance with his endorsements, the deal was already final. Come on, Mia, I'd be foolish not to take your dad's business. What would you expect me to do after getting fired by a major client like you?"

Mia couldn't argue with that. She twirled her fingers in her hair and nodded. "Heh, I'd expect you to take Daddy Max's coins and run with 'em."

"And did," Tanya chuckled, but then her expression turned serious, and she spoke earnestly. "Mia, look, I'm really sorry. I hate the way things happened."

"Me too. You knew my plans and what I was trying to do. This whole thing just blew up in my face. And I . . ." Mia's voice faltered. There was a boulder forming in her throat.

Tanya moved from the accent chair to the sofa next to her. "I'm with MJ. I don't like seeing you like this."

Mia mustered a feeble smile through the stinging behind her eyes. "Well, he's gonna talk to our dad, and everything will be okay soon."

At that precise moment, MJ strolled into the living room, with a cup of tea, as he'd promised. He placed it on the glass coffee table and took a seat on the other side of Mia. She turned her head to face him, finding his expression unreadable. There were still unspoken words between them. But that discussion would have to wait for another day. For now, she was grateful that he'd finally shown some compassion for her heartache.

"M & M, always, right?" Mia held out her pinky finger.

Without hesitation, MJ hooked his larger one around it. He gave her a reassuring smile and stated, "And forever, M & M."

CHAPTER 7

Troy exited the Raiders' sports facility and wiped his brow with the back of his hand. Another grueling week of practices and a win under their belt, his body ached in all the right places. The sun was still high up in the sky, but he knew that the night would come quickly.

"Yo, T, you comin' with us tonight?" Shawn casually slung his arm around Troy's shoulder, pulling him in close.

Troy arched an eyebrow. "And where you talking 'bout going?"

"Where else?" Romeo said shaking his head.

Shawn was grinning like a kid in a candy store. He then announced in his loud voice, "Nigga, Bleu Saffire!"

"What the hell did I tell you?" Troy playfully shoved him away. "I'm staying outta there. I'on need the distraction."

"Yes, the hell you do! We can get a couple of shots of Henny and eat some hot wangs. We ain't got another game or practice for a few days. That's plenty of time to flush our bodies. Come on, T. It's been a minute. I know my boy."

"You know me?"

"Hells yeah! You need to see sumn shake." Shawn winked and tugged on his arm.

Troy returned a blank stare for a moment. It'd been over a couple months since he'd arrived in Las Vegas. When they weren't on the road for away games, he'd been seeing Dr. Warren twice a week. Outside of that, he stayed home praying he would hear from Mia.

What would it hurt to hang out with his friends tonight? Troy thought to himself. He did need a break. "Aight, aight. Fine, let's go. But I'm driving, nigga. That way we go when I say so." Troy hit the button on his key fob to open his truck.

Shawn shrugged and bobbed his head in agreement. "Aight, I'm cool with that. I plan on being three sheets to the wind anyway. We'll meet up at your spot."

"I knew he was gonna wear you down," Romeo chuckled, shaking his head while dropping his duffel in the trunk of his sports car.

"No. He wasn't gon' be able to resist that shit for much longer. That nigga love ass." Shawn gestured with his hands, outlining the curves of a woman's body.

Troy chuckled and shot back, "Whatever. All I know is, y'all better not let me lay down. If I fall asleep, I ain't getting up to go nowhere."

"Nah, it's team no sleep. Rome, bring ya clothes. We getting dressed at his house. Nigga you gonna see sumn shake tuhnight!" Shawn yelled over his shoulder as he headed toward his truck.

A little over an hour later, Romeo and Shawn met up with Troy at his condo. After getting dressed and throwing back a couple of rounds of shots, they piled into Troy's Range Rover and headed out to Bleu Saffire. The sounds of "Thick" blasted through the speakers while Speedy talked about his past experiences visiting the popular gentleman's club.

"I'm telling you, T, the women in there ain't nothing less than a ten. That's why I'on have a problem dropping these bands on 'em. There's this one named Summer that I'd make my wife if I was ready to settle down."

"Nigga, why is you lying?" Romeo argued.

"I ain't lying. Did you see that trick she did with her pussy last week? Dead ass, she could be Mrs. Shawn Speedy Adams."

Troy observed from the rearview mirror the look of disbelief that Romeo shot Speedy. When their eyes met through the reflection, Romeo confided, "Man, T, this fool said the same shit 'bout these girls Destiny and Malaysia last month. Then there was another girl a couple of months ago. Nah, you know what? Vegas is perfect 'cause they gon' be sister wives fucking with this nigga. He'd be married to half of 'em in there."

"No, I wouldn't! Okay, maybe two or three."

Romeo howled. "See!"

Shaking his head, Troy returned his attention to the road. Shawn and Romeo continued with the banter on how much he would spend tonight. A few minutes later, a tall sign with the club's name came into view. Troy parked in front of the two-story, cream-colored building bordered in electric blue neon lights.

The three men exited the SUV, and Troy handed his keys over to the valet attendant, who stepped from behind the podium to greet them. Troy took his valet ticket from the young man then followed his friends up the pathway leading to a set of glass double doors. The booming music and the strong scent of cigar smoke hit Troy as he made his way through security and entered the lively gentleman's club. The sudden flicker of strobe lights temporarily blinded him, but his vision quickly adjusted. A rush of excitement coursed through him as he witnessed the dancers gracefully and seductively contorting their bodies around the polished poles on stage. Part of him was glad Speedy wanted to come. It'd been a while since Troy last went to see some good ass-shaking. He was right. As he observed the multiple platforms and the women working the floor of the expansive space, Bleu Saffire had a quality selection of shades, shapes, and sizes for their customers to enjoy.

"First round of shots on me," Romeo offered.

Shawn moistened his lips in a seductive way responding with a silent nod. Troy twisted his head in the direction that had drawn Speedy's attention. He had to do a double-take at the gorgeous woman approaching them, her brown skin radiating with cool, jewel-like undertones, and exuding the confidence of a model. When she stopped in front of his friends, Troy found himself gawking at her voluptuous curves filling out the cream corset top and split-thigh skirt she wore.

Shawn greeted her with a wink and a flirtatious smile. "Hey 'sup, Ky? Looking beautiful, as always."

The woman he called Ky made eye contact with all of them before nodding at Shawn. "Good evening, and thank you, Shawn. And as always, you're looking good too. I saw when you came in. No one reserved it this evening, y'all can—"

"So, you were watching me?"

Batting her lashes, she clicked her tongue. "No."

Romeo snickered.

Shawn shot him a scathing glance, but Romeo shrugged, completely unfazed. Returning his attention back to her, Shawn flirted, "Come on Ky, when you gon' stop playing games? You know I'd shut it all down for you."

Romeo covered his mouth and let out a playful cough. "Liar!"

"Nigga, shut up. I'm ready. Kiyah's the one that keeps playing hard to get."

Kiyah put a French-manicured hand in front of Shawn's face and spoke to Romeo. "As I was to about say before I was rudely interrupted, y'all are set up in the usual spot." Lowering her palm and tossing some of her honey-blonde tresses over her shoulder, she regarded Troy. "Well hello, handsome. You're new here. I see someone's being rude and didn't formally introduce us. What's your name?"

Troy didn't miss her biting into her bottom lip before proffering him a dainty hand to shake. Before he could grab hers or even answer, Shawn knocked Troy's palm down and wedged himself between them, giving Troy his back.

"Don't worry 'bout all that. And stop with the cappin', Ky. I already told you 'bout him. This my boy, T from Hotlanta. You know, the A, baby! He done been out here for a couple of months now. We brought him out tuhnight 'cause his wife been acting stank. She ain't so much as tried to reach out. That shit's been fucking with him. He needs to get his dick sucked or something."

Troy pushed him to the side. "Nigga, move. 'Sup, yo. I'm Troy and I'on need nothing. I'm good."

She narrowed her eyes at Shawn, but she extended a warm smile at Troy and spoke in a businesslike manner. "Well, it's nice to meet you, Troy. I'm Kiyah Graham. Welcome to Bleu Saffire. I hope you will enjoy your time with us. Bottle service and the girls will be over there in a few minutes. If there's anything else you need, let your hostess know. Now, if you all would, please excuse me. There're other customers I need to take care of. I'll check in with y'all later. Oh, I don't want any problems tonight, so make sure you keep a leash on that one, Romeo." Kiyah pointed to Shawn and gracefully pivoted in her red bottom stilettos, flicking her hair, which swished across his face when she walked away.

Shawn tapped Troy's chest with the back of his hand. "All jokes aside, that's future wifey right there."

"Didn't you say that about a couple of girls in here already?" Troy hiked up an eyebrow.

Romeo chimed in, laughing, "Yep, he sure as hell did. And that's exactly why she ain't been giving his ass the time of day. Why would she when he in here all the time watching other women twerk and pop their pussies?"

"Why not enjoy the entertainment she offers. I'm giving her club the money by coming in here."

"Hold up. This is *her* club?" Troy interjected.

"Yeah. She took over after her dad passed away unexpectedly last year. Since the section ready, I'm going over there for our shots." Romeo admonished Shawn when he brushed past him. "That shit you just said sounds dumb as fuck. What woman gonna be good with you being in here all the time? I know that's why she ain't studying your ass."

"Whatever yo. At least I ain't fucking none of 'em! She knows that." Shawn shouted after Romeo, but he'd already walked away.

Troy followed Shawn, dodging a sea of gyrating limbs from women doing lap dances and the clusters of people watching the dancers perform. They made their way to the rear of the club where Romeo stepped behind a reserved section that'd been cordoned off with velvet ropes. It was spacious with enough seating for a party of twenty. Troy thought it odd to have the large area for just the three of them. Since Shawn had stopped to speak with a dancer standing nearby, he questioned Romeo.

"Y'all expecting more people?"

"Nah, not tonight but don't worry. It won't be empty for long."

True to his words, Troy barely had time to settle into one of the leather armchairs before a swarm of scantily clad women overran the area. At the same time, one server came over with a tray of shots, while another had baskets of hot wings, cups, and bottles of Hennessy and Remy. Shawn leaned in close to the young girl holding the drinks, whispering something in her ear. She kept her eyes fixed on Troy before nodding in agreement.

When Shawn handed Troy his cup, he accepted it with a raised brow. "What'd you say to her?"

"That her job is to get you fucked up tuhnight! Sa-lute!" Shawn held up his shot to toast.

Romeo did the same, raising his. Troy hesitated. It would likely be a night he'd never forget messing around with his friends. Pushing aside any doubts, he lifted the mini red plastic cup in amusement. In perfect synchronization, they all downed their shots and tapped the closest surface, wincing as the fiery alcohol burned their throats.

Shawn then spoke to the group of women in a boisterous voice. "Aight ladies, y'all already know me and my boy Rome here. It's time to welcome my other boy from the A, Trouble T-Roy to Saffire. You know the rules. No hands! Lemme see sumn shake!"

The next few hours were a wild mix of shots, lap dances, and twerk contests with the dancers. Bleu Saffire was the strip club Juicy J referred to in "Bandz A Make Her Dance." However, the dancers did more than show their pussies. Some of them did tricks with toys, fruits, and each other. Troy could see why Shawn spent his check here. Even after the last dancer had left, the lingering scent of arousal filled the air, tempting and tantalizing.

"Having fun?" Romeo shouted above the music, which seemed to be much louder than Troy remembered.

"Yeeep!" He slurred, bobbing his head in response.

Troy didn't feel shit faced drunk, but the alcohol's effects had taken hold. A warm, numbing sensation vibrated throughout his body. He needed a minute to pull himself together before they came around with more shots. Relaxing into the plush cushions of the sofa, Troy let his head roll back, and he closed his eyes. He'd barely rested them when he heard Shawn's loud mouth carrying over Rae Sremmurd's "Throw Sum Mo."

"Yooo, T! Is that who I think it is?"

"Damn, I wouldn't mind meeting her. Ay, check her out, T." Romeo gave him an elbow to the ribs.

Troy's eyes fluttered open. He sat up straight when she came into his line of sight. The invisible string bikini and thong set did more than just enhance the beautiful woman's hourglass figure; it showcased her curves, highlighting her ample bosom and shapely hips. The barely-there two-piece sparkled with rhinestones, reflecting the light and drawing attention to her every move. Strutting with such grace, her clear platform stiletto sandals added to her elegant stride. Her walk was so damn sexy, he could admire her ass from any angle. The natural slant of her eyes, reminiscent of dark chocolate, and her jet-black hair that fell past her shoulders, reaching all the way to her waist without the help of any extensions, added to her captivating beauty.

Ain't no fucking way. Is that who I think it is? The alcohol clouded Troy's vision, causing him to struggle with telling Mia and the woman walking toward him apart. He knew it wasn't her, but Troy thought she could be his wife's doppelgänger. The only distinguishing features that stood out to him from Mia's were the woman's honey-colored complexion and slightly thinner lips.

Approaching the sofa, she leaned forward and purred in Troy's ear. "Hey, lover boy. You look like you could use some company. Mind if I sit here?"

My lap or my face? Shit, yeah! Wait, no! But the words didn't come out. They were stuck. He was stuck. A chill ran through his entire body as she caressed his arm, leaving him speechless and in awe. Troy hadn't seen her in over a year, and she looked good. Too damn good. The moment Troy inhaled, the intoxicating fragrance that filled his nose overwhelmed him. She smelled like mangoes and coconuts with a hint of cinnamon. It was a distinct aroma in the air, different from the other women who were there minutes ago. Troy's sexual desires were triggered by the familiar scent. Shifting in the seat to alleviate the pressure building in his crotch was pointless. Suddenly, hearing his friends' cheers snapped Troy out of the trance he'd been in. He whipped his head to the left.

Shawn raised his glass and shouted, "Yeah, Trouble T-Roy! You done hit the jackpot tuhnight! Sinnamen brought her ass all the way from the A baby! You've got an exclusive treat, my nigga!"

Sinnamen whispered, "That's right. I'm here just for you, Trouble T-Roy."

The way she rolled the nickname Shawn gave him off her tongue had his dick jumping for joy. Yeah, he remembered her too. Troy refocused on Sinnamen, her face mere inches from his. Her eyes, filled with desire, stayed trained on his lips. He looked at hers, admiring their perfect heart-shape. When he peered up, time seemed to stand still as their gazes locked in a silent exchange. No introductions were necessary.

Troy gulped hard and stammered, "Wh-what the fuck are you doing here, Sinn?"

"I just told you, lover boy. I'm here for you."

"How did you know I was here?"

"Word gets around fast when fine-ass ballers like you are in the building. I was in town and well, I was tryna see if you wanted to hook up for old times' sake."

Troy fought the urge to devour her mouth when he caught a whiff of her cotton-candy-flavored breath. He shook off the temptation, determined to maintain control. "I uhh . . . I umm, no, I can't. You can take care of my boys though. I'm good."

"Oh, I know, Trouble T-Roy." Sinnamen slid her body on top of him, straddling his lap. She rolled her hips and grounded on his erection before leaning in. Her breath tickling his ear as she whispered, "You're still the best I ever had."

All of sudden, Sinnamen hopped to her feet and twirled around, giving him a view of her thick derriere. She bounced, making her plump cheeks jiggle and smack together, appearing as if they were chewing on the thin fabric of her thong wedged between them. It was then Troy heard the song "Round of Applause." Sinnamen did as Waka Flocka Flame chanted in the chorus: dropping her ass low, making it clap, and coming up to twerk it back down into a full split. They'd brought in a new twerk team to perform for them. But Sinnamen had Troy's undivided attention with her lap dancing. He reveled in watching Sinnamen contort her body in ways he'd seen no other stripper humanly do. She shed her two-piece and threw the pussy at him. Her thick ass gyrating on his dick had him bricking up.

Fuck! Troy's groin began to ache. It had been over two months since he was last intimate with Mia, and he hadn't had any sexual release. Jerking off was getting old. Because of the excessive use, he was positive that his right arm had developed more muscle than his left. Being around all this ass and pussy, Troy could feel his resolve slipping away.

After another hour and more shots, Troy's cognitive state deteriorated to the point of complete obliteration. His vision was blurry, and he couldn't focus on anything for longer than a few seconds. He finally made out Romeo waving in his face. It took another minute for it to register that Romeo had asked for the valet ticket.

"Whatchu mean? Where we goin'?"

"Home. 'Cause y'all niggas is done. Speedy done said his prayers to the porcelain god. You probably next. Come on. Let's go."

"Okay. Hol' up. I'm coming."

Troy's head was cloudy, making the music and people chattering around him feel muted and distant. He'd gone too far with the drinking. Even though he sat still, it seemed as though he was swaying back and forth. He pushed himself up. When he took a step he stumbled, almost falling. Troy leaned against a wall, trying to regain his balance. Romeo was right. He was done. It was time to go.

Troy dragged his feet, but eventually he caught up with his friends, and stepped out of the club into a cool breeze. It was as if the city had slowed down just for a moment, allowing him to catch his breath. The sound of cars honking and the occasional burst of laughter from pedestrians could be heard in the background. Romeo called out to him to climb into the truck. Troy eased himself onto the backseat and let his head settle against the headrest. That was the last thing he remembered before passing out.

BEEP! BEEP! BEEP! Half-asleep, Troy scrambled for his phone and turned off the annoying alarm. He ran his tongue over his teeth, making a smacking noise with his lips. His mouth tasted like an ashtray, and he didn't even smoke. Just then, he heard the deep snoring and felt the pressure of a leg on top of his own. Calmly, he dislodged himself from underneath the supple limb. As he turned over, Troy's eyes almost bulged out of his head when he recognized the owner of the body part was Sinnamen. But the heavy breathing that sounded like a chainsaw wasn't her. His eyes swung to the other side of the bed.

Speedy? What the hell? Troy shifted to the edge of the bed and rose to his feet. He was staggering a little, but he managed to make it over to Shawn's sleeping body.

"Nigga, get up!" Troy hissed and gave him a hard shove.

When he didn't budge, Troy resorted to slapping him upside the head a few times. Shawn grumbled but pulled himself up into a sitting position and rubbed where Troy had hit him. He peered at Troy in disbelief, almost whining.

"The hell you smack me like that for, T?"

Troy's eyes bounced from Shawn down to Sinnamen, who stirred but remained asleep. His expression twisted in confusion as he stared back at Shawn, worry lines forming on his forehead.

"What the fuck did we do?"

CHAPTER 8

He didn't even want to go to Bleu Saffire. But Shawn had worn him down with the constant reminders that Mia wasn't reaching out and the fact that he wasn't getting any ass. Still, he shouldn't've been so easily persuaded. *Fucking peer pressure.*

"I'on know why I let your ass talk me into going." Troy grumbled, dragging a hand down his face.

"I ain't talk your ass into shit. You went 'cause you been wanting to see sumn shake."

He and Shawn both glanced back at the bed, then their eyes met. Shawn's lips turned upward into a playful grin, his eyes shining with mischief.

"Ain't shit funny. Why is she here? Y'all know I'on bring hoes to my house."

"Welp, for her you bent that rule."

"The fuck you mean?" Troy frowned.

Shawn smirked, slipping a hand underneath the cover. He gave himself a good tug before announcing, "Nigga, you the one who told her she could come."

I did? When? Troy's memory failed him when he tried to piece together the events from the previous night. It all ran together in a blur of lap dances and more alcohol than he should've consumed. Troy realized Sinnamen could've easily talked him into letting her come back to his place. With the well-known exotic dancer naked in his bed, he could only imagine the wild and kinky things that his dick and Shawn had done. The problem was he drew a blank of everything after hopping into the truck.

"I-I can't remember shit." Troy ran a hand across his dome, feeling the prickly stubble that was just starting to grow in. "What the hell did we do?"

"Shhhid nigga, everything."

"Ugh, you know I didn't need this shit, Speedy."

"Yes, the fuck you did." Shawn lowered his voice to a hush whisper, but his tone was stern. "Two months, T. Two fucking months and she ain't even tried to call you. What's up with that? It's obvi, her daddy done got into her head. What would she expect you to do? Keep jacking yo' dick when pussy like this is getting thrown in your face er'day? And—"

Troy threw up his hand. "Yeah, muthafucka under the circumstances, she would. I shoulda kept beating my dick instead of fucking with *her*. Of all people." He cringed, turning away to gather his thoughts. Troy didn't want to accept he'd been so careless again. But this was the proof. And now he needed to get Sinnamen out of his bed and his house.

Shawn pulled the covers back, announcing, "Shit, I gotta piss."

"Not in here. There's a full bathroom in the hall. And both bedrooms up here have one too." Troy stole a quick glance at Sinnamen. Memories of their past encounters flooded his mind. He twisted his head, mumbling in frustration, "Shit, I need a cold shower."

Troy padded toward the master bathroom. After relieving himself, he went to the sink and splashed water on his face, allowing the cool liquid to fully awaken him from his groggy state. Aware of the impending effects of a hangover, he popped a couple aspirin and headed to take care of his hygiene. He scrubbed away the remnants of his indulgence last night and let the hot water from the shower cascade over him, leaving him feeling rejuvenated.

By the time he emerged from the bathroom almost an hour later,

Sinnamen was up and moving about in his room. The faint scent of an unfamiliar soap wafted from her freshly showered body. Instead of her birthday suit, she now rocked a two-piece athleisure set with confidence. The vibrant shade of pink perfectly complemented her brown skin. Troy checked her out, noting how the fabric clung to her body. The barely-there bikini from last night popped into his mind. He shook his head, trying to erase the image. *Damn.* Her likeness to his wife was almost uncanny.

"Good morning, Trouble T-Roy," she purred and sashayed her curvy hips his way.

Unable to meet her flirty gaze, Troy looked around the enormous master bedroom instead. The king-size bed was neatly made now, but not too long ago, Sinnamen had been tangled in the sheets with him and Shawn. He silently made a note to himself to swap out the linen.

But she shouldn't've been here in the first place. The thought echoed in his brain. Troy was no longer under the influence of alcohol so there would be no justification if he'd allowed her to seduce him. He needed her to leave. Now. It wasn't him who should've been given the nickname. Sinnamen was more than a temptation. She was trouble with a capital T. When she stepped into his space, the scent of mangoes and coconuts threatened to engulf him.

Troy maneuvered around Sinnamen, sidestepping her, and made a beeline for the bedroom door. "Yeah, uhh, morning. Where's Speedy? I need to ask him something."

"I passed him on my way outta the bathroom. I was gonna ask you—"

"I need to hydrate after all that drinking. I'mma head down."

"Okay. Lemme finish getting ready. Want me to fix y'all something to eat?"

Troy didn't bother responding. He was already out of the room and at the landing for the stairs in a couple of strides. The pang of thirst struck him when he reached the bottom step. He hadn't lied. With the amount of drinking they'd done, hydration was necessary. Troy stopped by the kitchen and grabbed a sports drink from the fridge. While chugging the lemon-lime flavored beverage, he peered across the spacious layout and noticed Romeo sprawled on his stomach across the leather sectional, a wastebasket next to him. Troy went to the living room to check if his friend had woken up during the night and missed. He checked, thankful there weren't any signs of vomit. The trash can was empty too. Just then Shawn's thunderous voice filled the room before he appeared.

"Ay yo, T! I need one of them showerheads. Man, I could've stayed in there for another hour."

Romeo lifted his head, scrunching up his face. He rubbed his eyes and grumbled, "Nigga can your mouth be any louder."

"Yeah, but my head knocking right now. Where's the coke and them BC powders at, T?"

Troy settled onto the accent chair beside Romeo and gestured in Shawn's direction. "Door of the fridge and right there on the kitchen counter."

"Ugh, I swear I ain't never going out with y'all niggas again." Romeo sat up, yawned and stretched his arms above his head.

Shawn took a seat in one of the high-back bar stools at the breakfast island. "Ha! That's a lie. Nigga, I peeped how you was all up in Ky's girlfriend's face. I can put in a word for you."

"Hell no! Don't nobody need you as their spokesperson. Your ass start talking and ain't no telling what the fuck you gon' say."

Shawn shot back, "At least you'll get the pussy."

"Exactly the reason I don't need your help. I wasn't even going for the pussy. At least not yet." Romeo smiled to himself. He let out a long sigh before continuing. "I'm actually diggin' her. Baby girl's a smart one. She's into commercial real estate. I'mma see what she talking 'bout."

Troy mumbled, "I know your ass needs to see 'bout some mouthwash and toothpaste doing all that heavy breathing on me. You 'bout bad as that nigga over there sounding like a chainsaw."

"Ay, I don't snore. *If* I was, blame it on the al-al-al-alcohol."

Romeo joined in, cracking up. "Ha! Ain't no alcohol. Nigga, your ass snores without it."

"Damn, yo! You like a fire-breathing dragon." Troy waved a hand in front of his nose and pointed. "Go brush your teeth, nigga!"

"Man, fuck you." Romeo shot him a middle finger as he got up from the sofa.

Troy pointed upward and whispered, "And hurry up. We need to talk about our guest."

Right as Romeo made it to the edge of the living room, Sinnamen walked in. He gave her a once-over, then exchanged a secret knowing look with Shawn and gave Troy a subtle nod. Sinnamen dropped a bag adorned with the phrase, *WAP loading* from her shoulder onto the floor. She casually rested a hand on her curvy hip.

"So, now that everybody's up. Do you have anything in there I could whip up for us?"

Troy's eyes bounced from Shawn, who shrugged and spun around on the stool, to Romeo, who made a swift exit up the stairs. He refocused his attention on Sinnamen, studying her with intent. Even if he did invite her last night, she'd overstayed her welcome. No. This was not going to be like that morning with Sadé and Carla. There wasn't going to be any breakfast or brunches being made in here today.

"Nah, you ain't gotta do all that." He peeked down at his watch, the second hand ticking away the precious seconds. Then, Troy lifted his gaze to meet hers with a smooth and practiced lie slipping off his tongue like honey. "We gotta be up at the stadium in an hour."

Sinnamen cast a cursory glance at Shawn, whose back remained to them. He appeared to be engrossed in his phone, but Troy knew better. His boy was staying neutral.

"Oh. Okay then. Umm, well, how about this? Maybe we can all hook up after you're done. I can come back and fix y'all dinner. Even dessert." Sinnamen offered, coyly raising her brow.

"We'll see." Troy pushed himself up from the chair and walked over to her.

Sinnamen did a seductive spin and bent over to retrieve her bag. Her perfectly sculpted ass was no work of a plastic surgeon. She was cornbread fed, just like Mia. And dangerously too close to his dick. Troy discreetly adjusted himself and shifted his focus straight ahead.

"Listen, er'body got their eyes on the new guy. I'on need no distractions. And your *ass* is definitely one."

When Sinnamen straightened her posture and looked back at him, she flashed a devious smirk. "But you used to love this distraction. From what my spidey senses picked up, you're gonna need it again. I put my number in your phone."

And now I gotta delete it. Troy kept a straight face while shaking his head. "Come on, girl. Lemme walk you to the door."

Sinnamen pulled the bag strap across her chest and strutted in front of him putting an extra twitch in her walk. Troy couldn't help fixating on the round bubbles, bouncing like they were two basketballs, until he heard Shawn's loud throat-clearing. Troy willed his eyes up and saw that Shawn had turned around. Troy's shoulders lifted in a shrug, betraying his guilt for being caught in the act.

Shawn waved. "Ay yo, it was nice to, uhh, see you again, Sinnamen."

In return, she gave him a cordial smile and winked. "Yeah, you too, Speedy. Hopefully we'll see each other again real soon. Make sure you tell that other fine ass friend of y'all's, Romeo, that I can't wait to see him too." Sinnamen stopped by the door. Batting her lashes, she placed her manicured hand on Troy's chest and purred, "I'll be expecting to hear from you, lover boy."

"Uh huh. See ya, Sinn." Troy opened the door and shot her a lopsided grin.

She stepped outside and walked down the sidewalk, swaying those wide, voluptuous hips. Troy resisted the urge to watch her go. The moment he closed the door and locked it, Shawn was on him. He swiveled around in the stool and hopped off.

"Nigga! You got it bad for her. I knew that shit years ago, but after last night, I definitely see it now."

"Think I'on know that." Troy shuffled back over to the accent chair and plopped down. "She was the last person I expected to walk up in there last night. You gotta tell me, Speedy. I need to know. What the hell did we do with her?"

"First of all, you need to feed me. The fuck you lie fuh? We ain't got nowhere to be today. She was gon' fix us something to eat."

"Greedy muthafucka. What did I just say about her? She was gon' try and feed us more than food. That's why she needed to go. You better order something from Door Dash. The menus in that organizer against the fridge."

While Shawn sifted through the options for their lunch, Troy pulled his phone out and checked his messages. Right away he saw one pop up from Sinnamen, but he didn't bother opening it. He skimmed the other texts from Mark, Brenda, his brothers, and finally his dad. But nothing from *her*. Troy's mind was in turmoil. Why hadn't Mia tried to reach out to him? She'd promised to stand by his side, no matter what anybody said. But as he thought about it more, doubt seeped in. Maybe Maxwell had manipulated her into thinking they were better off without each other. What was the point of fighting for their relationship if Mia didn't believe in it anymore?

Troy struggled between wanting to fight for their love and accepting that she may have already given up on it. The thought of not being involved in their child's life tore at his heart, but so did the idea of being unwanted by Mia. If she didn't want him near her or the baby, it would crush him. And he knew that with every encounter with women like Sinnamen, the temptation to give in could easily lead to his downfall. He needed his wife bad.

"Ay T, this spot looks straight. They got some good stuff." Shawn's voice yanked him out of his mental musings. He held up a menu. "You want this teriyaki chicken rice bowl?"

"Yeah, I ate there before. Make sure they gimme brown rice and extra broccoli."

"Aight, I'm getting the same. I'mma get Rome this grilled salmon since he on that no chicken and red meat shit again."

Troy went back to his phone while Shawn placed the order for them. He responded to Mark about the progress of his last session with Dr. Warren, followed by another request for Mark to get in touch with Maxwell about Mia. Troy replied to Brenda with his usual "okay" and asked how much she wanted for the wire transfer she requested. Next, he confirmed with his dad and brothers the exact date of the game they planned to attend. Romeo strolled into the living room just as Troy opened Sinnamen's message.

> Lover boy last nite was fuckin amazin! I be reading bout this kinda stuff all the time. Tell Romeo and Shawn I'm down for a reverse harem if and whenever y'all are. *Clit kisses* – Sinn

"Yo, will somebody tell me what the fuck happened last night!" Troy shouted, dropping his phone in his lap. "'Cause now her ass talking 'bout some reverse ha-hare—the fuck is a harem?"

A low groan escaped Shawn. "See, I knew that damn girl switched my drink. That's why I'on fuck with rum. Had me calling Earl." He was coming out of the kitchen with another Coke and Romeo gestured for him to stop.

"Ay, grab me a bottled water. And you idiot, a harem is not liquor."

"Then, what was it, smart guy? 'Cause my ass was fucked up." Shawn opened the door of the refrigerator. Before Romeo could respond, he called out to Troy. "You want anything while I'm in here, T?"

"Nah, I'm good. Got my Power-Aid."

Shawn came into the living room and tossed the bottle to Romeo, then flopped down on the other side of the sofa. "Oh yeah, we ordered lunch. Got you the salmon."

"Good looking out." Romeo said after chugging down half the contents. He placed the cap back on the bottle and spoke to Troy. "As I was about to say, a harem is basically when a guy is fucking with multiple girls at the same time. They know each other and everybody's good with it. Basically, it's that sister wives shit."

"Say what now?" Shawn perked up, leaning in.

"Yeah, I'm sure your ass done heard of polyamory. The way you be about them damn strippers you could have a harem of them. Well, only if all of 'em are okay with sharing."

Troy grabbed his phone and quietly read Sinnamen's text again. Shifting his gaze to Romeo, he arched an eyebrow with curiosity. "Aight, what's a reverse harem then?"

"Pretty much the same, 'cept the girl would be fucking with a bunch of guys."

Shawn blurted out, "Hold up. Niggas be good with this?"

"I don't know. But my little sister and her friends be talking 'bout it for their book club." Romeo said, after taking another gulp of water. "It be in them smutty romance books."

Shawn leaned back, folding his arms across his chest. "Yeah, must be 'cause I ain't sharing shit. I'm good with it being just me and my strippers."

Troy and Romeo shot disbelieving glances at him.

"The fuck y'all looking at me like that fuh? Ay, I'm good on not seeing niggas' hairy asses or balls in my face. Last night was perfect with us taking turns."

Troy let out a low moan.

Romeo shook his head, but still held out his hands and spoke with a tone of genuine concern. "What's up, T?"

"I already told Speedy I'on remember nothing. I got in the truck and that's it. So, what he means taking turns? What the hell we do with her?"

Troy listened as Romeo recounted the events that took place after they left the strip club. He described how Sinnamen approached them and proposed an orgy involving all three of them. Romeo confirmed what Shawn had mentioned earlier, that Troy agreed to it and invited her to come over.

"Fuck! No wonder she sent this crazy-ass text." Troy squeezed his brows together and pressed his lips into a thin line.

Romeo got Troy's attention and pointed to his phone. "What'd her text say?"

"She's down with a reverse harem if y'all are."

"Heh, she got a taste of all of us and now she wants that poly shit." Shawn clutched his dick, snickering.

Romeo scoffed. "But you ain't down for seeing our hairy asses and balls."

"Shit, neither am I." Troy was back on his phone rereading the text. He could feel Shawn and Romeo's curious gaze on him, waiting for him to speak, but his mind was a whirlwind of conflicting thoughts and emotions.

His friends were clueless about the battle he fought inside. He tried really hard to stay faithful to his marriage, determined not to give in to any temptation. But he couldn't deny the overwhelming attraction he still felt toward Sinnamen. It was a perpetual struggle between his desires and his loyalty, leaving him torn and burdened with guilt. Troy finally looked up and blew out a deep sigh. "Speedy already knows this, Rome. Me and Sinnamen got a past, a real messy one. Long story short, she tried to break me and Mia up."

"And now she's offering to be a permanent distraction," Shawn reminded him.

"Exactly why I'on need her around. For real, you think I'm trouble. Nah, Sinn is. I need to steer clear of her and Saffire for that matter."

Romeo clapped his hands together. "Well T, if it makes you feel any better at least you ain't actually stick your dick in her."

"Huh?" Troy frowned at Shawn. "But . . . but, earlier you said we did everything. And just now you said we took turns."

Shawn pointed from himself and Romeo. "Yeah, *we* did. Man, you was talking mad shit but your ass was knocked out after that gluck gluck *3000* performance."

Romeo let out a throaty laugh. "Damn sure was. Fuck a chainsaw, you was calling them hogs."

"Fuck you, dragon mouth," Troy teased throwing a balled-up paper towel at Romeo that he caught.

Relief washed over Troy when he realized he hadn't slept with Sinnamen. It didn't completely erase what he allowed to happen, but it made him feel less guilty. For sure, he needed to stay as far away from Sinnamen as he could.

"Okay, I feel you on keeping your distance. But you got me rethinking this harem shit. Look at her IG page, Rome." Shawn handed his phone to Romeo.

"Dayum!" Romeo's jaw dropped.

Ogling her page, Shawn declared, "Following. 'Cause shawty bad as fuck."

"Why do you think her name's Sinnamen?" Troy gestured with air quotes. "She's a fucking *sin* to *men*."

CHAPTER 9

"I'm officially in my second trimester. I've been able to keep food down the past couple of days. So, hopefully this is it for me being sick 'cause I'm over it." Mia checked over her shoulder for oncoming cars before merging onto the sparsely populated I-75 highway. She was happy her appointment had ended sooner than expected, allowing her to avoid the usual afternoon traffic heading toward Buckhead.

"And baby?"

Mia glanced at the iPhone screen, watching her mother, Mai, move around the kitchen. "She's fine. The doctor says she's the right weight and size."

"You-you having girl, MiMi? Oh my god, lemme get your father." Mai's voice reverberated through the SUV's speakers as she exclaimed, "Max!"

"No, Mama, calm down," Mia chuckled while pressing the button on the steering wheel to lower the volume. "I don't know what we're having yet. I'll find out at my next visit. I'm just manifesting my mini me. Ain't nobody trying to deal with no bobble-head replica of Troy."

Mai let out a giggle. "But he would be handsome, bobble head just like his daddy. And I come with you, mkay. I wanna see too."

"Uhh . . . well—"

"Oh, I'm sorry. Is it surprise? You don't wanna know?"

"Of course, I do. And yeah, Mama, that's cool. You can come. I'll let you know when. I gotta go. See you in a few."

"Mkay, be safe. See you soon. Love you."

Mia ended the call and glanced over to the passenger seat at Angela. She heard the stifled laugh.

"Did I say something funny?"

"Yeah, why did you rush Mama off the phone? You're not even planning to be here for the next appointment."

"She doesn't have to know all that right now. Besides, I can always fly her out there."

"Okay, whatever you say." Angela's attention went to her phone. She kissed her teeth and typed out a message at light speed.

"Damn, who are you cussing out?"

Angela finished keying in her text, placed the device on her lap, and announced, "I think Jamal's cheating on me."

How you got him, is how you'll lose him. Mia fought to keep that thought from escaping her lips. She focused on the road ahead, but questioned, "Now, why on earth would you think that?"

"Just a gut feeling. He's in New York at this medical conference. Every time I try to FaceTime with him, he keeps making excuses why he can't."

"Ang, he's probably around other people."

"Even at night when he should be in his room . . . alone? He's been texting me and even talking to me over the phone just fine. But he won't turn his camera on." Angela shifted her body in Mia's direction. "And there's something else, but I'm kinda embarrassed to tell you."

"Embarrassed, why? What happened?"

"Nothing. It's just, well, I-I don't think Jamal's attracted to me anymore."

"What? Girl, bye. Y'all be fucking like jack rabbits."

"Not anymore. Ever since Tré, it's . . ." Angela's voice trailed off. She let out a deep breath. "It's different between us. Since I've been home, we haven't really had sex. Not like we used to. It's more cumbersome to get things started. And when we do get things initiated, it's all awkward. He's tiptoeing around me now. I just want it to go back to how it used to be."

"Try not to take this the wrong way. As much as you want it to go back, that's not going to happen. Tragedy changes you. Death will have an effect on your relationship. Either it's going to make y'all stronger or tear y'all apart." Mia glanced at her best friend for a split second, observing the tears pooling in Angela's eyes. Choosing her next words carefully, Mia continued, "You spiraled, Ang. You pulled away, isolating yourself from him and everybody else. None of us realized how much you were suffering until it was too late. Just like you, I'm sure it's been hard on Jamal these past few months too. Yes, you're better now, thank goodness. But it's not going to be the same as it was. This is the new normal for everyone."

"I didn't think losing my brother would've put this huge wedge between us," Angela whimpered. She wiped her face and sniffled. "I don't wanna lose Jamal too, Mia. I couldn't help that this happened to me."

"Aww, of course you couldn't, Ang. Look, you're probably overreacting. Didn't you say he's getting ready to take over as the head surgeon up at Northside?"

"Yes, but—"

"Girl, that man is going to be busy. If he's speaking at this conference, he's probably schmoozing with those companies for research and grant money. That's what they do."

"Or picking up nurse practitioners like me. Then spending the rest of the week fucking them." Angela sat back in her seat with a pout and folded her arms across her chest.

Yeah, you're probably right. Once more, Mia refrained from saying what popped in her mind. When Angela first told her that Jamal was a married man, Mia tried to get her to leave him alone. But Angela was adamant about continuing the affair after Jamal promised to end things with his wife. Even though he did end it, Mia still had her reservations about the good doctor. Something always rubbed her wrong about Jamal. But with all the mess going on in her own marriage, Mia couldn't focus on Angela's problems.

Mia exited the highway onto West Paces Ferry Road. She rolled to a stop at the traffic light and twisted her head to look directly at Angela.

"You have to figure out a way to rekindle that spark. When Jamal gets back, talk to him. You need to tell him how you feel. After what you've gone through, you need your man. Head of general surgery or not, he can make time for you. Wasn't that his gripe about his ex-wife?"

Angela perked up. "Yeah, it was! I'll talk to him. I'll remind him why he chose me."

"There you go." With the light changing, Mia shifted her attention back to the traffic in front of her.

For the rest of the ride, Angela excitedly shared her plans for Jamal. Mia hoped it would help move things in the right direction for the sake of her best friend staying on the road to recovery. She knew how much losing her brother, Tré, had affected Angela. Mia couldn't imagine what would happen if Angela lost Jamal too.

Making a left turn, Mia guided her Mercedes G-Wagon into the gated subdivision of Wynter Fells, the entrance embellished with fancy ironwork and flanked by tall, perfectly pruned hedges. The lawns were a lush green, with colorful flowers swaying and dancing in the breeze. Recognizing her, the security guards at the booth opened the gates and let her in. She drove along the meticulously maintained streets lined with opulent homes that seemed to compete for attention. Each house showcased stunning architecture, with towering columns, elaborate windows, and big yards, while luxury vehicles gleamed in the driveways.

"Wow, they've done some major renovations. When was the last time I came out here?" Angela's head swiveled around.

"It's been a minute. I think it was that party they hosted the year before last. Girl, with all these people relocating down here, Daddy told them to expand. There are more houses on the other side of the neighborhood. Girl, they're just as gorgeous."

Angela gazed out the window, her voice full of admiration. "Well, they've done a hella good job. It's so beautiful."

Mia nodded in complete agreement. "Yeah, that's what I love about Wynter Fells. It's so peaceful and serene out here."

She made a right turn down the winding private road that led them onto the sprawling twelve-acre estate, nestled within the exclusive subdivision. The grand structure of her parents' home loomed before them, an unparalleled masterpiece unlike any other property in the area. Its impressive fourteen thousand square feet housed seven luxurious bedrooms and ten full bathrooms. Mia parked and exited with Angela right on her heels. Walking through the threshold and standing in the grand foyer of her childhood home, Mia felt a sense of awe wash over her. Even after years of living there, every time she entered its doors, it still took her breath away. The vaulted ceilings stretched high above her with extravagant chandeliers that sparkled like precious gems. The marble floors reflected the warm light from the sconces lining the walls.

Running her hand along the console table with its arc-shaped base, Angela praised, "I'll never get over how gorgeous your parents' house is. Your mom always keeps it so clean and up-to-date on the furniture. I feel like we're on a HGTV show. It's no surprise, that's where you get it from."

"Yep. And I always love shopping with her. We find the most unique pieces. She was the one who taught me colors like navy blue and burnt orange work really well together. Whereas orange and purple are an absolute travesty together. I would never." Mia turned up her nose.

"I hope not. I taught you better 'bout color palettes, yes."

Mia spun around to see the shorter, petite, and older version of herself standing a few feet away. A wide grin spread across her face. She snapped her fingers. "Okay Mama, come through then."

"What?" Her mom frowned.

Mia chuckled and pointed. "Your outfit, Ms. Fashionista Wynters."

"Oh please, this nothing. I just threw on and make run to grocery store."

"You wore that to the grocery store, Mama?"

"Yes. And don't look at me like that. It's not over top like most times."

"Uh huh, if you say so." Mia smirked but leaned in, giving her mom the tightest hug.

Mai Wynters was a woman with an eye for style and fashion, from the smallest home décor details to the latest clothing trends. It was obvious that her love for fashion extended beyond just her wardrobe. As Angela observed, their house was always meticulously clean, thanks to their trusted cleaning service. But it was Mai's keen sense of style that truly transformed their home into a modern marvel, with classy and contemporary furnishings adorning every room. Even stepping into her mom's closet felt like entering a high-end boutique, with racks upon racks of designer clothing that could rival that of the most renowned stylists in the world. No matter what the occasion or if she was staying at home, Mai always seemed to be impeccably dressed. On this particular day, she sported an oversized top, paired with slim-fitting capri jeans and designer sandals.

"I say so. And how you have my other daughter and not tell me." Releasing her, Mai moved around Mia and held her arms out. "Angela, darlin' c'mere."

"Surprise, surprise!" Angela greeted her jovially.

Mia looked on and smiled as her mom squeezed Angela, rocking them from side to side.

"You are surprise for me. Sooo good to see you."

"You too, Mama."

"MiMi said you better now. Good, good. And how is your mom?"

Angela stepped out of Mai's embrace and took hold of her hands. "I am much better. My mom is doing good too. I'll let her know you asked about her."

"Please do."

"I told Nigel I heard other voices in here," A gravelly voice boomed from the other end of the long hallway.

With each stride, Maxwell Wynter's tall, imposing figure commanded their attention as he strode down the corridor toward them. Nigel Lowe, their trusted family guardian and his best friend, accompanied him. Maxwell came to a stop beside Mai. He placed his hand at the small of her back. Mai looked up, her gaze meeting his in a private, wordless connection. A devilish grin spread across his lips as he gave her a naughty wink. Mai's cheeks flushed a deep shade of crimson.

"Ewww, you two. We're standing right here." Mia groaned playfully at her parents' flirty display. The way they smiled at each other, it was like they were teenagers in love all over again. It was a beautiful thing to witness, but in that instant Mia felt a twinge of envy. She missed Troy.

Nigel let out a deep chuckle and dipped his head in her direction. "Mistress Harris, Ms. Washington, it's always a pleasure to see ye. Please accept my apologies for taking off so abruptly, but I'm needed up at the club. Max, I'll send a text once I get everything handled. Mistress Wynters, good day."

Once Nigel left, Maxwell greeted them, starting with Angela. "Hello, young lady. It's been a while, but I trust things are going well. How are you?"

"I'm good, thank you." Angela gave a genuine smile and nodded.

Mia's dad swung his eyes over to her. "Hey, Ladybug. You're looking beautiful as ever. Your mom said you had a doctor's appointment today, and all is well with the baby. But how are you feeling?"

Ladybug? I know what you're up to Maxwell Wynters. Like MJ, it was typical for her dad to use the affectionate nickname he'd given her as a little girl when trying to make up for upsetting her or as a tactic to control her. Not this time. There wasn't anything to say unless it was information on where her husband was.

Mia's tone conveyed the annoyance she felt. And like sandpaper, rough and abrasive, she responded dryly, "Hi, Daddy. I'm fine. But we both know I could be better."

"Let me go take care of our boss baby." Without taking his eyes off Mia, Maxwell pressed a kiss on top of her mom's head. "And then I'll take care of you, my love."

"Oh, Max stop. You make my face turn red." Mai giggled, fanning herself.

"Hmm, well if that made you blush, wait 'til I really turn the heat up."

"Ugh, we don't need to hear this." Mia rolled her eyes, but her parents ignored her, exchanging a quick kiss.

"Come, Angela. I finish lunch. You help me while they talk, mkay?"

Mai grabbed Angela's hand and whisked her away toward the kitchen.

Mia heard her mom's voice fade into the background as she excitedly rambled on about a new recipe that she'd found on TikTok she wanted to try.

"Alright, Ladybug, we've avoided each other long enough. Let's have a chat." Her dad turned in the direction he'd come from earlier and began walking away.

"Are you going to—"

"My office." Maxwell threw over his shoulder.

She wanted to scream but Mia knew throwing a tantrum with Maxwell Wynters wasn't going to accomplish anything. Balling her fists at her sides, Mia stomped behind him. They entered his large office suite at the end of the hall and her mouth dropped open. She hadn't seen her mom's latest upgrades. Mai had spared no expense designing her husband's professional space. The room had such a classy vibe, with trendy furniture and minimalistic décor fit for a senator of the modern world. A spacious desk with clean lines and a comfortable ergonomic chair took center stage. His laptop sat atop the glass surface, connected to a large high-resolution monitor that displayed crisp images and vibrant colors. The LED desk lamp emitted a soft and warm light, providing the ideal setting for focus and efficiency in his work area.

Pops of green from potted plants were scattered throughout the room, infusing it with a sense of vibrancy and vitality. Decorative items and books sat atop the floating shelves on the walls, giving the space a touch of personal charm. The soothing sound of ambient music filled the expansive area, courtesy of a Bluetooth speaker tucked away in a corner. Mia's eyes danced from one side of the room to the other, taking in all of her mom's work with a smile. She made a mental note to ask about a few items to incorporate into her own workspace.

"Sit down." Maxwell's authoritative voice made Mia flinch.

She eyed him as she sank into the plush leather chair on the other side of his desk. Her dad's intense, amber orbs remained fixed on her while he lowered himself into the seat customized for his large frame. His stare was so penetrating, so filled with emotion, that it sent shivers down her spine. It was as if he could see right through her, as if he knew every thought that crossed her mind. The silence in the room created an atmosphere thick with tension and unease. As the seconds ticked by, she wondered what swirled behind those piercing eyes.

Finally buckling, Mia whined. "Daddy, are you going to—"

Maxwell held up his hand silencing her. "Do you know why I gave you the name Ladybug?"

Mia was all too familiar with the story. Her mom had faced difficulties in getting pregnant, despite seeking help from top fertility specialists and going through expensive procedures. However, her mom believed it was a good omen when she saw ladybugs right before Mia's conception. Rolling her eyes, Mia nodded in agreement.

"Yes, Daddy I know and remember the story. You've told it to me like a hundred times. Mama kept seeing them. And then y'all were like Bey and Jay, drunk in love. You couldn't keep your hands off each other. Next thing you knew, she was pregnant." Mia blew out an impatient sigh.

Maxwell shot her a menacing glare but continued. "Your mom had been seeing ladybugs all week long. She believed it was a sign we would be getting some good news. I can remember how excited she was. But when we got to the doctor that Wednesday, we found out we'd been unsuccessful with the last IVF round. Mai wanted to take a break. And I get why. She was tired of the disappointment. So was I. But we weren't giving up. We just needed a day to forget about it all. One night of fun . . ." Her dad's voice trailed off, his lips curving into a wistful smile.

Mia could see the memories flickering behind his eyes, the lines in his face softening as he gazed off into the distance, obviously reliving those moments. She waited, watching her dad reminisce.

Another minute passed before Maxwell glanced back at her. "I think you might be right."

"About?"

"Bey and Jay. That night we were pretty drunk. We did a lot . . . and everywhere."

"Ewww, nope." Mia pretended to gag. "You can go ahead and skip. I'm good on hearing this part."

She could hear a low rumble of laughter bubbling up in his chest. Maxwell paused, taking a deep breath, and coughing to steady himself.

"Anyway, three weeks later we didn't have to go through another cycle because you were floating around in there, the sign of abundance and good fortune coming our way just as Mai predicted."

Mia leaned forward, supporting herself on her elbows against the smooth surface of his desk. Making a cup shape with her fingers, she propped up her chin. She studied him with intent, soaking in every detail of this chapter of her family's fairy tale. After finding out that Mai was pregnant, Maxwell received the final approval to begin construction on the subdivision where they would raise their family. She could practically feel the buzz of anticipation that must've filled their household during those months. By the time she was born, Wynter Fells Manor—one of many houses in the newly built Wynter Fells subdivision—stood tall and proud, ready to welcome its new residents. But it wasn't just a physical home that Maxwell had created, he'd even won a spot on the Atlanta city council that year, solidifying his success and status in the community.

"After you were born Mai told me to prepare for all the great things to come. I'm not going to lie. It went over my head. But sure enough, everything fell right into place for every business venture we touched. You were turning seven when I won a seat on the senate. Our year of completion. As Mai put it, she believed you were our good luck. I haven't lost a re-election yet, Bug." Maxwell tilted his head and gave her a knowing smile.

Mia's face lit up, feeling the satisfaction of being her parents' source of pride and happiness.

But then her dad's face transformed. Maxwell's features hardened, his mouth forming a tense line as tight as a high wire. His light brown irises bore into her with intensity and then he narrowed them in dismay. His next words came out sharp and cutting like the edge of a blade. "The moment Mai brought you into this world, I made a promise to her that I'd always protect you. When will you get it through that head of yours no one's hurting my daughter. Not on my watch. Not ever."

And when will you get it through yours Troy isn't going to hurt me? Mia understood her dad's natural desire to protect her. But she truly believed he had nothing to worry about. Troy wasn't going to do anything to harm her or their baby. She chewed the inside of her jaw while exchanging harsh looks with the man she had loved first. She was undeniably a daddy's girl, but she was also a capable woman who could handle herself. The hard part would be convincing him of it.

"Look, Daddy, I know you mean well, but Troy's not going to hurt me."

"You're damn right he won't. I'm not giving him another chance to. Is that why you're here, Bug?"

"You know that's why. Where is he?"

Maxwell sat back in his chair and folded his arms across his chest. "I'm not telling you."

"Why not? Troy's *my* husband? You need to accept that I'm sticking by him."

"Accept you sticking by a husband that cheats on and abuses you? Absolutely not. He's not good enough for you. I still don't get why you pushed Lamar away. He was the better man. Did you know he's the CEO of a successful and thriving biotech company that's on the stock exchange? And I know he's still pining over you."

She couldn't believe her dad would bring up her henpecked ex. Mia cut her eyes and grumbled, "How about I'm married. He can keep on pining."

"Hmph, at least he would've treated you like the queen you are. You needed to be with someone who would not only provide for you but respect you and your marriage. Not some hot-headed thug who doesn't know how to control his temper or his dick."

Mia felt a hot flush of anger rise to her cheeks. Troy made mistakes in the past, but he was working hard to change. She kept her voice even and under control when she responded. "Daddy, Troy is not a thug. He's a successful businessman just like you. Don't act like he's not out here with investment properties and his hands in other business ventures. You had no right to interfere in *our* marriage."

"Bug—"

"No, Daddy because I know Troy better than anybody else. He's not perfect, but neither am I. We both knew what we needed to do. We both wanted a healthier environment for the baby. None of y'all knew we were going to counseling to work on our issues. MJ told me y'all knew about our toxic relationship but stayed out of it. I just wished y'all would've kept that same energy and let me handle this."

"Let you handle it?

"Yes! Did you forget I was boxing Troy upside the head too? I didn't forget what Keeva taught me. I could hold my own!"

"Girl, you must think I'm Boo Boo the fool. What was the point of training with her if he still managed to whup your ass? Oh, that's right! You never finished!"

She returned a blank stare.

What could she say? Her dad was right. Mia hadn't kept up with her self-defense sessions with Nigel's daughter Keeva. She had been training Mia in mixed martial arts and boxing since the harrowing incident with Barron. Mia advanced through the levels faster than Keeva and Nigel anticipated. She showed great promise in the beginning. But then Troy came into her life. Once she became infatuated with their newfound romance, her priorities dramatically shifted. She began postponing their scheduled training sessions until eventually she canceled them outright. When Keeva confronted her after hearing about the domestic abuse, Mia hid it from her. She chose to stay wrapped in her love-filled bubble with Troy at the cost of neglecting her safety.

Mia kissed her teeth.

"Well, he did. Then you lied about it to Keeva. And what did I say?" Maxwell's palm met the desk with a loud thud. His voice boomed throughout the room. "Keep our name out of the fucking news!"

"And clearly, you keep forgetting my last name is *Harris*!" Mia shouted back. Her chest rose and fell as she glared back at her dad, but she lowered her voice. "It's not my fault my daddy is the senator of Georgia. Those reporter hacks are always reaching. What I have going on in my life with Troy has nothing to do with you or your precious re-election if that's what you're worried about, Daddy. I'm your lucky charm, right? I'll be more than happy to go on my social media platforms and let them know we good over here."

Clenching his jaw, Maxwell pushed back and got up from his chair. He strode over to the window. After pulling in a lungful of oxygen, he released it and turned to face her. "I know I taught you better. But I don't get your generation. Y'all love airing out your dirty laundry for everybody else to see it. And as soon as somebody says something you get mad telling them to mind their business. Make it make sense. Why would you do that dumb shit knowing I was going to find out? You know damn well I'm not about to sit around and let my daughter get her ass kicked! You're my fucking daughter, Mia! I didn't want to wake up one day and find out you were in a body bag because it went too far!"

Mia's shoulders slumped. She lowered her gaze avoiding his. Her dad mentioned the part she'd deflected, pushing it to the back of her mind. Troy's violent behavior had escalated to the point where she became exhausted and stopped fighting back. Mia had become nothing more than his punching bag. Countless times she remembered secretly wishing he would experience the pain of losing her. But deep down, Mia didn't want that for either of them. At first, her scheme to ruin Troy and leave him penniless seemed like the perfect lick back. He was obsessed with the money he made. And she knew it would devastate him if she took everything and walked away. In hindsight, her extreme tactic had a greater impact than she expected. Mia could have never predicted that it would reveal Troy cheated on her in their own home and potentially fathered a child outside of their marriage.

It should've been enough for Mia to leave him alone. Despite the pain and hurt, Mia still loved Troy deeply and hoped for reconciliation so they could return to the good times in their once happy relationship. Troy acknowledged his mistakes and got on his knees, humbly begging Mia's forgiveness. Once he agreed to attend marriage counseling and anger management for their family, she couldn't walk away from her husband. Mia straightened her back and raised her chin with confidence when she spoke to her dad.

"I hear and understand your fears, Daddy. But you have nothing to worry about. Why can't you see that we love each other and are committed to making this work. We made vows to each other. For better or for worse, so, no I'm not giving up on us."

"You really want to defy me on this. Well, if you want to throw your life away on that thug, go ahead. But don't come crying to me when he hurts you again."

"I didn't the first time!"

"Your mother will be ashamed of you," Maxwell retorted, his tone icy.

"Really, Daddy, ashamed of me? If there's anybody we should be ashamed of, it's *you*. I remember how much Mama cried when she found out about *your* affair."

"What?" Maxwell frowned, his face contorted in confusion.

Mia's heart raced with anger. She couldn't stop herself from lashing out. "You can stand there and judge Troy, but isn't that how MJ got here? Right. He's the product of you cheating on *my* mom. At least Troy doesn't have a love child out here on me that I'm forced to raise. So, you have no right to stand there and talk to me about loyalty or commitment."

Maxwell opened his mouth but snapped it shut.

"Yeah, let that sizzle in your spirit, Daddy."

"Know what, he can rot in Vegas for all I care. He better not come near you."

"Daddy!"

"No! You've got some fucking nerve, little girl. Coming in here accusing me of something you know nothing about. I know one thing, I never let you think it was okay to be with a punk ass-boy that puts his hands on girls. Forgot about Barron? Well, I didn't." Maxwell pointed a stiff finger and warned, "A man that puts his hands on a woman never stops that shit."

"And again, Troy will not hurt me or this baby."

"You're right. He won't. Not if I have anything to do with it."

"But, but y-you can't do this. He's *my* husband, Daddy! I will find him!"

"You know what. Go be with his sorry ass. Go ahead." He stepped toward her shouting, spit flying from his mouth, "Get. The. Fuck. Out!"

Her eyes grew wide. Mia jumped from the chair. They'd had arguments before. He'd even yelled at her, but not like this. She'd crossed the line. Likely to the point of no return.

Backing out of his office, Mia shook her head. "You know, Daddy I really thought you'd understand. I mean, you of all people. Mama stayed after all the shit you put her through with MJ."

"Shut up, Mia."

"Oh, now I'm Mia. What happened to *Ladybug*? That's right. I've pissed you off so there's no more buttering me up. I didn't come here for all of this anyway. I just wanted to know where my husband was. That's cool. I don't need you. I'll find him without your help."

"Look here, for your own good don't take your ass—"

The knick knacks on the console table across the hall shook from the door slamming shut. Mia angrily made her way back to the front of the house. "Ang, come on. Let's go!"

By the time she reached the grand foyer, Mai and Angela came rushing in.

"What all the noise for? You slam my damn doors, girl?"

Her ears burned and her eyes stung with tears. She regretted coming here. Her dad would never tell her where Troy was. She should've known that. Maxwell Wynters was a man of his word and stubbornness ran in the family. Mia had inherited it too. Her mother reached out, but Mia yanked away from her.

"Wait, I confused. You fine when you got here and now not okay. What's wrong? Max!"

"Ugh! No, Mama. I definitely don't need to see him anymore. I'm good on that. He said what he had to say."

"Well, I don't know what he had to say. What he say?"

Mia let out a sigh, rolling her eyes. Mai moved in closer and rotated her neck. She gave Mia the universal "mom look" that all children knew and understood. While Mai may have been petite in stature, and kind with a sweet nature, she was anything but passive. In fact, she was quite the spitfire and not to be underestimated. Mia didn't want to risk getting slapped for being rude.

"*Your* husband told me to get the fuck out after I asked him where *my* husband was. My husband that he had Beavis and Butthead beat the crap out of!" Mia cried out, pointing in the direction of her dad's office.

"And I'd do it again if that nigga even thinks he's going to breathe the same air as my daughter." Maxwell's voice thundered from behind her.

Mia spun around and shouted, "And you think you can stop me?"

Mai gasped, "Oh no, Mia Symoné. You respect Max. He's your father! He has your best interest at heart. He love you! You so disrespectful right now. And I no like this. You apologize. Right now!"

She turned to address her mom but spoke to her with a much quieter tone. "No, Mama, I'm sorry. But I can't apologize. And I'm not trying to be disrespectful. Daddy is overstepping. I need to go, okay? Call you later. I love you."

Without paying attention to her mom's continued protests, Mia dropped a kiss on her cheek and rushed out of their home. As Mia climbed into her truck, she tried to hold back the torrent of emotions threatening to overwhelm her. A lone tear made its way down her face.

Angela touched her arm. "Mia, are you okay to drive? I can if you want me to."

Mia swiped the back of her hand across her face and pushed the button to start the engine. "No. I'm okay. I just need a minute."

A couple of minutes passed before Mia finally lifted her head. She gazed at the looming double doors of Wynter Fells Manor. Memories of her childhood flooded her mind as she stared at the grand entrance. Mia pushed the gear into reverse and a sharp pain pierced her heart as it hit her: she never wanted to step foot inside that place ever again.

CHAPTER 10

Troy fidgeted in his chair. His hands were clammy, and the leather beneath him squeaked from the weight of his muscular frame. No matter how hard he tried to relax, his anxiety kept gnawing at him. Unlike his previous sessions with Dr. Warren, today would require him to confront both Desiree, the person he'd harmed, and his mother, Brenda, who'd harmed him. While trying to control his breathing, he stared at the sleeve tattoos on his arms. He focused his attention on one in particular: *I can do all things through Him who gives me strength.*

"Troy, are you ready to begin?" Dr. Warren's voice yanked Troy from his thoughts.

"Philippians 4:13."

"Excuse me?"

Looking up at Dr. Warren, Troy met his therapist's eyes and spoke in a confident tone. "I have to humble myself, Doc. I'm not the one in control here. But there ain't nothing I can't face as long as I have Jesus and believe in him. That and God making ways. I ain't into organized religion or nothing like that, but it's what my dad and Nana taught me."

"I see."

"Do you? 'Cause I'm finna call my ex that I spun the block and cheated on my wife with. Now she's pregnant by and gonna marry my best friend. We ain't got beef. I'm cool with it. But it's messy, right? And then you want me to talk to Brenda. Pfft, that woman a trip. Ain't no telling what's gonna come outta her mouth. Doc, I'mma need all the strength he can give me to get through this."

"Heh, you're right. Well, no need in wasting anymore time. Shall we get started?"

Troy peered down at his phone, his finger hovering over the screen. It'd been a few weeks since he'd last spoken to Derrik. Once he'd settled in at his new place, Troy called him. They had a long conversation about everything that'd happened after Derrik's birthday party. Derrik questioned Troy on why he didn't say anything about him and Desiree hooking up again. Troy didn't think it was worth rehashing the whole ordeal since it'd been months and Derrik had lost his memory in a car accident.

"Why didn't you tell me, T? You were in my face knowing that it would've come up. Your ass could've said something."

"Yeah, I could've, but what difference would it make? We squashed that shit months ago, D. You was all mad, but shit so was I when I found out y'all was fucking. We ain't never fought over no pussy. But I got over it. 'Cause you was right. I took my ass home to Mia where I belong. I was trying to stay there. I ain't want no more problems with her. So, to keep the peace, I didn't bring that shit up about Desi."

After that, they'd talked for hours. Troy wished he could fix things by going back in time. He'd cheated on and hurt Desiree. He wanted to apologize to her.

"I never said this was going to be easy Troy, but facing up to our wrongdoings is a crucial step to changing for the better. Isn't that what we're aiming for?" Dr. Warren's reassuring voice pulled him from his reverie.

Troy rubbed a hand across his smooth dome. "Yeah, I wanna apologize to her. I want her to know I'm sorry for how I treated her."

"Then you know what to do."

Swallowing hard, Troy swiped the screen, initiating the call. After a couple of rings, Derrik answered.

"Hey, what's up, T?"

"Ain't nothing, D. What's up with you?"

"Same ol' shit, different day but I'm good. How's Vegas been treating you?"

"Aight, I guess. Can't complain. It don't feel like home, that's for damn sure." Troy could feel Dr. Warren's gaze on him. Clearing his throat, he continued, keeping his voice steady. "Ay yo, uhh look, I know this might sound strange what I'm 'bout to say, well my reason for calling. But I uhh . . . I umm, I need to talk to Desi."

There was a lengthy pause before Derrik asked, "Talk to her, about what?"

Doubt began to seep into his mind, causing his anxiety to rise. He tried to calm his nerves, but it was no use. His eyes flickered over to Dr. Warren, who remained engrossed in scribbling notes on his notepad, completely unaware of the internal battle going on inside of him. Troy looked away, deciding to focus on the bookshelf on the opposite side of the room. Filling his lungs with oxygen, and releasing it slowly, he stated his case.

"I'm uhh . . . I'm in therapy, D. I been working on my anger and dealing with some stuff from my past. You know 'bout Brenda and some of that shit. But as far as Desi is concerned, I know I need to apologize for what I did to her. To make it right."

Derrik snorted. "Therapy, wow. Well, I'm happy to hear you're doing it. But ay, keeping it real with you, T, I don't know if Desi will talk to you."

He wasn't going to let Derrik answer for her. Troy pleaded. "Come on, D. Lemme talk to her, just for a minute."

His best friend was quiet for a moment and then he released an audible sigh. "Aight, I'll see what she says."

"Okay, I 'preciate it."

"Hold on."

There was silence on the other end of the line for several minutes. In the otherwise quiet office, Troy could only hear his own uneven breaths and the faint thumping of his heart. And then, he heard Derrik clear his throat. Troy sat up straight in the chair.

Derrik's tone was sympathetic. "I'm sorry, T, Desi doesn't want to talk to you."

Troy sighed, his shoulders slumping with defeat. He'd rehearsed his apology over and over in his mind, carefully choosing his words to express his remorse and regret.

"T, you there?"

"Yeah, uhh thanks, D. It's just, well, you know, I was hoping to make things right."

"Don't take it personal. She's trying to keep her stress levels down."

Troy's heart dropped even further into his stomach. He knew how important it was for pregnant women to stay calm and stress free for the sake of their unborn child. And Desiree had to do this for two babies.

"I didn't even think about that, D. My bad yo. No disrespect. I just want her to know that I'm sorry."

"Understood. But let's respect her wishes for now. When she's ready, she'll come around. Until then, good luck. I hope you're able to get through to Brenda."

"Shit, me too, D."

"Ay listen, I hate to cut this short. Gotta meet LMK at the studio. Matter of fact, they'll be in Vegas soon. I'm sure you'll run into 'em. But we'll get up later. I'll holla."

"Yeah, fuh sho'. Hit me back when you can."

After ending the call, Troy set his phone down. He peeked up at Dr. Warren, who observed him in silence. Troy attempted to mask his disappointment. He confessed with a shrug. "Welp. That didn't go the way I'd planned."

"Sometimes things don't. It's important to remember you can't control how others react. But what you can control is how you move forward." Dr. Warren stated calmly.

Troy dipped his head, acknowledging Dr. Warren's words. For a moment, he shut his eyes and sucked in a deep breath. Despite feeling discouraged, he knew he had to keep pushing forward. It was time to talk to Brenda. He released the air, opening his eyes.

"Aight. Let's get this over with."

"Okay. Be assertive, Troy. But stay calm. Stand by your points," Dr. Warren advised, nodding at his phone. "And be open to listening to her side of things."

It sounded easier said than being done. Even though Troy had divulged a lot about Brenda in his previous sessions, Dr. Warren didn't know his mom the way Troy did. Would she be willing to participate in this exercise on his path to healing? And if she was, would it do any good for their relationship? Troy wasn't sure if any amount of therapy could heal them. But he was willing to try. For the sake of his own sanity, and for the faint hope that maybe, just maybe, things could get better between him and Brenda.

Here goes nothing. Troy swiped his finger across the screen. Instead of making it a private call as he'd done with Derrik, this time he opted to use the speakerphone option. His muscles instinctively went taut. He braced himself for the confrontation.

"Yeah, hello?" Brenda's raspy voice was laced with a hint of irritation as it crackled through the speaker.

"Uhh hey, Brenda."

"Whatchu want, boy?"

"Umm, I wanted to talk to you 'bout something." Troy began, doing his best to stay composed. "I, uhh . . ." He hesitated and peered up at Dr. Warren, scanning his face for any sign of reassurance. Dr. Warren offered a small smile and a subtle nod.

"Boy, the fuck you want? I'm 'bout to get into this cypher."

The sound of her voice crunched like gravel underfoot, grating against Troy's ears. There was also muffled laughter over the music in the background which only added to his irritation.

Troy rolled his eyes to the phone and cleared his throat. "Brenda, can you go somewhere private? I'on need your friends hearing this conversation."

"Get on my damn nerves," She grumbled aloud. "Ay, y'all go 'head and finish rolling. I'll be back. Lemme see what this boy want." The shuffling of her house slippers on the floor and the fading sound of the extra noise proved she'd left her audience behind. A door closed and Brenda let out a sigh of annoyance. "Aight, the fuck you want? And hurry up. I got some loud from Neecy. I'm tryna be in space, T-minus ten minutes from now."

"Ahem, yeah so. Umm well, I . . . uhh I-I've been coming to therapy."

"Therapy? Ha! That's whatchu called me—hold up, for what?" Brenda scoffed derisively. "Wait, lemme guess, that bougie bitch made yo' ass go. Is her psycho ass in there too? And what yo' ass think that's gonna do for y'all? Yo' ass a damn tornado and she's a volcano. Y'all asses still won't keep yo' damn hands to yo'selves. Gon' fuck around and kill each other. That's cool though. Hold up, I'm still in the will, right?"

Ignoring her question, Troy could feel the frustration mounting at her callousness. He countered, "Brenda, this ain't 'bout Mia. I'm tryna work through some issues and make amends for the mistakes I done made."

"Pssh! Who you foolin', boy?" She taunted him, her voice dripping with disdain. "Whatchu think? Sayin' sorry gonna fix it now? Quit doing weak shit, Troy. This ain't a good look."

Anger boiled inside of him. There was no way to keep it contained. Troy snapped, "This ain't me being weak! I'm tryna take responsibility for what I did wrong. And-and I'm tryna heal!"

"Boy, who the fuck you yellin' at?"

Troy could feel the heat in his ears, but he lowered his voice. "Nobody, I'm just tryna explain to you—"

"Don't be wasting my time with this shit. 'Cause yo' ass ain't never gon' change. How I know? I raised you. You's a selfish, arrogant asshole just like yo' daddy."

"No! I'm not! And you know damn well why he's like that to you. I'm tryna make things right!" Troy found himself shouting again. He could see Dr. Warren's hands waving, but he couldn't calm himself. The desperation and hurt seeped through his words. "Why can't you see that?"

"I know one damn thing, yo' ass gon' stop yelling in my damn ear or I'mma hang this fucking phone up. And what's there to see, Troy boy? This lil' therapy session, you can do it by yo'self. I ain't gon' sit here and listen to yo' pathetic whining. The hell you thought? Ain't nothing gon' magically change just 'cause yo' ass said sorry."

He focused on his breathing, taking slow and deliberate inhalations and exhalations. The memories of her cruelty, both in words and actions, rushed back like a stormy downpour, overwhelming him with the pain and trauma he had endured. He closed his eyes and tried to push the memories away, but they were too powerful, too ingrained in his being. He couldn't let her continue to dismiss his feelings like it was nothing— not when the trauma of his childhood had left such deep scars on his soul.

"You knew and ain't do nothing 'bout it." Troy's voice shook.

Brenda spat back, her tone dripping with malice like a serpent's fangs, "Boy, what the fuck you talking 'bout now?"

"Pam. You, you knew she was touching me. She was . . . she was your . . . my, no *our* cousin."

There was a moment of silence, and Troy allowed himself to believe that she'd heard him at last. Yet, the moment he heard the mocking laughter, he realized calling her had been in vain. Brenda remained as cold, uncaring, and callous as she'd always been.

"Oh, my fucking god! Whatchu bring that up fuh? What did I tell yo' ass? Kissing cousins happen! Boy, do you see our genes? Ever wonder why you into big asses? Pam is what lil' boys' wet dreams are made of. And you better be glad it wasn't none of 'em niggas I was fucking with. If one of them touched you, yo' ass might be gay right now. You need to be thanking Pam. And I know she taught yo' nasty ass some stuff 'cause you was fucking on er'thang. But I can't believe you still hung up on that. Boy, if you don't get over that shit already! The fuck you in yo' feelings fuh?"

He peeked up at Dr. Warren. There was no hiding it. Brenda's crass words had shocked him as well. Troy's eyebrows slammed together. He reached out to grab the phone with the first instinct to hang up in Brenda's face.

Dr. Warren quickly gestured and mouthed, "No. Finish."

Troy lowered his hand, struggling to contain the raging storm of emotions swirling inside. He desperately wanted to keep a level head, but every fiber of his being was ready to explode.

"You there, boy? Calling my phone with this bullshit, and now yo' ass wanna be a mute."

With the boulder swelling in his throat, Troy swallowed hard and managed to keep his voice steady as he continued, "I'm here, Brenda. Maybe if you protected me—"

"Protected you? How? Witcho big ass. You been tall as a tree since you was thirteen. The fuck I look like protecting you. From who? Couldn't even keep a man around 'cause of yo' crazy, violent ass. You started knocking them niggas out. And I know damn well you ain't talking 'bout Pam. 'Cause didn't yo' ass start likin' it?"

That was a cheap shot. Brenda was fully aware of their secret and inappropriate physical relationship until Troy moved away to Atlanta. He avoided Dr. Warren's gaze, but he could feel his disapproving stare. Troy focused his attention on his device. Brenda's taunting laughter filled the office. Troy opened his mouth, but Brenda continued her rant.

"Right! You loved that shit! I done told yo' ass before, shit happens. Who else ain't dealt with this in their family? We ain't the first and damn sure ain't gon' be the last. So, let this shit go. You in therapy now, right? That shrink you paying better teach yo' ass how to relax, relate, and release. Woosah muthafucka! Matter of fact, you in Vegas now. Can you get me some medical weed?"

"Hell no! He ain't even that type of doctor, Brenda."

"Well, then lemme get back to mine. I'll call you Friday. I'mma need some extra spending money for this trip."

The fucking nerve of this woman. Troy didn't respond. He couldn't. He resisted the urge to hurl his phone against the wall, severing all contact with Brenda. Then there would be no way to reach him for that money. She would have to go back to her old tactics for getting it rather than leeching off of him.

"Now I know you ain't in yo' lil' feelings. Don't be disrespectful. I'm yo' mama. You ain't gotta like me, but I'm the only one you got. Ya hear me, boy?"

"Yeah, aight, Brenda. I heard you."

"Good. Just make sure you answer the damn phone when I call."

Without a goodbye, Brenda hung up. Troy closed and opened his fists in a repeated motion. The rage coursed through his veins as he grappled with his mother's disregard for his feelings. He blinked at the phone several times in utter disbelief. Her mocking laughter still echoed in his ears.

Dr. Warren leaned forward in his chair. "Troy, I know what you're thinking. Listen to me. You can't change her. It's not your responsibility to make her understand or accept your feelings. Your journey is about healing yourself, not trying to change someone else. She has her own personal traumas to address that are not yours. Give yourself the grace and forgiveness you deserve."

Troy pulled in a lungful of oxygen, steadying himself as he absorbed Dr. Warren's words of guidance. "Yeah, right," he whispered, giving him a slight nod. "I have to focus on my own healing, not her acceptance."

"Exactly. You've made incredible progress, Troy. I know if this was three months ago, your phone would've been thrown against a wall and my desk flipped over. Don't let today discourage all the work you've put in. You're much stronger now than you know."

With a shaky breath, Troy rose from his seat. He'd made strides in confronting his past and refused to let Brenda's mockery of it derail him now. Troy's voice was firm and confident. "I won't let her words drag me down. I'mma keep fighting. I got this."

Dr. Warren smiled. "Good man. You know I'm here to support you every step of the way."

Long after Troy had left, the heaviness of what had unfolded in that office continued to weigh on him, a blend of sadness from Desiree's rejection and anger at his mother's reaction to therapy. His hopes were crushed, but he still felt proud for trying and reminded himself of the progress he'd made.

Troy said aloud with conviction, "There ain't nothing that can stop me now."

CHAPTER 11

As he and his teammates exited the sports facility, Troy emerged with his head down. Shawn and Romeo were in a back-and-forth banter about the afternoon's practice, but Troy was too preoccupied to join in. He was lost in his thoughts. That talk with Brenda had been over a month ago. Troy ignored her derisive taunts about him remaining in therapy despite her opposition to it. The day before, she'd succeeded in getting under his skin by asking if it was helping with him and Mia's relationship. He would rather eat crow than tell her the truth: that Maxwell was pulling all the strings, exiling him to Vegas and forcing him into therapy, and—worst of all—he hadn't seen or heard from his wife in four months. Troy's musings switched to the conversation he'd had with Mark minutes after hanging up with Brenda.

"When Mark? 'Cause I'm 'bout to lose my fucking mind. Now he's blocked me. I wanna talk to my wife!"

"Okay. Okay. I'll call Max. In the meantime, don't let this be a distraction."

"Don't let it be—what? You know how the fuck that sounds, Mark? How do you expect it not to be? I wanna know how she's doing. Man, how's my baby doing?"

"I understand. But you also have a job to do for both of them. For all of you. Don't you want to make sure Mia and your baby still have a comfortable life when y'all are reunited?"

"Of course I do."

"Alright then. I need you to keep your head in the game. I'll do what I can from my end. Call you later."

Troy shifted his duffel bag from one shoulder to the other and pulled out his phone. He couldn't wait any longer. It'd been four months—four long, torturous months since he'd arrived in Las Vegas. He'd done as Maxwell instructed and now, another month without seeing Mia wasn't something he was going for. He swiped across the screen to unlock it and call Mark.

When Troy's thumb hovered over Mark's name, a sudden breeze picked up, blowing a familiar fragrance right into his nostrils. The scent, a mixture of jasmine and vanilla, stopped him in his tracks. Shawn gave him an elbow to the side just as he raised his head to search for the source.

It was *her*.

Mia stood beside his truck with her long, jet-black tresses dancing in the wind. Her outfit, a form-fitting white jumpsuit, accentuated every curve of her shapely figure. He couldn't take his eyes off of her.

"Damn," Troy whispered to himself, stunned but excited by her presence. Without a second thought, he shoved the phone into his pocket, dropped his duffel bag and rushed to her. The moment he reached her, Troy swept her from the ground, gathering her into a tight embrace. Mia met his lips in a flurry of kisses. His mouth devoured hers with hunger, desperation, and longing. After a minute he lowered her to the ground.

"Sym . . . baby . . . I've . . . missed . . . you . . . so much." Troy murmured between kisses. He moved his hands to cup her face, tracing the contours of her cheeks with his thumbs.

Mia pulled away some, her eyes shimmering with tears. "I've missed you too. I—"

He didn't give her a chance to finish. Troy's lips crushed against hers, claiming her mouth with another savage kiss. His heart had ached for the woman he hurt, the one person he couldn't imagine living without, his twin flame. She was back in his arms, and he could stay there with her for all of eternity.

"Ahem."

Troy knew it was likely Shawn clearing his throat. He groaned, withdrawing from the sweetness Mia supplied from her pouty kissers. Feeling the instant loss in the disconnect, he shook his head and lowered it. One of his arms snaked around her waist, drawing Mia closer. He ravished her without a care of who watched. His wife was finally here in the flesh. He couldn't help showing how much he'd missed her.

"Damn nigga, let her breathe," Shawn teased.

Troy waved him off and gave Mia short chaste kisses. He was about to turn to his friends when he hesitated and got in two more quick smooches. Amidst giggles, Mia reached out, cupping his face in her hands. His heart almost burst upon hearing her laughter.

"Lemme see what these fools want." Troy pecked her lips one more time. He spun around and barked, "What?"

"You forgot your bag over there, is what." Shawn pushed the duffel bag toward him.

"Right, heh, 'preciate it." Troy took it from him, placing it on the ground next to the rear passenger door.

"'Sup, Mia. We're glad to see you. Our boy was losing his shit not having his lady luck by his side."

"Shut up!" Troy gave Shawn a playful shove.

They all shared a good laugh. Mia peered up at him and Troy drew her into his side. It wasn't just talk; without her, Troy felt like he was going insane. "You damn right I was. But now my baby is here. I missed you so much," he whispered, pressing his lips to her forehead.

Mia squeezed her arms around him and echoed. "I missed you so much too, babe."

For the next several minutes, Troy enthusiastically caught Mia up, sharing details about his new team. While Troy discussed their upcoming games and practices, Mia listened, only interjecting with questions or comments relevant to the conversation. As they stood outside the stadium, other members of the team joined them. Troy took the time to introduce Mia to each one. They all warmly welcomed her into their group and even offered to connect her with their significant others so she could become an official member of their Wives And GirlfriendS (WAGS) club.

After a short while, Romeo extended a fist to Troy. "Aight, we gon' get out of y'all's hair. Holla at you later, bruh. See ya, Mia."

She waved. "Bye, Romeo."

"Fuh sho'." Troy pounded his fists with Romeo.

Shawn exchanged a quick dap with Troy and nodded at Mia before walking away. "See y'all two later."

"See ya, Speedy," Mia dipped her head and smiled.

Troy's full attention was on his wife as he gushed, "Damn, I still can't believe you're here. I swear I was just about to call Mark. Did he talk to Max?" He paused and glanced around. Troy arched a brow when he peered down at Mia. "Hold up. Where are the cameras? You ain't recording for that show no more?"

She first lowered her eyes and bit into her bottom lip. Mia then lifted her head, rocking it from side to side. "No. Mark didn't talk to him. And being estranged from your husband and sick as a dog for the past three months isn't exactly a trending topic on IG right now."

He frowned.

Mia grabbed his hands. "Listen, there's something I need to tell you, Troy."

His stomach clenched with anxiety, but he managed to give her a coaxing smile. "Aight, go 'head. What's up?"

She released his hands, taking in a deep breath. Mia cradled her belly before blurting out, "We're going to have a baby, Troy. I'm pregnant."

He smiled big and gathered her in his arms, squeezing Mia so tight they seemed to become one. Troy inhaled, filling his nose with her scent. He could never get enough of the jasmine and vanilla aroma that flooded his senses. Releasing a long sigh, he confessed, "Yeah Sym, I know. And you look sexy as hell carrying my baby. I can already see these hips are spreading."

Mia pulled away slightly and tilted her neck. She shot him a curious glance before shaking her head. "But how?"

Troy released her from his arms. "I've known since they brought me out here. Roscoe slipped up and told me."

"Fucking Beavis. Ugh! I can't stand that idiot." Mia rolled her eyes.

He'd forgotten about the names she called her cousins. Troy let out a hearty laugh, but then frowned. "Yeah, and that idiot, Beavis, started playing in my fucking face. He said Max wasn't gon' let me see you or the baby. Then I didn't hear from you. I started to believe it. Man, Sym, that shit's been killing me to think I wasn't gon' ever see you again—or even meet my baby." He stared at her for a beat. Emotions were communicated between them that could never be put into words. Troy tucked a stray strand of hair behind her ear. "I ain't never letting you go. I can't lose you again."

She nodded and grasped his forearms. "You won't. 'Cause I'm not going anywhere. And I wasn't giving up on us. My daddy and MJ weren't trying to tell me nothing. But as soon as I found out this is where you were, I came. You weren't here. Not the first time anyway. That was like, I think . . . "

"Four months ago." They said in unison.

Mia bobbed her head and continued, "Right after that I got so sick. I could barely get out of bed. I told them the moment I felt better I was hopping on the plane. I don't care what my daddy said. I would've kept coming here until I saw you. I'm so sorry they did this to you, Troy. No, to us."

"Baby, don't apologize." He cradled her face in between his palms. "Look at me. This ain't nothing you did. Do you hear me? Nothing. As much as we don't like how this went down, your dad, brother, and cousins did what they was 'posed to when it comes to protecting you. I get it now. God knows Sym, if that's my baby girl you carrying, I'd damn sure do the same thing. Let some punk ass lil' boy put his hands on her."

Mia's eyes widened.

Troy bobbed his head up and down, speaking with conviction. "Hell yeah, I'd fuck his ass up. Look, it's sinking in. A lot of things. I was wrong,

Sym. Dead ass wrong for what I did to you. I said it to you before. If you let me, I'm gonna make this up to you. Will you let me?"

"Yes, of course." She said with a slight nod.

He rubbed the back of his neck. "So, uhh I know we was gonna see a marriage counselor. But one of the things your dad made me do was see somebody about my temper. I've been seeing a therapist, tryna get through some stuff from my past and work on bettering myself."

"Really?"

"Really." Troy splayed his hands to cover her stomach. "I know it's been helping, Sym. I'on ever wanna hurt you again. Not emotionally, and definitely not with my hands. I wanna be the one you can depend on. You deserve love and loyalty. I'mma be the best dad and husband I can be."

Without saying a word, she nodded in agreement while tears rolled down her cheeks.

"I love you so damn much," he admitted, reaching up to swipe them away.

Mia replied through sniffles. "I'm so happy you did it. That's all I wanted . . . for you to get better for us. God, I love you too, Troy. More than anything else in this world."

"For real, you my everything, Sym—my rock, my ride or die. And I swear, things gonna be different."

"You promise?"

"Promise." Troy encircled his arms around her, lowered his head, and angled his mouth over hers, capturing it for another hot, searing kiss. A minute passed before he withdrew from her lips. "Hmm, hold up. How'd you get here?"

"A car service. I have a room at Arya."

"Not anymore you don't. You're coming home with me. We can swing by to get your stuff later."

Troy nuzzled his face into her neck. Mia squirmed and giggled. She gasped when he grabbed an ample amount of her thick ass, lifting her up off the ground. Her breasts bounced in his face. Troy recognized right away they were much fuller than before. His dick tapped against his thigh, alerting him that he could tell too. He squeezed the double bubble, pressing her against his growing erection.

He growled, his lips grazing her neck. "Sym, I need some pussy, real bad."

"And I need some dick, real bad." Mia purred.

Troy lifted his head, grinning. "Say less."

Lowering her to the ground, he whisked her around his truck to the passenger side and opened the door to help her inside. Once she secured herself inside with the seatbelt, Troy went back to get his duffel bag from the ground and threw it onto the backseat. He climbed into the driver seat and pushed the button bringing the engine to life. For a moment, Troy reveled in seeing his wife back at his side. He took his phone out and searched for the playlist they'd made for their road trips. His finger swiped across the display to set up the next few songs in the queue. Right as the opening notes of the first track, "Part II (On the Run)" blasted through the speakers, Troy shifted the Range Rover into drive.

Mia cheered. "You know this is our shit!"

"Oh, I keeps the Bonnie and Clyde playlist in heavy rotation." Troy took her hand and kissed the back of it. "This had to be a test. They just don't know. Ain't nobody getting in between this. Fuh sho' we was gon' find our way back to each other." He let go of her hand and rested his on her thigh, giving it a light squeeze.

She placed her hand on top. "Well, who wants a perfect love story?"

"Not us. 'Cause it's cliché, baby." Troy flashed a big smile and winked at her before focusing on the road.

Despite the afternoon traffic, they made it to the condo in under an hour. Troy held the door open and stepped aside, gesturing for Mia to enter. He then shut it with a kick, taking a moment to appreciate his wife in her form-fitting white jumpsuit, which hugged every curve, accentuating her voluptuous figure. Her sexy walk and the way her heart-shaped ass bounced with each step had his dick jumping for joy. He couldn't wait to get in between her thick thighs. Troy followed her into the living room. Mia was going to sit, but he stopped her.

"Nah uhn, c'mere."

Mia twirled around. A seductive smile danced on her lips while she strutted over to him, slow and sensually. Troy reached out and yanked her close, his hands roaming over her body as he kissed her passionately.

"Sym . . . you have . . . no idea . . . how much . . . I've . . . missed . . . you." He confessed between kisses.

Mia trailed her fingers across his smooth dome. "Hmm, I think I do. But you can show me."

Troy's hands moved to the zipper on the back of her suit, slowly unzipping it. He pushed the top down and over her hips. Once it pooled at her ankles, Mia kicked it off. He descended along her neck while caressing and squeezing her supple curves. She shivered, goosebumps forming under his wet smooches and touch. Troy eased her onto the plush cushions of the sofa.

"You're so beautiful."

Troy let out a groan at the sight of her swollen breasts threatening to spill from the lace black bra. Reaching behind her, he unfastened the hooks. He peeled the garment off, throwing it to the side.

"And so fucking sexy," he rasped, cupping her breasts in his hands. They were heavier and fuller. He latched onto a nipple, sucking it between his lips while he tugged and tweaked the other one.

"Trooooy." Mia whimpered, bowing her back to grant him better access.

He switched sides, giving that breast the same attention. Only when she started writhing against him did he begin his trail of kisses down to her abdomen. He came to a stop, taking a moment to spread his palms over the distended area that was once smooth and flat. Mia put her hands on top of his. Troy peered up at her before planting a kiss there. Her small, rounded belly was a symbol of the life they'd created together. It amplified his desire. His dick throbbed with need. Troy hooked a finger into her panties and ripped them off. Mia gasped. The corners of his mouth curved into a smirk as he drew her to the edge of the couch and settled between her thighs. He inhaled the intoxicating heady scent emanating from her pussy. Her arousal filled his nostrils. He nudged her thighs wider apart to grant him access to her glistening, plump folds.

"Pleeease, Troy. I need you." Mia begged, reaching for him.

Troy murmured against her vertical lips. "Patience, Sym. Can't rush me when I have this delicious plate of food in front of me. I'm gonna take my time eating all of it and lick my plate clean."

Mia clutched the edge of the couch and pushed her hips toward him when his tongue flicked over her clit. He swiped up and down, parting her slit to reveal the pink flesh already starting to cream. Her breathing became ragged while he teased her. He finally dove in, swirling his tongue through her slick heat.

"Oooooh fuck! Troy!" Mia cried out, her back arching off the couch.

Troy latched onto her swollen nub, sucking it between his lips before thrusting two fingers into her channel. She was gloriously wet. Her inner muscles clenched around his digits. He pumped them in a steady rhythm, curling them while nibbling on her clit. Her moans rose in pitch. He delved in some more, scissoring his fingers as he lavished more attention on her button. Mia convulsed uncontrollably, her thighs trembled against his shoulders. What began like a light trickle from a leaky faucet, became a never-ending waterfall.

"I-I-I'm . . . it feels . . . oooh fuck! I'm coming, Troy! I'm coming!"

"That's right, Sym! Come in my mouth!"

Troy went to work on fingerfucking and sucking even harder. He didn't want to come up for air. He wanted to drown in her liquid love. Troy ate her out like a man starved, growling against her flesh. Her pleasure was his. Her release his only goal. Mia shattered around his tongue with a broken cry. Troy gentled his strokes, lapping her through the aftershocks. When Mia rested into the cushions of the couch, Troy raised his head, his lips and chin dripping of her essence. Troy wiped his mouth with the back of his hand, gazing down at Mia's dazed expression with a smug grin. She blinked at him through half-lidded eyes, a blissful smile curling her lips.

"I need your dick . . . now."

Troy didn't need to be told twice. He scooped her into his arms, carrying her upstairs to the master bedroom. He laid her on the plush duvet, and in a hurry, he discarded his clothes. When he climbed onto the bed, hovering over Mia's supple figure, an overwhelming swell of devotion and protectiveness coursed through him, unlike any sentiment he'd ever known. Mia was his soulmate, and he would move heaven and earth to cherish her always.

"You're mine forever, Sym."

Mia reached down between them, gripping his heavy erection and guided him to her velvet prison. They both groaned when he breached her entrance. Troy sank into her tight heat one tantalizing inch at a time. Mia was his personal Eden, the slice of paradise he'd thought lost to him forever. He had to brace against the consuming need to plunge wildly into her depths. She deserved better than a quick fuck after being apart for so long. He wanted to savor this, needed to savor her and make the moment last. Troy gritted his teeth, forcing himself to go slow. Mia's slick walls clenched around him, enveloping his hardness in sublime pressure that made Troy see stars.

"God, you feel so fucking good. This my pussy, Sym?" Troy grunted.

Mia nodded in response. "Mmhmm."

"No. I need to hear you say it. Say it, Sym! Whose . . . pussy . . . is . . . this?"

"Y-y-yours, Troy!" she moaned as he moved, his hips grinding against hers in a rhythm that they only knew the tune to. Her muscles repeatedly contracted around his shaft.

"You're mine, Sym. You hear me? Mine! And you ain't going nowhere!" Troy exclaimed, his thrusts growing more urgent.

"Yes! Yes! Oh god, yes!"

She clung to him, and he continued to pound into her. Her body thrashed about the bed. Troy slipped his hands under her thighs. Mia's legs dangled over his arms. She moved her hands around his neck. His circular hip motion stretched her walls, making room for him. Troy then picked up the pace while angling to hit that sweet spot inside. He gave her what she needed, what they both needed, thrusting deeper and harder. The rich and earthy scent of teakwood mingled with the musky tang of sweat and the aroma of sex, a potent combination that hung heavily in the air. Their harsh breathing and the escalating slaps of skin echoed throughout the room.

Her body bowed. Nails digging into his back, Mia cried out, "There, Troy! Right there! Oh my god, right there! I'm 'bout to come!"

"Me too, Sym. Me too! Here . . . it . . . ahhh ffffuck!"

Closing his eyes, Troy gripped her ass tight. Fireworks exploded in his mind. While he emptied his nuts of hot cum deep inside of Mia, the sensation was so intense it was as though lightning bolts were flashing behind his eyes.

When Troy came down from his orgasmic release, he eased them onto their sides, drawing Mia close to his chest. Their legs remained tangled together, and his dick which had softened, stayed nestled inside her. For a moment, they lay there, their breathing ragged, clinging to each other through the aftershocks, hearts pounding against each other's chests.

Troy whispered against her lips, "I love you so damn much, Sym."

"I love you too, Troy. Always have, always will."

Overwhelmed, Troy crushed his mouth to hers, pouring all his love into a searing, passionate, and sloppy kiss. When they finally broke apart, Mia settled more firmly against him. Within minutes her breathing deepened. She drifted off to a peaceful slumber. Troy stayed awake a bit longer, watching her sleep.

She was finally with him where she belonged. And he'd walk through fire before letting her slip through his fingers again. Troy pressed a kiss to Mia's forehead, closing his eyes.

CHAPTER 12

Mia emerged from the master bathroom and slid back into bed. Troy wrapped his arm around her waist, pulling her close so that they were spooning. His warmth enveloped her, chasing away the chill on her skin. If it hadn't felt like the baby was standing on her bladder earlier, she wouldn't have moved from this comfortable spot. Troy's half-hardened pole pressed against Mia's back. She jutted her ass out in a teasing invitation.

"I missed being with you like this." Troy brushed his lips across her ear.

Mia rolled over to face him. "Me too, especially waking up to *him* poking me."

Even after a long night of passionate lovemaking, they hadn't gotten enough of each other. Mia ran her hand down his sculpted abdomen, exploring the solid ridges of his muscular frame. She grabbed his rigid length and gave it a tug, feeling its weight in her palm. Her fingers glided back and forth along his shaft. Troy let out a grunt, pumping into her grip. His dick jerked at her soft touch, leaking a bead of pre-cum that she swiped away with her thumb.

Mia seductively placed the moist digit in her mouth, enjoying the salty flavor. She then lowered herself until she was face to face with his erection, planting a wet kiss on the engorged mushroom tip. Through half-closed lids, she peered up at him. Troy returned a look that said he wanted more. Mia smiled, encasing every inch within the warmth of her mouth. Her tongue swirled around the helmet while giving him a slow blow, loving every strangled moan he made. His taste was like no other, a unique blend of masculine saltiness that left Mia intoxicated. Their combined scent of musk filled the air around them, mixing with the lingering aroma of sweat from their earlier session.

She sensed the tremors coursing through Troy's body, his face contorting into an intense expression of pleasure. An involuntary gasp escaped when she grabbed his shaft, her fingers sinking just a little into the heated flesh. His enjoyment fueled her desire to take it further. With a glint in her eye, she opened wider to accommodate his girth. She focused on creating a vacuum, applying more pressure. Mia's throat muscles relaxed, allowing her to take in more of him, feeling the forceful pulse of his arousal with each heartbeat.

Troy hissed, gripping a handful of her hair. "Shhhit, baby! You 'bout to pull this nut outta me."

"Mmhmm," she murmured around his blooming helmet.

Mia bobbed her head up and down, working her jaws to earn every ounce of the cum building up in his balls. She knew he was on the brink of coming. With tender care, Mia massaged them, squeezing while she suctioned as hard as she could. Seconds later, his muscular frame went taut. His dick swelled in size. Mia squeezed his nut sack. She noticed his eyes rolling back as the massive muscle twitched against her cheeks. He was about to unload inside her eager throat. Mia came off his dick to catch the first few spurts of his thick cream before resuming her bobbing. Troy's hips bucked against her face. He tangled his fingers in her hair, growling with pure satisfaction.

"Ahh fuck, Sym. This shit feels so good."

The room reverberated with Troy's heavy breaths and the audible slurps as Mia continued, devouring him whole, taking in every rope of nut he shot into her throat. When it seemed like there was no more cum left,

Mia slowed down, enjoying every last drop of his seed before licking him clean. She peered up and Troy smirked. Then, in an effortless move, he switched positions.

"Now, I need some pussy too."

Mia's giggles turned into a series of low moans as Troy's lips traveled from her neck to her breasts, leaving a trail of wet kisses and gentle bites. His calloused palms glided over her skin, his index fingers and thumbs tweaking her nipples. Troy took his time, teasing the peaks until they were taut. Mia shivered, arching into his touch with a soft purr. Leaning in, his tongue traced moist circles around her brown-tipped areolas.

"You like how that feels."

"Mmhmm . . . yesss."

He dipped his head. His pillowy kissers continued their downward journey, pressing a tender smooch to the rounded swell of her belly. By the time he settled between her thighs, Mia was writhing against the sheets, her pussy weeping with need. Troy slipped a hand between them, rubbing her clit with firm circular motions.

"You gon' come for me, baby."

Mia pushed her mound closer to his face. He removed his thumb and latched onto the protruding, sensitive nub, alternating between sucking and licking. His long, slick tongue plunged into her steamy heat, swirling around her meaty walls. Troy spread her vertical lips and commenced devouring Mia. Pleasure rocketed through her. The orgasm hit like a freight train. Mia screamed, her back bowing off the bed.

"Oh . . . my . . . Trrrrroy!"

While still in the throes of her climax, he prowled up her body. Troy supported his weight on his forearms, gazing down at her. He nudged her trembling thighs wider apart using his own muscular ones. Reaching between their entwined bodies, he gripped his thick, veined shaft. He teased her opening with the swole mushroom head, positioning himself to slide inside her heated depths. With a gradual and deliberate push, he eased inside, eliciting sighs of satisfaction from them both. She felt full and stretched around him, her pussy gripping him tight. Mia's lips parted in a low moan as their gazes locked. His hands found hers and he laced their fingers together, holding on as he took control of the pace. It felt so good to be dominated by him like this. Mia felt cherished and desired all at once. Out of nowhere Troy shook his head.

"I'on deserve you, Sym."

"Yes! Yes! Yes, you . . . doooo! It-it . . . oooh . . . feels so gooood! Harder, Troy! Harder!"

They maintained eye contact as Troy withdrew until only the tip remained inside. He threw her legs over his shoulders and then like a piston sliding into well-oiled machinery, he plunged in, making her cry out. Troy rotated from left to right. His hips slapped against her ass cheeks with each push inward, making a sloshing sound that echoed in the room. The headboard banged against the wall with their rhythm, creating a steady beat that matched their hearts' pounding. Her moans rose in pitch, and her thighs trembled against his shoulders.

Troy huskily whispered. "Damn Sym. You so fucking sexy. I love seeing you like this."

"Oh my god, Troy! I-I-I'm . . . 'bout to . . . ooooh fuck!"

Leaning in, he pressed her knees up toward her ears. She noticed Troy's gaze fixed on her as he continued thrusting. In and out. In and out. Mia tossed her head from side to side on the pillow. His strong hands clamped onto her calves, plunging so deep making Mia feel as though he tapped against their baby's sac.

"Owww!"

"Sorry baby. But you said harder. You got a greedy pussy. And you doing that trick . . . ahhh shit! It's so fucking juicy. Wet this fucking bed up then!"

Mia's toes curled, and warm, gushy liquid spurted with each stroke Troy delivered. He groaned, thrusting wildly while her vaginal muscles spasmed repeatedly around his dick, milking his own orgasm from him. Troy stiffened and then jerked hard, letting out a loud roar of satisfaction. "Arrrgh!"

They clung to each other during the aftershocks, their chests rising and falling with heavy breaths. When their breathing calmed down, they separated, and Troy lay on his back, taking in deep breaths. Mia's long, black tresses cascaded across his tattooed chest.

"Mmm, can we stay like this forever please?" She asked, snuggling closer to him.

"Hell yeah. I told you, I ain't never letting you go again."

Mia smiled, her hand reaching up to cup Troy's cheek.

"Hey, remember when we first met?" a lopsided grin played on his lips.

Mia's eyes lit up with amusement, and then she laughed aloud. "How could I forget those cheesy pickup lines?"

"But didn't I pull the baddest and most beautiful woman in the room?" Troy boasted, winking at her.

Their intimate moment was cut short when Mia's phone rang. She eased out of Troy's arms and moved to sit up on the edge of the bed. Mia grabbed her cell from the nightstand and grumbled seeing the display but answered it anyway. "Daddy?"

"Where are you?"

"I'm uhh . . . out. Why?"

"Out where?" Maxwell demanded.

She glanced back at Troy. "I'm busy right now, Daddy. Can we talk later?"

"No. We need to talk now. And you don't have to tell me where you are. I thought I told you to stay away from him, and yet you defied me. Why would you—"

"I love him, Daddy. And I'm not leaving him. Period."

Maxwell scoffed. "Love? That doesn't excuse violence and infidelity. I tell you what, forget Roscoe and DaeDae. If you don't leave, I'm sending Kieran, Aidan, Brendan and Niall to handle him this time."

Her blood ran hot at the mention of Nigel's sons. "I don't believe you. Really, Daddy? You'd send them crazy muthafuckas?"

"For my daughter? Yeah."

"Do you really wanna go there with me, Daddy? If they so much as lay one finger on my husband, that'll be the day your luck runs out," Mia warned.

There was a tense silence on the other end of the line, and for a moment, Mia thought her father had hung up. But then he spoke, his voice sounding defeated.

"Who am I kidding? You're just as stubborn as I am. MJ said your mind was made up months ago. Dammit, Bug, I'm your father. The first man in your life to love you. And I thought you loved."

"You are, Daddy. But this man I'm lying next to . . . he's my family now. And I have enough love for the both of you."

"I just don't want to see you get hurt in any way."

"I know and I appreciate your concern, Daddy. For real, I really do. But can me and Troy will get through this our way, together and without outsiders. Just trust me to do this, please."

"Fine." Maxwell said, resigned. "But I'm not making a promise to you that I won't handle it my way if I hear about him touching you again. Remember that I only want the best for you. I love you, Ladybug."

Mia swallowed the lump rising in her throat. "Okay, and I love you too, Daddy."

She hung up the phone feeling emotionally drained. But at the same time, she felt proud of herself for standing up to her dad and asserting her independence. Mia scooted back on the bed and leaned back on the propped-up pillows.

"He's just looking out for you." Troy lowered his gaze and placed a protective hand on her belly.

Mia put her palms over his. "I know. But I need to make my own choices. And I believe in us, Troy. I really do."

Troy brought his eyes up to meet hers. He reached up, brushing a lock of hair away from her face. "Me too. We're a team, Sym. And I'mma do whatever it takes to make this work. For you. For our baby. For us."

"I know you are. And I love you so much for that."

Mia smiled, feeling a sense of hope wash over her. Everything wasn't perfect—far from it, in fact—but she knew that they could face whatever came their way as long as they had each other.

CHAPTER 13

It was the week following a home game. Troy had another meeting scheduled with Dr. Warren, but today was different. This time, Mia was joining him for their first marital counseling session. As Mia made herself comfortable in the plush chair next to Troy, she stole a quick glance at him. Troy had just finished sharing his thoughts on their marriage, and Dr. Warren encouraged Mia to give her perspective. Troy remained silent and attentive while Mia described how their once-passionate love had decayed into an emotionless indifference, and their strong communication had corroded into painful silence. Where mutual understanding used to live, distrust and resentment occupied the space like unwelcome guests. Mia articulated the grief she felt watching their bond unravel leaving them isolated rather than the united front they used to be.

"The Troy that I married was gone. I knew how much football meant to him. Not playing cast a dark cloud over him. No more being goofy, laughing, or having fun. This version of him was depressed and always so angry. I tried everything to bring some light into his world. But no matter what I did, he just wasn't happy. I'm sure you can imagine how pissed I was when his mama, Ms. Brenda, called spewing her negativity. He doesn't know this, but I overheard everything she said to him. She told

Troy that he better hope his knee healed because if it didn't, his looks and his . . . well, what's between his legs wasn't going to pay the bills. And if he even thought about coming to her house, he would have to get rid of his bougie, gold-digging wife."

Mia's eyes bore into him. Troy averted his gaze to the other side of the room. He had no idea that she'd overheard Brenda's angry tirade that day. He'd been in his office with the speakerphone on, but he assumed Mia was in her own workspace. Troy lowered his head, shrinking down in his chair as she continued.

"Anyway, after her call things only got worse. He started drinking more and coming in later. One night he was so drunk, he passed out. Thankfully, I made it downstairs before he started choking on his vomit. When I took off his clothes, I found a gold card in his pocket." She paused for a moment and twisted her head to look at him.

Troy felt in his gut what she was about to say. Once again, he didn't make eye contact, unable to meet her penetrative stare.

Mia snorted. Her words were thick with sarcasm. "Instead of being at home with me living out his fantasies, he was up at Club Infinity, my daddy's and brother's playhouse of hoes. When I confronted him about it, we got into an argument. He backhanded me and walked away like it was okay. Troy knows I have hands. We fought. Well, until I picked up this sculpture from the sofa table and knocked him out. That was the first time and the beginning of it all. Troy would be slapping, pushing, or choking me, or I would be doing the same. Yeah, I would fight him, especially if I heard rumors about him cheating on me. It was like that for a while with us, the fighting. Until I couldn't take it anymore. I got tired, Dr. Warren. I was tired of the disrespect. It's not what I wanted our marriage to be. We were so good before his knee injury. He told me he didn't hate me, but I couldn't tell anymore when all we did was fight."

Mia's sobs echoed in the small suite. Troy flinched at the anguished sounds, but he didn't move. He couldn't. Paralyzed by guilt, he sat helpless as his wife's words told the story of their marriage with him as the villain. There was no denying he'd done the unthinkable to his wife. Perhaps there was some truth in Brenda's harsh condemnations. His apologies wouldn't take it back. Troy kept his head bowed in shame. With a sympathetic murmur, Dr. Warren plucked a few tissues from the box on his desk and held them out to Mia's trembling, outstretched hands. She accepted the offering, dabbing at her reddened eyes and blotchy cheeks.

Her voice was barely above a whisper. "Thank you."

"No, thank you for sharing that. I know it isn't easy for you to relive any of those hurtful moments. But it's therapeutic to release and let the other person know they've wronged you." Without letting Troy off the hot seat, Dr. Warren posed another question to her. "Mia, is there anything you would like to ask Troy? It can be anything that you need clarity on moving forward in repairing your marriage."

"How did things change between us? And why did *I* become your punching bag? I was there with you every step of the way to get you back on your feet. Why was I the one you took everything out on?"

Troy squirmed in his chair, his eyes darting around the room as he struggled to find the right words. He could feel her gaze on him, burning into his skin. Admitting defeat, he shrugged his shoulders and shook his head, unable to come up with a satisfactory answer.

Mia continued with a firestorm of new questions. "Why did you do it? Why did you cheat on me? And in our house! You brought her to our house! How could you?"

Troy let out a frustrated sigh, his shoulders slumping. "I'on know, Sym, okay? It was stupid. I was stupid."

"I thought you were happy with me. Wasn't I enough?"

He finally looked up and his words tumbled out. "Yes! Of course you were, baby. You've always been enough. It was just . . . it's just . . . I-I . . . I'on know."

He did know. Troy couldn't articulate his truth: he'd been seeking power and validation through his infidelity. He was trying to prove something to himself and others. He'd been emulating the men who always used violence and control to get what they wanted from Brenda.

Dr. Warren's tone was gentle but firm. "Okay, let's try a different approach. Troy, we've talked about this. You owe it to yourself and Mia to be honest."

"Aight."

"I want you to think about this for a moment before you answer. What happened in your past that impacts how you perceive relationships?"

Troy hesitated, unsure if he could handle the rush of memories that would surely come flooding back. Part of him wanted to confront them, while another part wanted to bury them and forget. But he knew he couldn't keep running from his past forever.

His breathing became shallow as he closed his eyes. He remembered the fear and helplessness of watching Brenda endure endless abuse from different boyfriends. Even though he was just a kid, Troy tried to protect her, but he often became a target of her aggression. Discovering later on that Brenda was a teen mother, Troy realized she'd been through a lot in her young life, both mentally and physically. She always seemed lost in her own chaotic thoughts and emotions. Her detachment from him was like a heavy weight that caused more pain than the physical injuries he'd sustained. Then there was Pam, Brenda's first cousin, the woman who'd taken advantage of him.

Pam's behavior greatly influenced Troy's growth and development into adulthood. He resented her manipulation, but also felt grateful for Pam's presence as a substitute mother in Brenda's absence. Troy battled between the two conflicting emotions and how they shaped his sense of self. He wondered if things would have been different without Pam in his life. Troy opened his eyes.

He took his time to get the words out. "Brenda always blamed me for why my dad didn't wanna be there no more. Never understood why 'cause he said that was all on her. Anyway, every time one of her boyfriends would beat her up, she would do the same to me. She'd tell me to quit being weak, man up and take it like she did. Funny thing. After a while I didn't cry no more. I started knocking them out when they put their hands on her. But that didn't stop Brenda from hitting me once they left. No appreciation for me keeping them from beating her to within an inch of her life. Nah, 'cause according to her, I made another man walk out on her. Then she knew her cousin, Pam—" his words faltered. His eyes went to Dr. Warren, who nodded, coaxing him to continue.

That was when the first one fell. Troy tried to wipe his face. But more tears rolled down his cheeks as he struggled to speak, "Pam, uhh . . . well, umm . . . she-she was touching me. I think I might've been thirteen or maybe fourteen when it started. She said I wasn't like the other boys my age since I was tall for my age and built like my dad. I was her special boy, and she would treat me like the man I would become."

"Oh my god, Troy." Mia gasped, covering her mouth.

The way she looked made him feel ashamed and dirty all over again. He never wanted anyone to know what Pam did to him especially after Brenda's warning. Troy kept it to himself. He could see the condemnation behind Mia's shocked expression.

She's judging me. Troy let his head drop. He fixated on her French tip stiletto nails.

"I'm so sorry that happened to you, sweetheart." Mia grabbed his hand, squeezing it tight. "But it's nothing to be ashamed of. It was wrong of her to prey on a little boy."

What about when I became an adult? Pam pumped up his ego by hinting that he would have women chasing after him with an NFL career, handsome looks, and a big dick. Troy battled with the fact that he gradually grew to love what they were doing, even though he knew it was wrong.

"Go ahead. Continue, Troy." Dr. Warren encouraged.

Filling his lungs with oxygen, Troy raised his gaze to meet Dr. Warren's and started speaking.

"Pam did all kinds of stuff to me and showed me things to do to her. This went on until I left Boston. Brenda knew. She told me not to tell nobody. She said if I did say something, everybody would think I was gay 'cause what boy wouldn't want Pam? Told me to consider it a rite of passage. But I knew it was wrong. And I was mad at myself. Mad at Brenda. Mad at Pam. So fucking mad all the time." Troy finally turned his attention to Mia. "Then I kept hurting the one person I love most in this world when I got mad 'cause shit got hard for me. I took advantage of what we had. I swear I didn't mean to, Sym. It's just I'on know how else to deal with all this I got bottled up in me."

Dr. Warren spoke sympathetically. "But you can't keep using your anger as an excuse. You have to learn to deal with conflict and challenges in a healthier way."

"I know, Doc."

Mia rubbed his shoulder, her touch gentle and reassuring. Troy knew he didn't deserve her forgiveness, but he was grateful for it, nonetheless.

"Okay, this was good." Dr. Warren clasped his hands together, his gaze moving between them. "Now, before we finish up, I want to remind both of you about the importance of ongoing communication and support. This isn't going to be an easy road, but as long as you're both willing to put in the work, I have faith that you can make it through."

Troy bobbed in acknowledgment, a sense of determination washing over him. He stood up, offering Mia his hand. "Thanks, Doc. We'll see you next week."

Troy and Mia exited Dr. Warren's office, their bodies lightly touching as they strolled down the hallway.

"Damn, that was intense, huh?" Troy mumbled, running a hand over his bald head.

"Yeah, it was. But we needed it."

They made their way out of the building and to the parking lot. The bright rays of the sun pierced through the tall buildings, casting harsh light and long shadows across the concrete pavement. The sound of cars zipped by on the busy street, leaving behind trails of exhaust fumes. Unaware of what lay ahead, Troy felt confident in their ability to overcome it together. Their love was unstoppable.

Troy reached out and took Mia's hand, giving it a squeeze. "Hey, I meant what I said in there. You're the Bonnie to my Clyde, Sym. You and me, we're in this together."

She peered up at him and nodded with a small smile. "I know. And this ain't no perfect love story."

CHAPTER 14

Other than the fifteen minutes it took to figure out what they would have for dinner, the ride from Dr. Warren's office was mostly quiet. Mia fidgeted behind Troy while he unlocked the door to the condo. She couldn't wait to begin their house hunt next week. She was craving a new project to lavishly design and embellish. Her hands twitched, restless for the chance to transform the mundane spaces into opulent oases that reflected her creative vision. Troy stepped aside so she could enter first. Mia placed her Chanel purse on the console table and made a dash for the bathroom. The pressure on her bladder had been unrelenting. When she emerged a few minutes later, Mia found Troy sprawled out on the sofa, his legs extended and crossed at the ankles. He'd just taken a deep swig from his protein shake. Her gaze drifted over his athletic frame before shifting to the coffee table.

"Thanks, babe."

Mia went for the tall bottle of coconut water, feeling the condensation on the label. She plopped down next to him, fluffing the pillows for extra comfort.

"You really like that stuff now, huh?"

With a smile, she took a long sip of the chilling, invigorating beverage before answering. "Mmhmm. It's so good." Mia twisted the cap back on, set the container on the coaster and tucked her feet underneath her butt. "Your baby kept me from eating. But that stuff right there kept me hydrated. Now I can't get enough of it."

"Then I'mma make sure we keep a supply of 'em."

"Good. And while I was in the bathroom, I went ahead with ordering dinner. It should be here within the hour."

"I figured your greedy ass was in there doing that or talking on the phone." He chuckled, sitting up straight and inching closer to her.

Troy's calloused hands slipped under her dress and caressed her growing baby bump. His fingers traced the curves of the pudge. He'd been doing it every day since she arrived. Mia closed her eyes momentarily, loving the sensation of his touch. When the rubbing motion stilled, her lashes fluttered open, and she studied him for a few seconds. The furrow between his brows smoothed out when he released a heavy sigh, the quietness of the moment enveloping them both. She spied the faint wrinkle lingering on his forehead, evidence he remained lost in his thoughts. Mia punctured the wordless void between them by giving his arm a gentle tap.

"Hey, are you okay?"

Troy looked up at her. Other than the day he thought he'd never play football again, Mia had never seen such sadness in her husband's eyes.

"Yeah. I'm straight."

"But babe, like you said, today was intense."

"Yeah. I know."

"And remember Dr. Warren advised us about the importance of ongoing communication and support. Both of us have to be willing to put in the work, right?"

"Right." Troy repeated with a nod.

With determined eyes narrowed into thin slits, Mia stated, "I know you better than you think. You're not straight."

The air hung heavy with unease, each second feeling longer than the last. Finally, Troy released a long, shaky breath.

"I'on know, Sym. This shit is . . . it's embarrassing as fuck. Doc says I shouldn't feel like this, but I can't help it. Then the way you looked at me when I told you what happened. You know, with Pam. And I know what you said but ... "

Troy's shoulders sagged, and his head drooped, chin nearly touching his chest. Mia's heart clenched with a pang of sadness, realizing his innocence had been destroyed by his own family.

In a drunken stupor one evening, Troy claimed Brenda should've never won sole custody of him. He didn't know the ugly specifics of the custody battle between his dad and Brenda, which ultimately resulted in her gaining full guardianship. However, he kept insisting she was an incompetent and unfit parent. The traumatic experiences he'd endured would leave lasting scars on any child. The pain and suffering inflicted upon Troy were unfathomable for someone so young. Papa Mike tried to intercede by trying to spend lots of time with Troy and remove him from the situation, but his efforts couldn't outweigh Brenda's cruel mistreatment.

Mia closed the distance between them, her fingertips grazing the coarse stubble along his jaw when she cradled his face. With a gentle nudge, she raised Troy's chin and waited until his sorrowful eyes found hers.

"Troy, listen to me. There's nothing to be embarrassed about. I'm sorry if the way I reacted made you feel some kinda way. I was in shock. That's all. You didn't do anything wrong. Now, your cousin, Pam. She was older. She knew better, but she still took advantage of you. I knew I didn't like that heffa for a reason. The way she would hug on you was always sus. I wonder if your other aunts knew."

"Aunts? I ain't never meet nobody else from Brenda's side 'cept Pam."

"What about those ladies at our wedding? At least two of them claimed to be your aunt, and there were those guys who said they were your cousins."

"They ain't my real family, Sym. Them Brenda's peoples from 'round the way. You know how we grow up with people and call 'em our play cousins." Troy formed exaggerated air quotes with his fingers and clicked his tongue against the roof of his mouth, swaying his head back and forth.

"I'on even fuck with half of them muthafuckas no more. The people there for me was my dad, Mama Krys, my brothers, and my sister. Oh yeah, and you know D and his family."

"Figures. And she has the audacity to call me a gold digger. All Brenda's ever cared about is your money. Meanwhile, her cousin was taking advantage of you!"

He pulled away, rejecting her words with a nonchalant shrug. "But what about when I started liking it?" Troy didn't look at her. He gazed straight ahead as he confessed, "I kept fucking her 'cause I wanted to. Nah, I loved that shit. It felt good. What does that say 'bout me now, Sym?" He turned to her with a pained expression that tore at Mia's heart.

She linked her dainty fingers through the gaps of his larger, solid hands, intertwining their palms together. Mia clung to Troy with all her might, hoping to express her feelings through this simple physical connection.

"It says you were an innocent boy who adapted to a situation beyond his control. Babe, have you ever heard of grooming? Did Dr. Warren ever bring it up during your sessions?"

His eyebrows slammed together in confusion. "Nah. What's that?"

This conversation would be like navigating a minefield. Mia knew she needed to approach him with sensitivity and empathy, while carefully leading him to confront the painful truth of his past. Sensing his grip tighten, Mia became more cautious about choosing her next words. She cleared her throat and began.

"Plain and simple, grooming is when an adult develops a relationship with a child to exploit and harm them. Pam was priming you for her ultimate endgame." Mia paused for a split second and thought about what Troy shared in Dr. Warren's office.

I was her special boy, and she would treat me like the man I would become.

She probed further, "When Pam said that you were her special boy, how did she treat you?"

Troy extricated a hand from her grasp and rubbed his smooth dome, heaving out a deep breath, his cheeks deflating like a popped balloon.

"Better than Brenda that's for damn sure. She was always too busy up in some nigga's face to worry about me. Pam did all the stuff a mother would."

A mother wouldn't be fucking on her son! Mia raised a curious brow but used a gentle tone coaxing Troy to continue. "Stuff like what?"

"Since Brenda wasn't 'round much, Pam made sure I had home cooked meals every day. She taught me about body hygiene, checking me on washing my ass and sweaty balls. She took me to school and helped me with my homework. I always rocked the freshest gear and the latest kicks 'cause she started buying all my clothes. Pam said I should look like the money I was gon' make one day. And she never missed a game. Instead of Brenda, it was Pam who showed me what it felt like to be loved, like a mother would. Stuff like that."

"You were a child who needed nurturing, Troy. She knew that. It would make sense that she manipulated you into trusting her."

Troy stiffened, his broad shoulders tensing as if bracing for impact. Mia noted the subtle shift in his strong frame and knew they'd dredged up painful memories, awakening feelings he'd likely tried to bury. She nodded in understanding, encouraging Troy to keep going. His eyes grew glassy when he spoke.

"I thought she cared for me in a way Brenda never could. But then it was confusing as fuck by what she started doing." His voice cracked with emotion. He averted his gaze. Humiliation and shame clearly visible on his face. "I guess I can see how it was all part of her plan," he finally admitted with a sigh.

Mia reached out a hand to Troy, offering him comfort in his moment of vulnerability. "Babe, it was natural for you to have an emotional connection with her."

His mind had wandered somewhere else. Mia could see the distant look in his gaze. He was lost in memories, transported to a different place and time. When he spoke, his forehead furrowed with deep lines.

"I remember the day Pam came to stay with us. My dad had just dropped me off. We walked in on Brenda smoking weed with Pam. Of course, that pissed him off. While him and Brenda was outside arguing,

Pam introduced herself. Like I said, I ain't never meet nobody else from their side of the family. I think I told you Brenda's mama threw her out after she got pregnant with Mikey."

"Yeah, you did." Mia nodded.

Troy pressed on, rocking his head from side to side. "All I know is, them Johnsons is dysfunctional as fuck. Glad she kept the rest of them muthafuckas from 'round me. Anyway, after my dad left, Pam started teasing Brenda. She said Brenda must've hated my dad's guts when she was pregnant, 'cause he was the one that spit me out. Why Brenda gon' say my big lanky ass was hung like him too? What mother would tell another woman 'bout her son's dick? Brenda, that's who. While her crazy ass had the nerve to be laughing 'bout it, Pam had her tongue out, giving me a thirsty look."

Mia's jaw dropped but she quickly pressed her lips together. She didn't want him to mistake her shock for judgment. Obviously unaware of her stunned reaction, Troy carried on, pouring out his confession.

"So, Pam got settled in. Everything was cool that first year. She took care of me while Brenda was being Thotiana on her hot girl summer shit. And then my birthday came rolling round. Pam talked to her 'bout it, but Brenda said she wasn't doing nothing. She made plans to go outta town with whatever nigga she was dealing with at the time. No sweat 'cause Pam already had everything planned. She took me, D and a couple of my other teammates to Six Flags. Then we went to Sully's for burgers and ice cream. After she dropped everybody off, I was still hyped 'bout the day. When we got home, I took my shower and came out the bathroom with just a towel on. I wasn't thinking nothing of it. I was running my mouth 'bout everything we did. Pam walked up to me and snatched the towel off . . ."

Troy paused. His eyes met hers. The corners of his mouth turned down slightly in contemplation.

Mia observed him gnawing his bottom lip, fully engrossed in his memories. "Babe?" She called out, trying to bring him back to the present moment. When he focused on her again, Mia gave him a small nod of encouragement, urging him to keep going.

Troy fidgeted with his hands while he recounted how Pam had taken his virginity on the night of his fourteenth birthday. He further divulged that a year later even after Brenda had come home early from a date and caught them in the act, Pam persisted in exploiting him.

Mia shook her head disapprovingly. "As a mother, I can't believe she was okay with that shit."

Troy bobbed his head in agreement. "They argued about it. But Pam didn't apologize for what she did. She told Brenda stop acting like they ain't never fucked their cousins too."

"What? Oh my god!"

"I told you, Sym. Them Johnsons is dysfunctional as fuck."

"No, Troy, that's just messed up on so many levels." Mia let out a frustrated sigh, running a hand through her hair. "How can someone say something like that? It's sick."

Troy leaned in closer. "Well, it didn't end there. Would you believe she was messing around with my uncle too?"

"Who?"

"Pam. She got with my dad's younger brother, Anthony, Uncle Ant. I found out before him and Brenda broke up, they all used to double date and stuff. They thought they was the shit for getting with the baddest cousins in OG. That's Orchid Gardens, them projects where Brenda and Pam used to live. Anyway, I was ear hustling on a conversation between my dad and Uncle Ant. Why was Pam fucking on both of us at the same time."

"Unbelievable. I don't know who's worse, Brenda or Pam. Neither one of them should've been around you."

"I know. But did I ever tell you what happened with Brenda and my dad? Why she's so mad about my relationship with him and Mama Krys?"

Other than the obvious that he was the better parent, Mia had no idea. She shook her head.

"It has everything to do with my brother Mikey."

"Well, I know they don't get along."

"Yeah, true. But I never told you this. He ain't my dad's son."

Mia's jaw dropped. Her eyes wide with surprise. Her brain couldn't catch up. Did she hear him correctly? The oldest brother she thought was also his dad's son wasn't. She grappled for the right words to articulate her shock, but they eluded her. Mia wasn't sure if she could handle any more shocking news, but she was just too curious. She maintained composure and asked, "Then who is Mikey's dad? The way he is with y'all it would appear he's Papa Mike's son too. Mama Krys even treats y'all as if y'all were her own. Oh yeah, I guess that's why. But does Brenda even know who his dad is?"

"Of course, her ass knows. And my dad and Mama Krys wouldn't ever treat him any different. Yeah, that's why Brenda stays mad. My dad loves Mikey. He thought that he was his son for almost two years. Brenda wasn't gon' tell my dad the truth and give up her meal ticket. But anyway, Mikey's real dad was some guy that lived right up the block. She had 'em all fooled. My dad fell for her lies while she was out thottin' and boppin'. He wanted to be a family but deaded that idea once he found out, and especially after dude made a scene to get his son. After that, they fought all the time. He told her she was for the streets, her and Pam too, for that matter."

Right at that moment the doorbell rang.

"That would be our dinner."

"Damn, I forgot we ordered."

Mia rubbed her stomach. "Not me. Your baby is hungry. It's time to feed us."

"I got something else I can put in your belly."

With a roguish grin spreading across his face, Troy rose from the sofa, bringing her up with him. Mia eagerly pressed her body against his, locking her legs around his waist, and holding onto his broad shoulders for support. Their bodies fit together like puzzle pieces, and she let out a satisfied sigh as he held her tight in his embrace. She could feel the heat of his breath on her neck and the hardness of his erection through his jeans, pushing against her ass.

"Troy! You've been tapping our baby on top of their head almost every night since I got here. Gimme a break so I can eat. Feed me now and fuck me later."

"How about I fuck you so good and then I feed you after?"

Mia let out a carefree giggle while Troy carried her to the front door. He gently set her down before opening it for the delivery person. While Troy signed the receipt, Mia sauntered off to the kitchen to get their dinner unpacked. By the time she opened the first sack, Troy's voice boomed through the space.

"Sym, I mean it! You giving me some pussy first, and then we eating." He yelled from the living room.

When Troy entered the kitchen, Mia froze mid-chew, her cheeks puffed out around a massive mouthful of eggroll. She held up a hand as he advanced steadily, backing her against the imposing marble island.

"You just couldn't help yourself?"

"Babe, I-I umm—"

"You what?"

Mia swallowed and smiled big. "Mmm . . . yum!"

"Yeah, it's about to be yum aight."

"Troy! What're you? Oh shh—"

He bent his knees, cupping her ass in his large hands, and lifted her effortlessly off the floor. With care, Troy placed her onto the cool, smooth countertop that was clear of the bags of their dinner. He pushed her summer dress up over her hips, exposing her now soaked thong. Gripping the delicate lace material, he tore it off her body in one quick motion. Troy snaked his muscular arms under her thighs, sliding Mia to the edge.

"I can't have my main course without an appetizer too." Troy's smoldering gaze locked on hers, his eyes darkening with desire as he inclined his head. Flaring his nostrils, he inhaled before a ravenous rumble left his throat. He moistened his lips. "It smells delicious down here. And it's been marinating. I want 'Sym Sum' tonight."

Mia quivered under his predatory stare, her nails digging into his toned forearms. Rocking her hips in invitation, she panted out in a desperate plea. "Then sate your hunger, babe. And indulge in me."

Like a savage, Troy dove into her pussy, eagerly licking and slurping, as if he wasn't going to eat actual food in a few minutes. He latched on to her clit, sucking hard and causing Mia to let out a needy moan. His strong fingers gripped her trembling thighs, spreading them wide for better access. Troy flattened his gifted tongue on her button, swirling and flicking it around with precision before moving to the crack of her ass to repeat the same actions. Mia's stomach caved in, her core clenching. She released his arms and instead held onto his clean-shaven head.

"Pleeease . . . Troy. Don't stop." Mia pleaded, digging into his scalp as he continued his assault on her sensitive bud.

Troy paused for a moment and peered up at her with a hairy chin dripping, glistening of her essence. He murmured, his breath hot against her wet flesh, "I'm draining you of all the 'Sym Sum' you got in here."

Troy's tongue darted out, circling and probing inside until Mia thought she couldn't take any more. As if sensing her nearing climax, he pulled back slightly, only to plunge deep inside her once again.

"That feels so good. I-I . . . need more."

Troy straightened his back, positioned himself at her entrance and penetrated her slick channel in one swift movement. Mia gasped at the intensity of the feeling. She clung to Troy, wrapping her legs around his waist as he began to thrust into her. Their rhythm became faster and more frenzied, the air around them thick with the scent of sweat and desire. Troy's mouth found her neck, sucking and nipping at her flesh as he drove deeper and deeper.

Troy groaned against her throat, "Just like a glove . . . fucking tight. You always feel so good around my dick."

"Fuck, yes! Hmm, that's it, Troy. That's it!"

Troy slid his hands down to grip her ass, pulling her closer as he pistoned his hips forward. Mia's breaths were jagged, and her chest rose and fell rapidly as she trembled beneath him, her inner walls gripping him. With a guttural cry, Troy's body went taut while his dick pulsed inside, filling her with his hot cum.

After a while he withdrew from her dripping sex. But he didn't want her moving. Instead, Troy insisted on cleaning them both thoroughly. Next, he reheated their dinner and brought it to the living room along with their drinks. He even set up the TV for them to watch their new favorite show on Netflix, *Lucifer*. As she took a bite from an eggroll, she couldn't help smiling. The day had started out tense, but Mia knew that their commitment to healing and to each other meant things were going to get better for them. Her gaze drifted over, connecting with Troy's. He gathered her into his arms and pressed his lips on her forehead.

"I love you, Sym."

"I love you too, Troy."

CHAPTER 15

The sun beat down on the football stadium, casting its harsh rays on the players as they began their pregame warmup. Troy felt the warmth against his skin as he stretched his arms. The atmosphere was bursting with energy; fans dressed in black and silver were shouting and holding banners, ready for the game to start. He looked around at his teammates, Speedy and Romeo among them, their faces set with determination.

"Aight, boys," Troy called out, clapping his hands together. "Let's show 'em what we're made of!"

As the game kicked off, the Raiders' prowess was evident from the start. Their offensive line bulldozed through the opposing team's defense, creating ample space for Speedy to sprint downfield. Troy, always the charismatic leader, motivated his teammates with loud cheers and high fives, his own adrenaline pumping, as he'd already scored one touchdown with perfect execution.

"Okay I see you, Speedy!" Troy shouted, after Shawn intercepted a desperate pass from the opposing quarterback and scored. The crowd roared in approval, sensing the Raiders' dominance. At the half, the scoreboard displayed 21-7 with the Raiders in the lead.

However, as the second quarter of the game unfolded, the pendulum of momentum began to swing in their opponents' favor. Troy could feel the shifting tide as their previously struggling adversaries found their footing and started clawing their way back into the game. The stadium's atmosphere grew increasingly tense. The once jubilant cheers of the Raiders, fans were now replaced with anxious murmurs and sporadic bursts of encouragement.

"Come on! We can't let 'em take this from us!" Troy shouted, his voice almost hoarse from exertion. His teammates nodded, sweat pouring down their faces.

"Watch your blindside, Troy!" Romeo warned, just as an opposing linebacker charged towards Troy. He barely managed to sidestep the tackle, feeling the rush of air as the player narrowly missed him. The crowd gasped, sensing the precariousness of the situation.

"Damn, that was close," Troy muttered under his breath, his heart pounding in his chest.

Romeo pointed to his helmet. "Focus, man! We've got one last shot at this."

Troy nodded, preparing himself for the final moments of the game. The scoreboard showed the Raiders trailing by two points, leaving them with just one chance to either tie or win. "Let's do this," he shouted. As the huddle broke, Troy took his position, ready for the crucial play.

"Green 19, green 19 set hut!" Romeo barked out the cadence, his teammates springing into action. The ball was snapped, and he dropped back, scanning the field for an open receiver.

Troy held his hand up as he ran into his position the way they'd practiced all week. Out the corner of his eye, he spotted Shawn cutting across the field. Romeo launched the ball in Troy's direction.

"Come on, come on," he whispered, leaping into the air and stretching out his arms to make the catch. Unfortunately, the ball slipped through his fingers, bouncing onto the turf below.

"Damn it!" Knowing that their last chance in the game had just vanished before his eyes, Troy was visibly frustrated.

When they met up mid field, Troy apologized, hanging his head in defeat. "Sorry, man. I should've had that."

Shawn lifted his helmet partially off his head and shrugged. "Shit happens. Any given Sunday, right?"

"Right." Troy forced a smile. He knew that they had all given their best, but sometimes that wasn't enough.

As the final whistle blew, signaling the end of the game, Troy's emotions were a whirlwind—anger, sadness, and above all, disappointment. With his dad and siblings watching and his team losing, he felt so embarrassed. As the team walked away from the field, the cheers from the crowd gradually subsided, leaving behind a weighty silence that reflected the bitter reality of the Raiders' defeat. Fans in the stadium stared in disbelief at the scoreboard, some shaking their heads while others slumped back into their seats. A handful of disgruntled spectators started to leave, their faces contorted with anger. Some of them voiced their frustration.

"Can't believe it. All that hype for what, just to lose."

"Thanks for nothin', Raiders!" another shouted, her words dripping with venom as she threw her hands up in frustration.

A roar of disappointment aimed at the defeated team echoed from the more belligerent section of the audience. "Boo! You guys suck!"

On the sidelines, Troy stood motionless, his fists clenched and jaw set, as he tried to process the loss. He could feel the weight of his teammates' eyes on him, each one searching for words of consolation that would never come. The anger and frustration bubbled up inside him like lava, threatening to erupt at any moment. However, he knew he needed to tame his temper. One of the techniques Dr. Warren advised him to try was repeating a calming phrase. Troy began chanting the chant under his breath: *Take it easy. Take it easy.*

The offensive coordinator called out his name, making his way towards him. "You did everything you could out there today, Troy. Don't let this eat away at you."

"Thanks," he mumbled, trying to force a smile but failing miserably. "I just . . . I guess I can't help but feel like I'm the one that let everybody down."

"Nah, every player on this team had a part to play today. And we win or lose as a team. Remember that, okay?" He advised, giving Troy a firm pat on the back before heading to join the rest of the team.

Troy trudged alongside Shawn and Romeo back to the locker room, keeping his head low like everybody else. Once he reached his locker, he peeled off his sweaty jersey and tossed it into a heap on the floor. A heavy sigh escaped his lips. Deep down, he knew that this loss didn't define him. And dwelling on it wouldn't change anything. He needed to focus on the next game. On winning. He made his way to the showers. Troy twisted the faucet to the highest setting, the steam instantly billowing around him. He shut his eyes, braced his hands on the tiles, and relaxed as the hot water pounded over his body. By the time he emerged, he felt grounded again, his confidence restored. They'd lost today. But it was far from over. Troy smiled, cracking his knuckles. The Raiders season had only just begun.

Several minutes later, Troy walked out of the locker room, scanning the nearly empty stadium for his family. There, a couple of rows behind the Raiders bench, he spotted them. His dad, Mike, stood next to his step-mom, Krystal, with his arm around her protectively. His brothers Mikey and Dorian lounged on the bleachers alongside their baby sister, Alana, Mikey's son, and Dorian's two rambunctious kids. Troy's gaze found Mia, her round belly proudly poking out of a Raiders t-shirt. At five and a half months pregnant, she radiated health and beauty. His heart expanded with love and pride as he jogged over to them.

"There he is!" Alana shouted, jumping up and down excitedly.

Mikey and Dorian came down from the bleachers with his two nephews to meet Troy halfway. Mikey held out his hand. Troy grabbed it and they gave each other a chest bump.

"Bro, you were awesome out there!"

"Thanks, man."

Dorian exchanged a fist bump with Troy, followed by a brief hug. "You did good, T!"

"Ay man, I tried." Troy shrugged it off and sighed.

Mikey's son tapped him. "Uncle T, I saw when you caught the ball. You were running so fast like this."

He laughed watching his nephew pretending with his arms.

"Me too! I saw you get a touchdown!" Dorian's son exclaimed.

Troy beamed proudly, giving his other nephew a hi-five. "Thanks, lil' D!"

His dad came over and pulled him into a tight bear hug. Emotion clogged Troy's throat. He whispered in Mike's ear, "I know we blew it, but I 'preciate you being here for me, Dad."

"I'll always be proud of you, win or lose. No matter what, remember that, okay? You played a helluva game out there today, X-Man," Mike, affirmed, giving him a hard pat on the back.

A sense of nostalgia washed over Troy hearing the nickname his dad used to call him when he was constantly bouncing off the walls as a kid. He didn't want to disappoint his dad, but that's exactly what he'd done today. Troy let out a heavy sigh, resigning himself to his emotions. "Yeah, thanks."

His dad released him and gripped his shoulders, smiling. "For real, you did great out there today. Keep working hard and those wins will come. Just know that we're always here for you. I mean it, X-Man, we're all proud of you, win or lose."

Troy lowered his head, a flush staining his cheeks. His dad's unwavering devotion had the ability to rip up his heart and reveal the hurt child inside, the one who'd always craved affection and belonging. He raised his head and nodded, blinking back the stinging behind his eyes. His attention shifted to his sister, Alana, standing between his dad and stepmom. At fifteen, she was blossoming into a beauty that resembled them both, with Krystal's tanned olive skin tone and heart-shaped face, and Mike's soulful brown eyes.

Krystal tucked a stray curl behind Alana's ear. "I agree. You were amazing, Troy! We're all so proud of you."

"Thanks, Mama Krys. And Alana, you're getting prettier every day. But no dating until you're thirty!"

Alana rolled her eyes, though she was smiling. "Ha. Ha. Very funny."

"I'm serious, girl! You're not allowed to date until I retire!"

"But I'll be an old maid by then!" Alana protested with a laugh.

"Exactly. I'm keeping them fuckboys far away from my baby sister. Right, Mikey? Dorian? They've been keeping an eye out while I'm not around." Troy winked, giving his brothers a pound.

"Ugh! Why didn't I get sisters?" she pouted folding her arms across her chest.

Troy laughed and turned to find Mia standing right beside him. She peered up at him with those slanted eyes, soft with affection. He snaked an arm around her waist, his hand settling on the soft curve of her belly. Their baby. The life they'd created together. He brushed a kiss on her forehead. "How's my baby mama doing?"

"Missing her baby daddy," Mia said with a teasing smile, covering his hand on her stomach with her own.

They shared a moment of intimacy amidst the clamor happening around them. Suddenly, the throng of reporters closed in around him and his family, barraging him with questions about the game and upcoming season.

"Excuse me, Troy," one of them said, shoving a microphone in his face. "Can you tell us about your thoughts on the game? What were the key factors that contributed to the loss today?"

Troy tensed, annoyance flickering. The vultures were always circling, waiting to pick the carcass clean. He knew how important it was to give a good interview, to speak eloquently and confidently. While calming himself, he breathed deeply. Keeping his shoulders straight and head held high, he kept his tone neutral. "Obviously, we ain't get the result we wanted. We faced a tough opponent today and well, a few things contributed to our loss: We struggled with consistency on both sides of the ball. On offense, we had some missed opportunities with key passes and third-down conversions. That stalled our drives. On defense, we had a few breakdowns in coverage that led to some big plays for the other team. We had some penalties that hurt us. That took away our momentum and yardage. Basically, we need to improve our execution and discipline. We got the talent and the potential to do better, so we gon' learn from this and regroup and come back stronger next week."

The reporters scribbled their notes and nodded their heads.

Amid the group of reporters, another reporter called out. "Hey Troy, we can't help but notice the protective hand on your wife's stomach. Is there exciting news you'd like to share?"

A smile tugged at the corners of Troy's lips, his expression softening as he glanced down at Mia's rounded stomach. He peered down at her and she nodded. "Yeah, Mia's just shy of being six months pregnant. We're both really excited 'bout our little one on the way," he confirmed, pride swelling in his chest.

"Congratulations!" another reporter chimed in, the small crowd around them erupting into applause and cheers. Troy felt the burden of the game's defeat lifting from his shoulders. It was replaced by the joy of celebrating this milestone with those around him.

"Do we know the sex of the baby? Any names picked out yet?" a different reporter asked, her pen poised above her notepad, ready to capture every detail of their story.

Troy exchanged another glance with Mia, the playful glint in her eyes reminding him of the recent late nights spent whispering about nursery colors and baby names. He grinned. "We're keeping that a secret for now," he teased, wrapping his arm tighter around Mia's waist. But I promise you'll be the first to know when we decide."

"Alright, everybody, big smiles!" the next reporter instructed as they snapped a series of photos. Mikey's son and Dorian's son and daughter playfully jostled for position beside their uncle, while Mike and Krystal beamed proudly, their arms wrapped around each other. Mia stood next to Troy, her hand cradling her swollen belly, the embodiment of radiant happiness.

After a few more photos were snapped, Troy signaled for the cameras to stop. He ushered his family out of the stadium. They parted ways with plans to meet in the morning for breakfast before his dad and brothers had to catch their flights home.

Once Troy and Mia made it home, Mia had a surprise of her own for him. She pulled the jersey off over her head and tossed it to the side. "Remember what Papa Mike said?"

"My dad said a lot today. Remind me."

"Win or lose, we're proud of you, Troy. You did the damn thang out there. I think you deserve some celebratory pussy." Mia unbuttoned her jeans, tugged them down, and used her foot to push them off once they gathered at her ankles.

Troy grinned sheepishly but yanked his shirt off and nodded in agreement. "I think I deserve some too."

CHAPTER 16

Lounging on the couch, his eyes fixed on the TV screen, Troy was watching highlights from the game the day before. They'd won back-to-back. It was a stark contrast from two weeks prior, when his dad, step-mom, and siblings had been in the stands as the team suffered a disappointing defeat, much to his disappointment. In spite of the loss, their outpouring of love and support had eased the blow to his wounded pride.

The doorbell rang, interrupting Troy from his musings. He checked his phone to make sure he hadn't missed a call or text from Shawn and Romeo to say they were stopping by. Mia was upstairs asleep. She'd started ordering stuff for the baby but didn't mention she was expecting any deliveries today. Troy frowned, pushing himself up from the couch with a grunt. Shielding his eyes against the glare of the afternoon sun, he opened the door and found himself face-to-face with his mother. Donning a casual two-piece, sleeveless, wide-leg pants set, her brown skin seemed to absorb the sunlight, casting an ominous shadow behind her. She tapped her long, painted nails against the doorframe, each click echoing like a ticking time bomb.

"Brenda?" He braced himself for whatever insult or demand she had in store.

A venomous grin spread across her face as she exclaimed, "Surprise, surprise!"

Surprise my ass. Brenda's sudden appearance was unexpected and unwelcomed. She shouldn't want money. Troy had already given her what she asked for weeks ago. There was only one explanation for why she was on his doorstep. The pictures of him, his dad, Mikey, and the rest of the family had been circulating on the internet, and she'd seen them. It never failed. Brenda would always flip out whenever his dad and the rest of the family were at his games. He never got why she cared when she never came to any. Troy wished he had the courage to slam the door in her face. Instead, he put on a fake smile and greeted her.

"You didn't say you were coming. What're you doing here?"

"Can't a mother visit her child? And since when do *I* have to announce myself? Move, boy." Brenda pushed past him and barged into the house.

Troy looked heavenward with a silent prayer. *If anybody is up there listening, please help me not to cuss this woman out today.* He closed the door and followed Brenda's trail as she explored his home from the kitchen to the dining room and now into the living room. She stood in the center of the luxurious space and spun around with a sly smirk that immediately put Troy on high alert. He knew his mother well enough to know she was up to something.

"Nice place. But it ain't nothing like that big ass mansion you got in Atlanta. Quite the downgrade, don't ya think, Troy boy?" She let out a wicked chortle, picking up a curved ceramic sculpture and pretending to examine it.

She was right, the two-story rental with three bedrooms and four full bathrooms was nothing in comparison to the home he owned. But she knew this was where he had to be for now. "You know this ain't permanent, Brenda. Our realtor is looking for something else since I'mma be here for a minute."

Brenda glared up at him, her words dripping with disgust when she sneered. "Speaking of that, I seen them pics of y'all and *Mommy 2.0.* Cute. Y'all the perfect family, huh? Too bad it's all just for show."

Typical. She wasn't there to spend time with him as a mother who'd missed her son. No. Brenda's heart was filled with bitterness, and it knew no end. Her visit would most likely be filled with toxic rants about his dad and stepmom or about how his brother Mikey never called her. While everyone else in Troy's life showed him unconditional love and support, she remained an outcast. And rightfully so. When he was growing up, she hadn't shown him an ounce of the nurturing that a child needs. And now it stung that his own mother seemed more consumed with bleeding his finances dry than providing even a drop of the affection he found freely given by others.

Troy took the statue from her and returned it to the shelf. "Brenda, can you not go there 'bout them today?"

"Oop, did I hit a nerve?" She taunted as she made her way over to the wet bar. "Whatchu got in here to drink? Oooh, Belvie. Good boy. You know what to keep around for yo' mama. Got some olives?"

"Yeah. You know I do."

"Well, go get 'em." She shooed him away while grabbing the bottle of Belvedere and a glass from the cabinet. "You know I like my martinis dirty."

Troy did as he was told, chuckling to himself. She only liked this drink of choice as of late. It used to be brown liquor. Straight, no chaser. But his mother tended to tone down the ghetto fabulousness when she was surrounded by luxury. Courtesy of his money, Brenda could now afford designer clothes and lavish trips around the world. Recently on a trip to Spain, some woman told her martinis were a status symbol of wealth and status. Troy silently handed her the jar and stood off to the side while she made her beverage. Along with the best weed, martinis had become her new favorite indulgence.

"Hmm. Perfection," Brenda said aloud, sauntering further into the spacious living room.

She eased down on the L-shaped sectional and crossed her right leg over her left. The corners of her mouth curled upward. "Mike wasn't always so devoted to Krystal. He loved me once, ya know. I remember a time when he couldn't stop spinnin' the block with me."

I knew it. Here we fucking go. Troy did everything not to roll his eyes. It was no secret Brenda still harbored feelings for his dad, but bringing up their long-dead relationship served no purpose other than to stir up trouble. Troy placed a coaster on the oak coffee table before going back to the bar and returning the vodka bottle to its rightful place in the liquor cabinet.

He spoke over his shoulder, "And how long ago was that?"

"Not that long ago."

He turned around with his lips pursed and rocked his head from side to side. "You and I both know that dad's happy with Krystal." Troy folded his arms across his chest and leaned against the wall.

Brenda took a sip. Then she scoffed, dismissing him with a wave of her hand. "That's what he wants y'all to believe. Trust me, boy, yo' daddy ain't happy. He will never get over me or this—"

"Nah. Keep that shit to yourself, Brenda."

She cackled, setting her drink down but not on the square he'd put there to keep from leaving a mark on the delicate surface. Troy pushed off the wall. He picked up the tumbler and placed it on the coaster.

"Why're you here, Brenda?"

"Didn't I tell yo' ass when I was at the door? I can visit my child. Wasn't Mike here? Mikey too? Why I ain't get no invite?"

"You know damn well why. Remember last time you and Krystal was in the same room."

"I can't help it if she's intimidated by me. I will always be first. Hmph. What Ricky Bobby daddy say?"

Troy cut his eyes as she actually recited the words from the movie, *Talladega Nights.*

"If you ain't first, you last. Fuck that high-yella bitch and the raggedy horse her yella ass rode in on. Never could stand that ho. Them Trini bitches always think they better than everybody else. I'm yo' mama! Invite me next time, boy."

He never understood her fixation on his dad when she was the one who messed up. Despite all of her efforts over the years to earn back Mike's love, he remained unforgiving and distant. His dad made it clear that he would never forgive Brenda for her betrayal. But Brenda continued to dwell on the past. It was a lost cause, and Troy didn't know if she would ever give up. He didn't really care. It wasn't his responsibility to fix their broken bond.

With a shake of his head, Troy dismissed her rant and request. "Even if I did ask your ass to come, you wouldn't've. So, knock it off."

Brenda reached for the glass with a shrug and smirked. "I'on even watch that nonsense anyway. You know they said them knocking yo' head 'round like that all the time ain't good. They gotta be knocking some of them screws loose up there. Yo' ass crazy enough as it is. And then you already done fucked up yo' knee. If football didn't pay so well and got us a way outta the hood, I sure as hell would've told yo' big ass to go get a job with yo' daddy. Do you know how much money he makes as a journeyman?"

Of course I do. You never let me forget what I was worth. "Yeah, I know, Brenda. What's your point?" Troy decided he needed a shot. He went back to the liquor cabinet.

Brenda uncrossed her legs and rotated her neck. "Boy, who you poppin' yo' funky attitude with? I swear every single time you get around Mommy 2.0, yo' ass come back on some new shit. Did you forget who fucking raised you?"

Troy knocked back the shot of Hennessy and didn't waste time refilling his glass with another. He had to calm his nerves. The tension in the room was growing. "No. I couldn't even if I tried, Brenda. You'd remind me."

"Boy, I swear y'all some ungrateful muthafuckas. Mikey ass act like he can't even answer the phone. He'd rather pretend that simple bitch really gives a fuck 'bout him."

"You just don't know when to quit, do you?"

"Quit what? Pretending that y'all muthafuckas wasn't playing house with another bitch when yo' mama was right here. We 'pose to be a family, boy, but Mike fucked that up letting that ho come around and brainwash y'all."

You can't be serious right now. Troy didn't bother refuting Brenda's claims and reminding her that Mike left because he didn't trust her. It would lead into an all-out argument with Brenda accusing Troy of choosing sides again and wanting to see their family divided versus together. He shook his head.

"Nobody was playing house, Brenda. It was pictures, okay. Just pictures. You know damn well them vultures gon' snap whatever they can, especially with Mia being pregnant."

Brenda spoke in a singsong voice, her words oozing with fake sincerity. "Ohhh, that is right! I almost forgot to congratulate you on her pregnancy."

"Thanks," Troy replied, bracing himself for whatever other nasty remark was sure to follow.

"Where is that bougie bitch anyway?"

"Brenda, watch your mouth. She's my wife. And upstairs taking a nap."

Once more Brenda waved him off dismissively. "Don't tell me what to do, boy. Her ass bougie as fuck. And I know if she carrying a big headed boy like yo' ass, she needs all the rest she can get. Lawd, y'all big ass head boys had my thick ass wide as all outside. But Mike said he couldn't get enough of this gushy—"

"Brenda!"

"And then I had that snap back! Ayyy!"

"TMI, damn!"

Brenda laughed maniacally and threw up her palm with an eyeroll. "Stop acting like you don't know how it is with pregnant pussy. This ain't even yo' first time being a daddy."

"Huh?" Troy scrunched up his face in confusion.

"Ain't no 'huh.' I know yo' ass heard me. When you brought up that whole Pam thing, I told her. See, I ain't know y'all hooked up when you came home after the draft. But it started to make sense when I put two and two together."

"Whatchu talking 'bout, Brenda?"

"Don't play dumb, Troy. That adorable little boy of hers, why he looks just like you."

Images of that brief encounter with Pam flooded Troy's mind, bringing with them a tidal wave of emotions. He'd been reckless, but he'd never considered the possibility that there could have been consequences beyond that fateful night. Could it be true? Troy's heart pounded in his chest, his breath hitching as he tried to maintain a poker face.

"Brenda, that's not possible. I-I . . . we—"

"I-I we what? Y'all fucked." Brenda shook her head and chortled. "Now, Troy, I know yo' ass ain't out here with a baby by yo' cousin. Ewww, I swear you's a nasty lil' boy."

A million thoughts raced through his mind, but only one mattered—the implication this revelation could have on his relationship with Mia.

With barely contained anger, Troy stated in a low voice. "I'on know what you're up to, but I swear to God, Brenda if you're lying about this, I'll—"

"You'll what? Yo' ass ain't gon' do nothing. It ain't like you been the most responsible when it comes to yo' . . . uhh . . . extracurricular activities. Don't act like yo' ass ain't been out here fucking on other bitches behind Mia's back."

Brenda stood from the couch, her flawless brown skin seeming to radiate under the sunlight streaming in through the window. Even though she was much shorter than him, she appeared to tower over him with a sense of power and intimidation. Troy clenched his fists at his sides. He searched for the right words, for some way to regain control of the situation, but they eluded him. Staring down into his mother's emotionless eyes, Troy felt rage and terror.

She leaned in. Brenda's voice was threatening and reeked of deceit. "Here's the deal. You give me five million, and I'll keep my mouth shut. No one has to know, especially not yo' bougie ass wife."

Troy tightened his jaw, fury simmering beneath the surface. The audacity of her demand left him reeling. *Five million dollars? Was she out of her mind?* He snapped, his voice straining under the weight of his frustration. "Are you insane, Brenda? I'on have that kind of money!"

Brenda countered, her eyes narrowing into slits. "Figure it out, Troy boy. I know with this trade they're paying you a lot. Or maybe yo' spoiled ass wife can ask her daddy to help you out. That senator's trifling ass got money."

"Even if I did have that kind of money, why would I give it to you just 'cause you coming in here with this now? How do I know if any of this is true? Why Pam ain't saying shit 'bout it?"

"Boy don't fucking play with me. If you don't, I promise. I will make yo' life a living hell. Yo' wife, her family—er'body will know what you did and what came of it. Then where will you be? So alone. Ashamed. Worthless."

Troy swallowed hard, feeling the walls closing in on him as the reality of the situation began to sink in. As much as he wanted to deny it, he knew his mother held all the power. If she chose to reveal this secret, it could very well destroy everything he'd worked so hard to build.

He took a deep breath, trying to steady his racing thoughts. He needed to find a way out of this, a way to protect Mia and the life they'd created together. But how?

"Fine," he ground out through gritted teeth. "I'll get you the money. But you better keep your damn word. Now can you get out?"

"Why of course, darling. And you know me—always a woman of my word." Brenda paused at the door. "Remember, Troy boy, one week. If you don't come up with that money, I'll make sure the world knows about yo' dirty little secret. TMZ, The Shade Room, Baller Bizness ... shit, any and er'body that'll listen."

He stared into Brenda's cold, calculating eyes. A shiver ran down Troy's spine. Even after she'd walked out, his gaze remained on the closed door. He knew all too well what Brenda was capable of. There would be no stopping her. All Troy could do was pray that he would find a way to come up with the money.

"Is it true?"

Troy spun around. His heart dropped when he saw Mia at the bottom of the stairs, her face contorted with disgust.

"Mia, I—" he began, struggling to find the right words. He couldn't lie to her. Troy gulped. Realizing he couldn't stall any longer, he finally admitted, "Yes. And no. I went home after I was signed. I saw Pam, and we messed around. That part is true. As far as a baby, I didn't know. I swear to you, Mia."

Mia stared back at him blankly. After a long pause she asked, "Are you going to pay her?"

Troy hesitated. His mind raced. He knew ignoring Brenda's demands would only bring more chaos.

"Answer me, Troy," Mia demanded, her voice shaky but insistent. "Are you going to pay her to keep quiet about . . . *your baby?*"

"I-I-damn it, I'on know! I'on know what to do," He admitted, dragging a hand across his shaved head.

"Well, you need to start thinking dammit! 'Cause this . . . I didn't sign up for this part, Troy."

Troy stepped closer to her, the distance between them heavy with unspoken tension and fear of what the future held. "I know, Sym. But whatever it takes. We gon' figure this out."

Troy promised, though even he wasn't entirely sure how they would manage. Because if any of what Brenda said was true, their lives would never be the same again.

CHAPTER 17

"Make love to me, Troy."

Troy smiled against her neck, his breath tickling her skin. "Anything for you, Sym."

He pulled back some. His eyes darkened as he met her gaze, before swooping in to claim her lips. Their kiss became more urgent, more demanding. Hands roamed freely over each other's bodies, seeking out pleasure and giving it just as freely. Mia could feel his erection pressing against her. Breaking their sloppy connection, Troy continued his descent, leaving a trail of wet kisses and gentle nips. Mia tilted her head, exposing more of her throat allowing Troy better access. His calloused palms slid up her body, cupping her swollen, throbbing bosoms, molding and reshaping them with satisfaction.

"Fuck, baby."

"Yesss!" Mia hissed, feeling him graze her sensitive kernels.

Troy took a nipple into his mouth, sucking hard, as he rolled the other between his fingers. Mia bowed her body, moaning softly in delight as the sensations coursed through her. Needy moans escaped as Troy kept moving lower until he reached her most sensitive spot.

"You're so fucking beautiful," he murmured, kissing her inner thighs.

Mia's hips bucked off the bed when his warm breath tickled her. He parted her folds, teasing her swollen clit with his thumb. She gasped and shuddered against his touch.

"Please, Troy. I need—" Mia didn't finish her sentence. She couldn't. Troy pushed two long, thick digits inside her tight channel, eliciting a satisfied hum. His gifted tongue flicked her bundle of nerves in rapid succession while his fingers continued thrusting in and out, in and out. The sounds coming from her pussy were almost obscene, as if Troy were sloshing through muddy puddles. Mia let out a little cry and then her body went taut. Just as she was about to reach her climax, Troy flipped her over onto all fours. Without any instruction or coaxing, she put a dip in her posture, giving him the perfect 'face down ass up' pose. Mia peeked over her shoulder, her eyes meeting Troy's as he positioned himself behind her.

Using one hand to hold her open and the other to guide his heavy erection, Troy penetrated Mia's slippery softness with a low groan. He began to move, thrusting into her with a rough, punishing rhythm that sent shockwaves of pleasure through her entire body. Mia met him stroke for stroke, the slap of his thighs against her ass was in perfect sync. Troy smacked Mia's right cheek, causing her to yelp. She clutched at the sheets as her legs shook uncontrollably from the powerful strike. Before she could recover, Troy delivered another blow to the left side. The intense sensation was almost too much for Mia, and she buckled.

"Nah uhn, Sym throw that shit back!" Troy instructed, popping her butt once more.

"Oooh, Troy! Fuck!"

He plunged deep and steady, hitting all the right angles. Mia's body responded to his every move, building up to another climax. She pushed back against Troy, matching each thrust of his with her own. The bed creaked beneath them as they rocked in sync, a primal and arousing dance bringing them closer and closer to the edge.

"Ahh fuck! I'm close," he groaned as his grip on her tightened.

"Yes! Oh god yes, Troy! Come for me!" She begged, dipping lower and undulating her hips toward him. "Fuck! I-I'm 'bout to—" She couldn't complete the thought. Mia exploded around him, her orgasm shaking her to her core. Mia buried her face into the pillow, biting down to hold back the scream threatening to escape.

"Here. It. Comes. Arrrgh!" Troy grunted as his shaft pulsated inside.

After a few moments, he rolled off of Mia and lay beside her, catching his breath. They lay entwined, descending from the high of their passionate session. Troy whispered loving and reassuring words into Mia's ear while his gentle hands caressed her body. Mia ran her fingers lightly over his chest, feeling the firm muscles beneath her touch.

"Damn, Sym, that was fucking amazing. They ain't lied. Pregnant pussy is the gushiest," Troy exhaled against her forehead as he massaged her stomach.

"You're the one who made it gushy."

Mia smiled up at Troy and hummed while slipping her hand below his waist. Troy's dark brown gaze met hers and he hissed. His hips bucked forward against her hand, straining against the firm grip she had on his half-swollen package.

The sudden ringing from Troy's phone interrupted the intimate moment they were sharing. He shrugged it off, but then it rang again. With a curse, Troy untangled himself from Mia to reach for the device on the nightstand.

"Hello? . . . Yeah, this me . . . Ay 'sup, Diesel? What's good? . . . Nah, I ain't spoke to him . . . He did what? . . . Nah, nah you good. 'Preciate you for calling me. I'll be there as soon as I can."

Mia watched as he hung up, but Troy didn't say anything. Instead, he swiped across the screen to place another call.

"Come on, man. Pick up," he muttered to himself while getting up from the bed.

Mia's senses were heightened as she regarded Troy. After the unexpected news Brenda shared almost a month ago, anything was possible. Mia sat up and pulled the sheet around her, trying to make sense of what was happening. Troy had tried to call someone, but they didn't answer. He turned to Mia with a frustrated shake of his head and let out a heavy sigh.

"They can't get a hold of Rome and Speedy up at this club showing his ass. Lemme go get him before he ends up in jail."

"Troy?"

"Sym, she doesn't know where we live now. And didn't MJ get Brendan to handle everything else? Promise I'll be right back."

Mia studied his face, searching for any signs of deceit. She finally nodded her assent. Troy was right. They had nothing to worry about. Fearing Brenda's threat, Troy had teamed up with their realtor, working tirelessly to expedite the search for a new home. By the end of the week, they'd moved out of the condo. Meanwhile, Mia got MJ to enlist the help of one of Nigel's sons, Brendan, a skilled cybersecurity engineer who could prevent or effectively counter any of Brenda's attempts to expose information about Troy.

After taking a quick shower, Troy threw on some casual clothes before rushing out the door. Watching him leave, a pang of unease settled in Mia's gut. Half an hour later had gone by and her phone rang. Angela's name lit up on the display. She could hear the panic in her best friend's voice before she could even answer.

"Mia, I told you! I knew it! I fucking knew it! Jamal—he was cheating!" Angela spoke fast, her words tumbling out in a panicked cascade. "But this? Hell no! I didn't see this coming! And it wasn't with another woman!"

"Ang, I'm gonna need you to breathe. Slow down and explain what happened."

"LaLa and Sisko with their messy asses is what happened! Jamal wasn't even at a fucking conference in DC. He was in Paris parading around with some buyer from Gucci named Christian! He's fucking gay, Mia! Gay! But do you wanna hear the fuck shit? I hope you're sitting down for this."

She wasn't sure if she was prepared for the bomb Angela was about to drop in her lap, but Mia nodded even though Angela couldn't see her. "I am. Lemme hear it."

"Why was he married to the same ho that was fucking on Troy and Derrik!"

Out of nowhere, it was as if the room began spinning off its axis even though she was sitting still. *Did she just say Jamal's ex-wife was Desiree?* Mia knew she couldn't have heard her best friend correctly. "I'm sorry come again."

"You heard me. Jamal's ex-wife fucked your husband and his best friend. Sisko said the math wasn't mathing. But you said Troy doesn't have twins running in his family, right?"

"No, he doesn't. Not on either side. But wait, Ang, back this up. You found out Jamal is gay and that his wife is Desiree all on Baller Bizness? When?"

Angela blew out a deep breath. "A couple of hours ago. They talked about Troy playing for the Raiders, you not being online anymore and the rumors around your pregnancy. But it was brief. Since LaLa knows Troy, she said she was gonna be calling for an exclusive. I would've called you already, but I've been trying to get in touch with Jamal. Here he was acting like it was just Tré when he—"

An incoming text from Mia's cousin, Roscoe caught her attention. She squinted at the display. The image seared her eyes with its implications. Mia was torn. Of course, she wanted to assist Angela in any way she could, but she had her own troubles to deal with. She was in the eye of the storm that was her life with Troy. Her loyalty to her husband was unshakable, but it wouldn't be true to his character if he didn't test it.

"Ang, listen, I need to make a quick call. Let me get my head wrapped around what we can do about Jamal. I'll think of something. Just relax and stay put. Don't do anything! Do you hear me?"

"Okay, fine. I won't. But hurry up."

"Alright. I'll call you back."

After ending the call, Mia punched in a quick message. She went back to the text her cousin sent. Her fingers tightened around the device as she studied the incriminating photo. "Troy, you fucking idiot!" she exclaimed through clenched teeth.

There he was, her husband—muscles taut, tattoos on proud display—leaning close to Sinnamen, the ho that'd been trying to infiltrate their marriage for as long as they'd been together. His full lips curved in a way too familiar and too intimate, while Sinnamen's painted red mouth hovered close to his ear.

In that moment, her determination solidified like ice in her veins. Protecting her marriage wasn't just about standing by her man. It was about facing threats head-on, especially when they slinked out of neon-lit corners. She got up from the bed and dressed in record time. By the time Mia made it to the front door, she was greeted by Keeva Lowe. The striking beauty with raven hair and intense blue eyes was dressed in her usual attire: a black fitted vest suit and sturdy lug-sole boots. Sometimes, Mia regretted not completing her training with her family friend and hired henchwoman. However, Keeva had taught Mia enough self-defense techniques to hold her own and even throw a few punches if needed.

"We're going to Bleu Saffire."

"Copy that. Your chariot awaits," Keeva grinned, outstretching her arm to an all-black, Mercedes Benz G63 AMG SUV with blackout windows.

Mia returned an even bigger smile that split her face. "My oh my, how I've missed you, Keevs! I love it!"

"I knew you would. Now let's go see what trouble the mister has gotten himself in."

Mia carefully settled into the back seat and let out a deep sigh. "Ugh, if that ho is in his face just be ready. 'Cause I know I'mma have to put hands on her thirsty ass."

"Let's hope it won't have to come to that." Keeva pushed the button bringing the engine to life.

After being delayed by an accident on the highway, it took Keeva almost an hour to reach the strip, and another ten minutes to finally arrive at the gentleman's club. Before Mia and Keeva showed up, Roscoe confirmed Troy had already left with Speedy. Sinnamen was not with them. It didn't matter. Mia needed to address the other root cause of this recurring problem.

Mia's face was illuminated by the neon glow of Bleu Saffire's sign as she strutted through its glass doors. The club throbbed with life, the bass reverberating through the space. The air was heavy with a combination of perfume, sweat, and desperation, creating an intoxicating atmosphere. While the dancers followed the instructions to French Montana's "Pop That," Mia's eyes searched the crowded room until they landed on her prey—Sinnamen. The woman was dangerous, exuding a seductive aura as she lounged in a VIP booth wearing a revealing two-piece thong set. With Keeva on her heels, Mia cut through the sea of people.

She strode over to the table and leaned in, pointing a manicured finger right in Sinnamen's face. "You just couldn't wait to bring your funky pussy out here and twerk it on my husband could you? Did you smell mine on his breath, ho?"

"Hmph, but you the one up in here looking for him. Has it ever occurred to you that your husband came here for me?"

"I highly doubt that."

"Don't. 'Cause clearly, your pregnant pussy ain't wet enough if he's in here sniffing 'round mine," Sinnamen retorted, rising to her full height.

Mia stepped forward, her warning clear in her tone and the hostility laced in her words. "Stay the fuck away from Troy!"

"Or what?" Sinnamen sneered, moving closer.

Their faces were mere inches apart, their breath hot against each other's skin. Sinnamen's body lightly pressed against hers, a subtle but deliberate display of dominance.

"Or I'm gonna make your ho ass regret it." Mia shoved Sinnamen back. "And gimme fifty feet, you funky ass ho!"

Sinnamen stumbled, barely catching herself on the edge of the booth. Her eyes grew wide with shock, bouncing from Keeva to Mia. In an instant, she narrowed them and spat, "I don't give a fuck if you are pregnant. You're gonna pay for that, bitch!"

"Oh, I wanna see this. Make me," Mia dared, puffing out her chest in defiance.

Sinnamen reached out to push Mia, but she evaded her by dodging out of the way.

"Bitch! I wish you would try and hurt my baby!" Mia caught Sinnamen's wrist mid-air. Despite her protruding belly, Mia managed to maneuver Sinnamen's arm behind her back and spun her around, landing multiple punches to her face. Sinnamen tried to swing with her free hand, but Mia had the advantage, her grip strong and her stance unwavering.

"Let me go, you crazy—" Sinnamen's words were cut short by several blows Mia delivered to her mouth when she tried to yank herself free.

Keeva intervened, stopping Mia from using Sinnamen's face as a punching bag. Mia flung Sinnamen to the floor. While a bouncer from the club assisted a bruised and bleeding Sinnamen to stand, Keeva held back Mia. A couple of servers approached, one with a towel, offering it to Sinnamen. Rather than using it to clean herself up, Sinnamen spat out the blood onto the floor.

Her eyes glistened mischievously as she gyrated her body and provocatively taunted Mia. "Ya pussy's dry. And ya bitter. Ha! No wonder your man keeps coming back to get this WAP."

"Always a fucking sideline ho! I feel sorry for your thirsty ass. When are you gonna get it? Troy don't want you!" Mia laughed maniacally.

Sinnamen's frustrated outburst was reminiscent of a child's tantrum, as she stomped her feet and screamed back, "Well, if he didn't want me, why was his dick down my throat a couple of months ago? Where was you at when I was in his condo swallowing his other babies, huh? And we both know his diet is immaculate 'cause they was mmm mmm good."

Mia struggled to break free from the strong grip of her bodyguard, speaking through clenched teeth. "Lemme go, Keeva!"

Keeva leaned in, her voice lowered, but loud enough and stern over the music. "Let it go, Mia. You've done too much. We've got a crowd waiting. Brendan won't be able to clean this one up."

"Oop! Don't get mad. Just enjoy it sister! 'Cause I ain't going nowhere! Muuuah! Clit kisses!" Sinnamen continued to taunt Mia, playfully tapping her crotch region.

Keeva barked the order at the security guard. "Get her ass outta here already!"

Once he led Sinnamen out of the booth, Keeva guided Mia in the opposite direction. The commotion had caught the attention of nearby patrons, and the club's owner was notified. However, Keeva stepped in defusing the situation. Mia was sick and tired of the one woman that refused to stand down. Since she and Troy had been together Sinnamen had always been in the background waiting to slither in when Mia wasn't around. No matter that she'd already handed Sinnamen a thorough beating once before. The incident had taken place at an upscale gentleman's club in Atlanta, and Keeva's brother Brendan had taken action to eliminate any proof by erasing security footage from both the establishment and nearby street cameras. This safeguarded Mia from potential legal repercussions. As she faced Sinnamen for a second time, Mia wished they had been in a private VIP room instead. If that were the case, Sinnamen may not have left in one piece.

When Keeva pushed the door open, a sudden burst of light from a camera temporarily blinded Mia. As her vision adjusted, she was hit with another burst of light, and then another, and another after that. Mia shielded her eyes realizing this was the result of what Keeva had said moments ago: *You've done too much. We've got a crowd waiting.*

They were being "papped." The paparazzi and tabloids had descended upon the scene, their lenses feasting on the drama. Shouts from the nosey gossip bloggers pelted her like hailstones. A reporter she recognized from Baller Bizness called out, thrusting a microphone toward Mia.

"Mia, over here! Is your marriage back on the rocks?"

"Is Troy having an affair with a dancer?"

"Is it true that Troy has been seen with this other woman before?"

"Do you care to comment on the rumors surrounding your marriage?"

Mia's stomach churned with dread. Once again, her marriage was a spectacle for the world to consume. Keeva ushered her from the melee of snapping photos and hurling questions. They reached the SUV, and Keeva sped away, putting as much distance between them and the chaotic scene as possible. When they were some miles away, Mia turned to her bodyguard with a pressing query of her own.

"Keevs, do you think I have an embarrassment kink?"

CHAPTER 18

"Hey, y'all! Heeeeeey! What's happening? Welcome to another episode of Baller Bizness with yours truly, LaLa."

Clapping erupted from the audience as LaLa sashayed across the floor of the studio. With her signature afro, the tall, brown-skinned woman donned a denim jumpsuit and platform red bottoms.

"Annnnd your lovely co-host, Sisko!"

More cheering and applause ensued as Sisko entered from the other side of the studio. Sisko never failed to impress with his impeccable fashion sense, today sporting a light-brown Tom Ford Atticus suit. He spun around gracefully and took a bow.

LaLa laughed heartily and joined the crowd in the hand praising for her co-host. They playfully hugged and exchanged French cheek kisses before walking over to the large armchairs in the middle of the studio and taking up seats opposite each other. LaLa grabbed one of the coffee mugs from the table in between their chairs and took a sip before speaking.

"Mmhmm, yes indeed! So glad you could join us today as we dish out all the juicy drama going on with the ballers around the world. And if you're just tuning in, Sisko and I are fresh off a flight from the West Coast and whew chye! Do we have some drama for yo' mama! If you were here for the tea that we had the other day about Troy and Mia Harris, we have an update."

Sisko laughed, popping his lips. "Hold up, LaLa. Are we serving the baller babes a special peach brew?"

"You already know! And tuh-day it's piping hot. Matter of fact, what we got might just go down in the BGC Hall of Fame. For y'all that don't know, that's our very own Bad Guhl Club here on Baller Bizness where we honor our baddies from the A that ain't afraid to throw them bows and knuck if you buck."

"Wait. Somebody made the BGC Hall of Fame and you didn't tell me? See, it be your own people keeping stuff from you. Who, pray tell?"

"Yeah, LaLa. Who?" someone in the audience shouted, causing laughter to spread throughout the rest of the studio.

LaLa giggled and raised her hands in an attempt to calm their excitement. With a sly grin, she looked over at Sisko and leaned in conspiratorially, resting her elbows on the armrest between them. "Ahem. Mia Harris put the paws on the exotic dancer, Sinnamen."

Sisko brought a hand up to his chest. "I know you lying!"

"Am not. I've got it right here for our baller babes."

Sisko extended his hands in an enthusiastic gesture. "Well, LaLa honey, don't make us wait!"

"Okay then! Roll that beautiful baller footage!"

LaLa snapped her fingers and the giant screen behind them flickered to life. Grainy images showed Sinnamen rushing toward Mia. The video, though lacking clarity, was unrelenting in its portrayal of raw aggression. The footage was choppy, but then it showed Mia's hand gripping Sinnamen's wrist as she launched into her attack. Every punch that Mia threw was visible, her hair swaying in synchronization with her movements. The audience's raucous cheers and jeers added to the intense atmosphere of the fight. Mia's face was frozen in a moment of pure rage. Then the camera panned over to capture LaLa and Sisko, their faces lit up with excitement.

"Never thought I'd see Mia Harris, of all people, throwing down like this," Sisko muttered, his eyes never leaving the pixelated chaos.

"Neither did the rest of Vegas," LaLa added, her gaze also fixed on the spectacle. "But that wasn't just some random catfight. We know there's more to it."

Nodding, Sisko popped his lips. "Yeah, something big must've set her off. And with Sinnamen? 'Cause she threw them hands like she was fighting for her life—or love. You think it's Troy? Just saying, fidelity ain't exactly his strong suit."

"Well, she's definitely ride-or-die for Troy. Can't nobody say she don't fight for what's hers. But did you catch what Sinnamen posted after their lil' fight? Trouble in paradise?" LaLa quipped with a sly tilt of her head, peering at the screen behind them.

Displayed for the viewers were a few blurry photos of Sinnamen and Troy in bed, captured in various intimate positions. The images had been distorted to conceal Sinnamen's nudity. Meanwhile, a peaceful and unaware Troy lay beneath her.

Sisko let out a low whistle. "Now that right there is a grenade with the pin pulled out.

"Explosive doesn't even start to cover it," LaLa said with a click of her tongue. "The question is, did Troy invite the fox into the hen house, or is Sinnamen stirring the pot for her own reasons?"

"Talk about déjà vu. This ain't their first rodeo with rumors and scandal, but this time, things feel a bit different, don't they, LaLa? There's another human being involved. Mia's going to be having a baby soon," Sisko mused, arching an eyebrow.

LaLa's nod was slow, deliberate. "Fact. And we've seen them shine at charity balls, kiss-cam at the games, flaunting their love like it's bullet-proof. But now? Now, it's like watching a glittering tower teeter on the brink. Mia's always been loyal, a fighter for her man, but everyone's got their breaking point. And Troy? Yeah, he loves hard, but can even the strongest love survive back-to-back blows like these?"

Sisko popped his lips and gestured to their studio audience. "Alright baller babes, what's y'all's take on the latest chapter in the saga of Troy and Mia? Is this just another bump in the road to 'happily ever after,' or have we hit the end of the line?"

"Hit us up on our socials. Let us know if you think Troy and Mia can make it down the field, or if these latest revelations will be the game-ending play." LaLa's voice dropped to a low rumble, her gaze sharp with forewarning. "In this city of lights, when darkness falls, it hits like a blitz."

CHAPTER 19

Troy and Mia exited the chill of the obstetrician's office and stepped out into the blistering Las Vegas sunlight. Neither spoke, their silence hanging thick between them like the smog over the Strip. She walked beside him, her designer heels clicking assertively against the pavement, her long black hair whipping around her face in the desert wind. When they reached his truck, Troy unlocked it with a beep that sliced through the uneasy quiet. He held the door open, a gesture fraught with the weight of unsaid apologies. Without so much as a glance at him, she settled inside. Troy closed the door with more care than usual and circled around to the driver's side.

He began the moment he brought the engine to life. "Look, baby I know I've been . . . fuck, I can't even find the right word for it."

"A complete idiot works."

Okay. I gotta eat that. "I'm sorry, aight. What happened with Sinnamen . . . it shouldn't've happened. I let Speedy talk me into going to Saffire. I ain't even know she was gon' be there. I was fucked up after all them drinks. Speedy said she came to the house. I-I really don't remember nothing. That's the truth, baby. I was just missing you real bad."

Troy had tried to smooth things over with Mia about the night he'd gone to Bleu Saffire. He'd admitted to everything he could remember. Mia stared out the window, her expression veiled.

"You call being up in her face and letting that rancid mouth bitch suck your dick, missing me?"

Troy's grip tightened on the steering wheel. "Dammit, Mia! You know it's not like that. I was drunk! She knew that. Ain't nobody could ever take your place, not in a million years."

"Oh, so I'm Mia now that you're a little frustrated? Pfft. You weren't drunk the other night. And flattery don't erase betrayal, Troy," Mia replied, turning to look at him, her eyes wary.

"Sym, baby, I'd walk through hellfire for you, you gotta know that." Troy's voice held a raw edge of desperation. "What I did—it was stupid and weak, okay? And I hate myself for hurting you all these times. But I swear, baby, I love you more than life itself. I'm not fucking this up no more."

The truck slowed to a stop at a red light, and the buzz of the city momentarily filled the space between them. Troy's tattoos seemed to come alive as he flexed his hands, releasing the steering wheel briefly before grasping it again.

"Actions speak louder than words," Mia finally said, her voice soft yet carrying the weight of her pain.

"Then I'mma show you, every single day," Troy promised.

The light turned green, and Troy accelerated forward, his gaze darting to Mia who sat beside him with a placid expression. The silence was heavy and remained that way for the rest of the drive, broken only by the hum of traffic and the low purr of the truck's engine as they finally pulled into their driveway.

When they entered the house, the tension between them also walked in as an uninvited guest. The grand foyer felt too expansive, the high ceiling echoing their footsteps, mirroring the growing distance between them. Troy followed Mia into the kitchen where she went to grab a bottle of coconut water from the fridge. The moment he set his phone on the marble countertop, it began to buzz and vibrate, disrupting the uneasy silence with its high-pitched ringtone. Brenda's name flashed across the screen. His gut clenched.

Weeks had gone by with no word from Brenda since she unexpectedly appeared at the condo. They relocated to an upscale community in Clark County to avoid any more surprise visits from his mother. Troy was surprised that it'd taken this long for her to reach out to him again.

"Go ahead. Answer. And put it on speaker. I wanna hear what she has to say." Mia's voice held a sharpness now, her earlier calm evaporating.

Troy gave her a subtle nod. He reached for the device, his movements stiff, bracing himself for the verbal assault he knew was coming.

"Look, Brenda—"

"Yo' bougie ass wife thinks she can stop me! You think I'on know she used her rich family and their ties to block me, boy?" Brenda spat, her words sharp as shards of glass.

He gritted his teeth and shot a quick glance at Mia. Her fingers drummed impatiently on the countertop, a clear indication of her annoyance. Though she pursed her lips, she remained silent, leaving Troy to handle his mother.

"Nobody's blocking you," Troy countered, fighting to keep his tone even. "You spinning stories, as always."

Brenda snarled, "Stories? You know damn well this ain't no lie. I know you don't want this to come out. It will ruin yo' precious image. Don't worry. I'mma find a way to scream it from every goddamn rooftop in every city."

"I'on care what you do, Brenda. I ain't that scared lil' boy no more. Mia and our baby, they're my world, and I won't let you—or anyone—tear us apart."

"Aww shit! Ain't this something new. I guess them therapy sessions done gave yo' ass an even bigger head now," Brenda replied, her laugh devoid of humor. She stopped cackling long enough to continue her vicious rant. "Brave words. But bravery won't save you. Let's see if you keep this same energy when the truth comes out. Time's up, Troy boy."

Troy pressed the button, ending the call with a force that mirrored the

184 | LOVE ON THE SIDELINES

turmoil inside him. The phone screen went black, but the darkness of Brenda's threats still seeped through his mind like poison.

"Block her." Mia stared straight ahead, her beautiful face etched with lines of outrage that both awed and terrified him.

It felt as though the weight of his secrets were pressing down on him, threatening to crush the life they were building. He hated the distance between them, a chasm that seemed to widen with every beat of his desperate heart. Troy reached for her hand, pulling her to him, splaying a protective hand over her stomach.

"Can you do it now?" There was a challenge in her eyes, a flicker of doubt that he needed to extinguish.

He grabbed the device, swiped to Brenda's name, and did as his wife asked. Troy's gaze locked with hers. "I'll do whatever it takes."

"Damn her," Mia muttered under her breath.

"Everything will be okay, Sym," he whispered into her hair, breathing in the familiar scent of jasmine and vanilla. "I love you more than anything. You and our baby, y'all my everything. And I'mma fight like hell to keep us together. Ain't nobody coming in between this."

Mia lifted her head, her eyes searching his. "Promise me, Troy."

"Until my last breath," Troy scooped her up, He nipped at her earlobe, whispering. "I've got you, Sym. I've always got us."

Mia breathed, wrapping her legs around his waist, pulling him closer. "Then show me, Troy. Show me how much you love me."

CHAPTER 20

Mia tried to focus on Angela's tirade about her boyfriend Jamal, but her attention kept getting drawn back to the breathtaking, colorful sky. The heavens blazed coral, amber and magenta, bleeding into dusky violets and muted blues. The mountains were awash in the vivid hues, creating a brilliant canvas that captivated her. She wrenched her eyes away from the hypnotic vista and attempted to tune back into the litany of complaints, nodding along absently as Angela ranted.

"He just left, Mia. Jamal packed up his stuff and moved out while I was at work. Didn't even leave a note."

"Damn, girl, that's cold." Mia replied, but her sympathetic tone also held a hint of distraction.

Lurking beneath the surface of her composed exterior, a storm brewed within Mia. Sinnamen, that conniving dancer with moves as seductive as her name, had been inching her way into Troy's life while they were separated. The woman was like a parasite latching onto their marriage, feeding off their happiness. As if Sinnamen wasn't enough, they also had to deal with Troy's manipulative mother, who was siphoning off his resources while holding onto a dark family secret that could potentially destroy their lives. Mia couldn't fully empathize with Angela's problems when her own world was falling apart.

With a sigh, she pushed herself away from the kitchen counter and sought refuge in another part of their new home, somewhere that brought her joy and a sense of calm. Mia entered the baby's nursery. The room was filled with designer baby clothes and plush toys, a testament to her creative touch and lavish lifestyle.

Mia's fingers brushed against the soft cotton onesies, folding them with a precision that betrayed her inner torment. She slid the garments into the drawer, each movement a distraction from the thoughts that gnawed at her.

"After all that waiting around thinking it was gonna be us. When it was him the whole time in the closet. He was really with me *and* his wife *and* living on the DL the whole time." Angela's voice crackled through the phone.

"Men like Jamal—they're cowards. You're better off without him."

Out of nowhere Angela's breath hitched on the other end. "Wait— hold on."

"What, Ang? What is it?"

"There-There's an . . . we have an active shooter! Oh my god, they're up at Northside! That's where Jamal works! I have to go, Mia. I'll call you back."

As the line went dead, Mia felt a sense of urgency. There was no more time to waste. She couldn't hesitate now; not when she had her own battles to fight. Taking a deep breath, she approached the baby's armoire and let out a long exhalation. With steady hands, she slid her finger across the screen and dialed a number reserved for confidential conversations that could not be overheard by anyone else. Keeva's trustworthiness was never in question. She was more than an ally—she was Mia's executioner.

After a couple of rings, Keeva answered in her cool and collected tone. "Mia, what may I do for you?"

"Keevs, we need to handle a certain bug problem. Can you ensure this one will go away . . . and for good?"

"Are we talking about a complete extraction from your life? Not just a scare tactic."

Mia grabbed another neatly folded onesie, placing it atop its kin. Her eyes, though focused on the task, were distant. "Complete extraction. Elimination. She thinks she can slither into my world and disrupt everything I've built with Troy. I won't have it."

"Understood," Keeva said, the sound of keystrokes punctuating her words. "There are ways to make people disappear without a trace—change their priorities so they find . . . uhh . . . new interests. It could involve a job offer across the country. Perhaps a sudden need to care for a distant relative, or even a new romantic prospect that sweeps them off their feet."

"I don't give a fuck what it is. I want her gone, Keevs. And nothing traceable back to us," Mia insisted, moving to the crib and running her hand along its polished railing, her knuckles whitening with each word. "Clean. Permanent."

"Always," Keeva affirmed with a calm that belied the gravity of the conversation.

Mia's conviction resonated through the room. "Sinnamen's a pest that needs exterminating. Do whatever it takes."

"Consider this pest control of the highest order."

Mia hung up and stood still for a moment, staring at the empty crib. She imagined Sinnamen, oblivious to the sand shifting beneath her feet. Her lips curved into a malevolent smile as she contemplated. Like a hunter, Mia was biding her time and waiting for the perfect moment to strike and claim victory over her unsuspecting prey.

Mia's eyes gleamed with dark satisfaction as she spoke aloud. "There's only one way to deal with a pest. You make sure it's exterminated—for good."

CHAPTER 21

Troy shifted in the plastic folding chair, arms crossed so tight his biceps bulged. He didn't utter a word. He just listened, as one by one, the men peeled back layers of hurt with voices that wavered between strength and despair. He observed their interactions, the nods of understanding, the clenched jaws and hands that fought to remain still. They spoke of rage turned inward, of love twisted into something unrecognizable. Each confession echoed fragments of Troy's own life, bouncing around the sterile walls, a reminder of what brought him to this place. But Troy, known for his charisma and confidence, now held his tongue captive, sealing away the torrent of emotions threatening to spill over.

"Pops would come home, whiskey on his breath, looking for something to hit. If it wasn't the dog, it was me." The heavyset man with hands like wrecking balls gripped his knees, his voice a low rumble in the tense room. The words spilled out raw and unfiltered, each one landing with the force of a punch. "I swore I'd never be him, but hell, there I was, years later, throwing my own girl against the wall because she looked at me wrong."

The group's collective breath seemed to catch, the air thick with unsaid empathy. Troy's jaw tightened as the man's story resonated with a familiar ring. It was one he knew all too well. Dr. Warren's gaze lingered on Troy, silent yet piercing, an unspoken challenge hanging in the air between them. Troy felt it—a nudge, a dare to step into the arena and bare his soul.

"Troy? You've been awfully quiet. Remember, you said you would do whatever for Mia and your baby. The individual sessions are important, but these support meetings are equally important for your journey. Perhaps you'd like to share next?"

Share. Like it was that easy. His tongue stuck to the roof of his mouth like dried cement.

"Come on, Troy," the man to his left prodded, his own story of shattered relationships still hanging heavy in the room. "We've all laid it bare here, man. What's holding you back?"

Troy turned to meet the man's gaze, his eyes two flints striking sparks. "You think it's that easy?"

"Easy? Hell no," the man shot back, the muscles along his jaw jumping with tension. "But what are you doing here if you ain't gonna face your demons?"

"Face my demons? You don't know a damn thing about my demons!"

"Maybe not," the man conceded, leaning forward. "But I know a thing or two about screwing up. About hurting the one person who should mean the most."

"Cheating and beating on his wife," another voice chimed in, cool and accusing. "That's what I heard about you, man. What's all this for? To make good with the league? Either you here pretending or to make some real change. Which is it, Troy?"

Troy jumped to his feet, the chair crashing behind him. "You questioning my commitment? I love my wife more than any of you could understand."

"Love ain't enough, brother," the first man said. "You gotta show you're worthy of it. Own up."

"Troy?" Dr. Warren raised his hands.

Troy dismissed him. "Nah! They don't get it!"

"Getting it ain't the problem. It's what you're doing about it that counts," the man retorted.

"Actions, man! Where are they?" another voice joined in, the pressure mounting around Troy.

The circle of men stared up at him. Judgment. There it was again. Troy dragged a hand over his clean-shaven head, the familiar taste of self-loathing coating his tongue. What was wrong with him? He'd promised Mia, swore to her he'd get help. But how could he bare himself to these strangers? How could he share the ugliest parts of himself, the parts he'd spent a lifetime concealing?

He picked up the chair and placed it upright, then slumped into it, defeat bowing his shoulders. Mia deserved better than his broken pieces. Better than him. After all these years, he was still a little boy craving love from a mother who'd never given a damn. Troy's fists balled, tattoos stretching over his skin as if bracing for impact. "I'm here, ain't I? Putting in the work, tryna fix this mess!"

Before any of the other men in the circle could respond, Dr. Warren interjected, "This isn't about proving who's stronger or who's right. It's about understanding and healing." The older man's gaze, steady and purposeful, met Troy's stormy one. "Your journey, Troy, isn't about the acceptance from this group or even Mia. It's about accepting yourself, your past, and moving forward. Start by forgiving yourself."

Troy's shoulders, previously set rigid like the beams of a boxing ring, dropped a fraction. Dr. Warren's words were a balm, soothing the sting of raw emotions. Troy's jaw softened, the fight leaving him in an exhale that carried the weight of a thousand apologies never spoken.

"Speak on it, Troy," Dr. Warren urged softly, his voice a stark contrast to the simmering tension that enveloped the room. The invitation was more than words. It was a challenge, a dare to unearth demons Troy had danced with in the shadows for far too long.

"Man, Pam . . ." Troy started, hesitating as the name crawled out of his mouth, laced with venom and shame. His hands clenched into fists, knuckles bone white. The group leaned in, their own stories mirrored in the fragments of Troy's halting confession.

"She . . . she was supposed to be safe. My mom's first cousin and all. Played me like I was, I dunno, her puppet. Started when I was thirteen or fourteen. She'd touch me, say things—mess with my head. Made me think it was normal, that I wanted it. By the time I realized it was abuse, I was eighteen. She'd already—hell, she'd messed me up good."

"Talk to us about your mother, Brenda, Troy," Dr. Warren coaxed gently.

That name—Brenda—was a trigger, igniting a wildfire of memories in Troy's mind. He took a breath that filled his lungs with the stale air of vulnerability.

"My ma—ahem, I mean Brenda. Can't call her mama. She ain't even want nobody to know she had kids. Heh, what can I say? She was detached. Like I wasn't her son, just some burden she had to deal with."

The group was silent, each man seeming to understand that beneath Troy's muscular veneer lay a battlefield of emotional scars.

"She ain't never hugged me. Never asked about my day. Hell, the only time she spoke to me was to remind me I owed her, for life, for the food she put on the table."

"Is that why you turned to Pam?" Dr. Warren prodded gently.

"Yeah," Troy spat out, as if the admission left a sour taste in his mouth. "At least Pam pretended to care. Gave me what I thought was affection." He paused, and for a split second he was back there, a teenager desperate for a touch that didn't reek of obligation or resentment. The words poured out now, unbidden and raw.

"Because of Brenda's indifference, I looked for something, anything, to fill that empty space she left inside me. And when I saw men using her, treating her like trash, something in me snapped. It was like that was all women were good for, you know?"

He could feel their eyes on him, their judgment—or maybe it was understanding—weighing heavy in the air. "So, I used girls in high school, college . . . my whole life and acted out 'cause it felt like power, control. Things I never had at home."

"Tell us about the anger towards your mother," Dr. Warren pressed, a nudge to keep the past bleeding into the present.

Troy laughed bitterly. "Anger? That's too soft a word, Doc. I hate her. She tossed me into this world and just watched me struggle. Her coldness, her neglect . . . I see it now, how it twisted me up, made me think love was something you could just take."

"Man, you ain't alone in this," said a voice from the other side of the room. Their words reaching out to Troy like a lifeline thrown out from a boat into the abyss of his past.

Heads nodded, eyes no longer shrouded by judgment but softened by a raw understanding. These men, strangers brought together by their brokenness, now found solace knowing someone else had walked through the fire and came out scarred just like them.

Dr. Warren watched the exchange, his gaze steady and thoughtful. As the emotional tide ebbed, he cleared his throat, drawing the group's attention.

"Thank you, Troy. For trusting us with your truth. No, you're not alone. Your path to redemption isn't over, but in here this afternoon, you've laid another stone on the road to becoming the man you want to be. The courage it takes to face these demons, to speak them aloud in the presence of others, it's commendable. You've taken a monumental step today."

"Doesn't feel like it," Troy muttered, his voice lacking its usual defiance.

Dr. Warren insisted, "Believe me, it is. You've acknowledged the weight of your experiences and how they've shaped your actions. That's progress—real progress. And it's not just about making amends. It's about understanding the root of your hurt so you can start to heal."

The other men murmured their agreement, and one by one, they reached out—a fist bump, a pat on the back, a solemn nod. Each gesture signified a silent pact among them, a brotherhood forged in the crucible of their darkest truths.

"'Preciate it," Troy managed to say, his words a mere whisper in the charged atmosphere of the circle.

As Dr. Warren finished the session, the clock on the wall ticked its last tock, mirroring the shaky heartbeats of those in the room. Troy's chest rose and fell with each heavy breath, relieved to have finally shared his deep secret. The atmosphere had shifted, now thick with understanding and lighter with the weight of their shared burdens.

"Time's up for today. But remember, this is just one step. The real work happens out there." Dr. Warren gestured vaguely toward the door.

The men uncrossed their legs and shifted in their seats, the scrape of chairs against the floor sounding a reluctant retreat. Yet nobody bolted. Instead, they converged on Troy like iron filings to a magnet, each offering a piece of themselves in solidarity.

"Good stuff today, man," said a guy with a scar zigzagging down his cheek, his hand clamping on Troy's shoulder in a grip that spoke volumes more than words.

"Keep fighting the good fight, brother," another added, his eyes carrying the glint of his own wars fought and still waging.

Troy looked at each of their faces, these strangers-turned-comrades, and found his voice. "Umm, I uhh 'preciate it. Thanks, I—I won't give up."

"None of us will," came a chorus of determination.

As they filed out, the group formed an unspoken guard around Troy, nodding to him with a respect that didn't need voicing. It was in their straightened backs, the firmness of their steps. They were a band of warriors, flawed yet unyielding.

Outside, the relentless pulse of Las Vegas quickened, but Troy stood rooted for a moment, absorbing the newfound camaraderie. The Strip stretched before him, a gaudy vein of life threading through the desert, pulsating with energy that both enticed and repelled. But he wasn't the same man who had been exiled to these streets months ago, tempted by mirages of happiness in the neon glow.

"See you next week, Troy," Dr. Warren called out, pulling him back from the brink of the city's hypnotic dance.

"Yeah! Next week, Doc," Troy echoed, affirming the promise to himself as much as to his therapist.

CHAPTER 22

"Show me what you've done with the place," Mai urged, leaning closer to her screen.

Mia obliged, panning the device around the room. "I went with the Princess Tiana theme. See the mural? That's hand painted. And I've got matching decorations for the shower. It's gonna be magical."

"It's beautiful, MiMi. I love it. And the food? Please tell me you don't get those God-awful weenies in a soggy-ass blanket like your cousin, Steffie did."

"I would never let those near our guests, Mama. We're going with veggie sushi, puffed pastries, mini quiches, shrimp cocktails, and Troy insisted on Kobe sliders. You know him," Mia playfully rolled her eyes.

"And who coming?" Mai asked, her eyes narrowing.

The underlying current of her question was clear: *was Brenda Harris going to be there?*

"You don't have to worry, Mama. Ms. Brenda will not ruin this day for us. She's not coming. She doesn't even know where we live. Nigel's son, Brendan has been keeping a watchful eye on that. We're not worried about her."

"Good. I don't need her stressing you out. And absolutely not. She cannot ruin this day."

"She hasn't and no, Mama she won't."

Mia flipped through the satin-bound photo album, a collection of baby shower inspirations she'd been compiling since the pink lines appeared. With shared enthusiasm, they continued discussing every aspect of the event.

Mai poised her pen in anticipation, ready to cross off the next item on her list. "Okay and what about games? What we playing?"

"So, I've decided we're gonna have baby bingo, but with a twist—mini designer bags for the winners. No cheesy prizes at my shower!"

"And what about your gifts? You finished the registry? Anything specific you want for baby?"

"Actually, yes, there is something I want for her." Mia paused, biting her lip as she contemplated. "Something timeless. I was thinking of a charm bracelet, starting with a charm for her birth. Then something we can add to throughout her life."

"Perfect. I love it. I find something." Mai nodded, approvingly.

"Oh, we gotta make sure they have enough streamers and balloons, Mama. You know how I feel about empty spaces," Mia said, her eyes darting to a stack of parenting books and a pile of stuffed animals.

Mai's pixelated nod bobbed on the display, her voice crackly but enthusiastic through the FaceTime call. "Trust me, MiMi, it'll be wall-to-wall with pink, green, and gold."

The drone of a news anchor drifted from the living room like white noise, filler sound between the mother-daughter banter until "Sinnamen" pierced the bubble of baby shower bliss. Mia's hand froze mid-air, a tiny hanger clutched tight.

"Hold up, Mama. Can you go over to the TV and turn the volume up?"

Mai did as Mia requested, moving closer to the big screen. The anchor's sculpted face swam into focus, and Mia hung onto his every word:

"Welcome back to Atlanta News Now, I'm Rick Spanoli here with some breaking news. We're now learning the name of the woman whose body was found over the weekend at Lake Lanier after spending the weekend out with friends. Tonight, in Forsyth County, Atlanta News Now's, Kai'Lani Bryant is live near the scene of that tragic drowning. Kai'Lani?"

"Rick, this happened about a quarter mile back in that direction. Officials told us that Kimberly Sinclair, also known as exotic dancer, Sinnamen, was out on the lake with Atlanta socialites, Camila and Porsha DeVine, and friends enjoying a party. Sinclair had been dancing when a fight broke out between other partygoers. According to one eyewitness's claim, Sinclair was accidentally bumped, causing her to fall over the side of the boat and into the water. Sinclair's friends attempted to rescue her as she swam back toward their boat, but the lake's swift undercurrent of the lake pulled her under. Sinclair never resurfaced. Georgia's game warden recovered her body further up the lake. Officials are still investigating, but from early reports we're getting, this appears to be a freak accident. They are warning families and other that are visiting out here at Lake Lanier to always use caution. Wear their life preservers and, of course, do not go where there's an undercurrent. Right now, we are live here in Forsyth County at Lake Lanier. Kai'Lani Bryant, Atlanta News Now. Back to you Rick."

"Every year that lake take lives. The locals say it's haunted. Yet, they say this a freak accident. Interesting, isn't it?" Mai's inquisitive gaze locked with Mia's.

"After all the shit Kim has put us through. Maybe karma decided to take her for a swim."

"Maybe this is universe's way of balancing things out. No worries. That lake keeps its secrets well," Mai replied thoughtfully, her eyes reflecting understanding.

Mia moved toward the drawer. Wanting to steer the conversation away from the murky depths of the haunted lake to safer shores, Mia suggested, "Let's just focus on the shower okay, Mama?"

"Yes, of course. I have another idea about what we can put on the tables."

Mai rambled on about the party favors, but Mia was only half-engaged. Her mind was still processing the fact that her pest problem had finally been taken care of. The weight of the situation pulled her back to reality, and she finally felt a sense of relief. They eventually wrapped up the call with promises to touch base later. Standing amidst the soft hues of pink and sage green, Mia rested her hand on her belly. She silently made a vow to the life growing inside of her that she would do everything in her power to keep their family safe.

Mia whispered, more statement than question. "Life goes on, right."

CHAPTER 23

"Playoffs, baby!"

A deafening chorus of cheers filled the room, causing the walls to vibrate. Troy's fist pumped the air as another round of backslaps and hollers came his way. The suite, high above the dazzling Vegas strip, pulsed with the kind of electricity that only a playoff berth could ignite. Troy's team had secured the win.

"Babe, you crushed it out there," Mia murmured against his chest. She pulled away just enough to flash him a proud smile.

Troy pressed a kiss on her forehead. "Couldn't've done it without my Bonnie."

"Damn straight," she giggled and gave him a celebratory high-five.

Around them, the suite buzzed with elation. Amongst the chatter and clinking glasses, Troy spotted his brothers, Mikey and Dorian, rough-housing like they hadn't aged a day past ten. His dad and Krystal approached them.

"Good game, X-Man. You played your heart out there."

"Thanks Dad."

Krystal smiled at them both, "Let's toast to family," she suggested, lifting her glass, "To new victories and old ties that keep us bound."

"Family!" they echoed.

Shawn hollered from across the room, "Yo, Trouble T-Roy! You comin' to celebrate or what? I know this lil' spot—"

"Speedy got ass on the brain, but we've got classier plans tonight, right?" Romeo cut in, his flirtatious grin spreading wide across his face as he sidled up beside Shawn.

"Well, classy's my middle name." Shawn pointed his thumb at his chest.

Romeo coughed. "Liar!"

After laughing at his friends, Troy rocked his head from side to side. "Thanks, but no thanks, Speedy. Y'all go 'head. I'mma stay right here to celebrate with the fam and friends."

"Look at our brother, making history all over again!" Dorian exclaimed, wrapping an arm around Troy's shoulder.

"Like there was ever any doubt," Mikey chimed in, leaning against the wall with a smirk pulling at his lips.

Shawn's voice boomed over the music and chatter as he declared, "None whatsoever. Y'all know we 'bout to take the whole damn thang!"

He and Romeo exchanged a friendly fist bump before bringing Troy into the circle and doing their secret handshake. The trio of friends howled in boisterous laughter. As the suite erupted into another round of cheers, the door swung open with such force it seemed to suck the joy right out of the room. A collective gasp rippled through the crowd as Brenda, clad in a form-fitting dress that hugged her toned figure, entered the celebration with confidence. But she wasn't alone. Pam, entered alongside her, also sporting a tight outfit that seemed to be molded to her curvaceous body. Gold bangles clacked against Brenda's wrist as she strolled in, scanning the room with intense eyes that eventually locked onto Troy.

"Guess I missed the invitation." Brenda's voice was a knife, cutting through the moment of silence, sharp and unwelcome.

The atmosphere shifted, the air thickening with tension as guests exchanged uneasy glances. It was a stark contrast to the camaraderie that had filled the space just moments before. Brenda moved with predatory grace. The crowd parted as if she wielded some magnetic power, her presence alone dictating the movement of those around her. Brenda finally reached Troy. Pam lingered behind her, unable to meet his gaze as he fixed her with an intense and questioning stare, full of suspicion.

"Enjoying ya lil' shindig, boy?" Brenda questioned while scanning the room of party goers, her eyes landing on Mike and Krystal. Her lips curled in disgust.

"I was," Troy stated, bringing Brenda's attention back to him.

Pam let out a nervous chuckle. "Umm, hey Troy. You did good out there. Congratulations."

"The fuck you congratulating him fuh? We ain't come here for all that. Stick to the script," Brenda scoffed, rolling her eyes.

"Didn't know I couldn't tell the boy I was proud of him. Damn. My bad," Pam held up her hands in a surrendering gesture, apologizing.

Brenda then turned to Troy, sneering, "You think you so high and mighty dontcha? Mr. Football Star." Her painted nails gestured dismissively at the crowd before pointing accusingly at him. "But they don't know the real you, do they?"

Troy's jaw clenched at her provocation. Silence suffocated the room, every pair of eyes fixed on the unfolding drama. His teammates, his brothers, they didn't need this—not now, not ever.

Troy felt Mia's grip on his arm tighten, but still he growled. "Shut your mouth, Brenda."

"Or what? You gonna let them know about that dirty little secret you got with yo' cousin Pam here?" Brenda challenged, inching closer.

"Don't do this."

"Don't do what? I told you I was gonna shout it from the mountaintops. How you knocked up yo' cousin!"

A hush fell over the room, the weight of Brenda's words falling like a hammer. The guests exchanged shocked looks, the festive atmosphere curdling under her announcement.

Pam stepped forward, her face a mask of disgust aimed squarely at Brenda. "Know what Bee? I can't, boo. I ain't with this kinda drama. I'm out."

Brenda laughed, the caustic sound made Troy's hands ball into fists. "Guess lil' Pammy don't wanna play along anymore."

Pam shook her head, making her decision clear as she backed away from Brenda's toxic orbit. But before making her exit, Pam declared, "No, Bee. I don't. My baby ain't Troy's. For the record, his daddy is Anthony Harris. And he takes damn good care of his son."

With that, Pam cut through the crowd, leaving Brenda to her own self-made chaos. Troy could feel the heat rising behind his eyes, the muscles in his arms tensing as if preparing for combat. The mention of a secret love child, however false it might be, was a low blow—one that could unravel everything he'd worked so hard to build.

"Well, whatever. Everybody else here might be buying yo' bad guy turn good act, but I know better." Brenda taunted, her eyes locked onto Troy's. "I've always known—"

"Just leave, Brenda. You've got no business here."

"Or what? You gon' throw another one of yo' famous tantrums? Oh, I remember those days," she mocked, pushing every button she could reach.

The tense standoff seemed to hang in the balance, one wrong move away from erupting into violence. It was a moment fraught with years of emotional wounds and rejection from family. However, it was the honesty in Pam's confession that ultimately broke Brenda's hold on the situation.

"Your lies don't live here. And neither do you. Leave now. Before I forget you supposed to be my mother." Troy warned, the word 'mother' sitting on his tongue like poison.

Brenda's harsh laugh ricocheted around the luxurious suite. "Mother? Boy please. I stopped being that a long time ago. Face it, Troy. You was always just a ticket—a way to get us up out the mud."

Troy's breaths came out as ragged snarls, his glare smoldering with a heat that could scorch the very air between him and Brenda. The muscles in his jaw twitched, a primal instinct urging him to attack. However, before his anger could take over, two large figures appeared at his sides. Kieran and Niall grabbed Troy's arms with a firm hold that showed their experience in handling volatile situations.

"Easy, big guy. This ain't the play." Kieran murmured.

"Let me go!" Troy's voice was a guttural growl, his body a coiled spring ready to release. But no matter how he twisted and turned, trying to shrug off their hold, Kieran and Niall were unyielding walls.

"X-Man, look at me." Mike's authoritative tone sliced the charged atmosphere as he stepped forward.

"What, Troy boy? You gon' do what yo' ass always do—throw a punch?" Brenda taunted, her eyes glinting with challenge. "You were always good for that. Therapy ain't gon' change yo' worthless ass."

"Just let me tag her in the mouth one good time."

"Man, don't do this. She ain't worth it," pleaded Kieran, his eyes searching Troy's.

Brenda sneered, her dark eyes flickering with contempt. "Come on, Troy. You can't be surprised. I've always been about my coin, and yo' ass was my golden ticket."

"Get away from my son, Brenda! You've done enough damage." Mike stepped forward, his likeness to Troy apparent despite being an inch shorter.

Her lip curled in disdain. "Yo' son? Tuh! Damage? No, Mike. The damage was done when we decided to bring this muthafucka into this world. And what would you know about—"

"You left him alone, Brenda. Alone and scared in that nasty fucking apartment until child protective services had to step in. Okay, I couldn't deal with losing my mom but you, what you did—" Mike paused, and his next words were laced with accusation and old guilt. "You lied about Mikey being mine for two years! My namesake! But he wasn't even mine! Why would I stay? And because I didn't want you, you left *our* son, our baby alone, Brenda? How could you? How did *you* let him get taken? So, he wouldn't end up in a foster home somewhere or lost in the system I lied for you. Maybe he woulda been better off with somebody else other than your sorry ass. But I'm to blame for your neglect? Your absence? Pfft."

A collective gasp swept through the room, the revelation hitting like a gut punch. Troy, still held back by Kieran and Niall, felt the ground shift beneath him. The betrayal, the abandonment—it all crystallized in that moment, a jagged truth he couldn't ignore.

Then there was a slow hand clap. It was Brenda.

"Always playing the martyr. Is that what you tell yourself at night? That you're the savior, Mike?" Brenda's laugh was bitter, devoid of warmth.

Mike countered, unwavering, "Truth doesn't need any telling. It stands on its own." He then turned to address Troy. "X-Man, I don't care what she's told you. I never stopped wanting you in my life. I've always been here. Always."

The sincerity in those words reached Troy, pulling at the emotional scars branded into him by neglect. For years, the chasm between father and son had been bridged by half-truths and outright lies. Now, with each word from Mike's mouth, the foundation of those falsehoods crumbled away. His heart swelled. Here was Mike, whom he knew loved him, but asserting a claim that Brenda had always denied.

"Always?" Troy's voice broke, the single word heavy with the weight of doubt and hope intertwined.

"Every damn day." Mike stepped closer, his eyes locked on Troy's, reflecting a shared dark brown hue—a mirror of lineage and now, perhaps, understanding.

Brenda's mocking laughter cut through their moment, sharp and jarring. "Weak muthafuckas. If this ain't the bootleg version of *Madea's Family Reunion* I'on know what is."

"On God, I'mma fuck her up," Troy spat, muscles tensing as he fought against Kieran and Niall's steady grip. They were statuesque, pillars holding back his tornado force.

Brenda's eyes narrowed at Troy. "Boy, please. You ain't doing shit 'cept running me them coins. Same as you been doing."

"Brenda," Mike interjected.

She ignored him and continued in her tirade. "No, Mike. I shoulda swallowed him. I tried but I scheduled the abortion too late. You left and I was stuck with his retarded ass. Somebody need to pay me for my pain and suffering."

"Somebody better get her the fuck outta here!" Troy demanded.

"Oh, I ain't going nowhere until you come up off my money, boy."

Troy's gaze never wavered, but his mind raced. "You think you can just walk in here and demand—"

"Money, Troy boy. Now." Brenda spat, her hand diving into her purse with predatory quickness. The metallic glint of a gun emerged, sending a ripple of panic through the onlookers. Gasps echoed off the walls, the crowd parting like the Red Sea, their faces etched with shock and fear.

"This is for raising yo' ungrateful ass all these years. You owe me, Troy! I want my cut and I want it now!"

Troy's voice was a low growl, betraying the calm he fought to display. "Owe you? You've taken everything from me!"

"Put the gun down, Brenda," Mike pleaded.

"Hell no! This is all yo' fucking fault. I ain't want him! I wanted it to be us, Mike! Just us! It was never about that muthafucka! And you can't save him if I pop one in yo' ass." Brenda's curled lip matched the malice with which she gripped the weapon. She aimed it toward Mike, a clear threat in her intentions.

In the midst of chaos, Kieran and Niall sprang into action, their bulky frames a blur of motion. Keeva, the most unassuming of the trio, silent as a shadow, circled behind Brenda, her presence unnoticed amidst the chaos.

"Back off!" Brenda barked, her finger twitching on the trigger.

But it was too late. Kieran and Niall had closed in, creating a barrier between her and Troy. Their eyes locked onto hers, unflinching.

Keeva seized the moment, her arm snaking out to grip Brenda's wrist. With a deft twist she hadn't seen coming, Brenda's hold on the gun loosened. In an instant, it clattered to the floor, harmless.

"Get yo' fucking hands off me!" Brenda screeched as Keeva's other arm secured her in a vice-like embrace, pulling her away from the stunned crowd. Despite Brenda's writhing and kicking, Keeva navigated through the throng with a practiced ease, her grip unbreakable.

With Kieran and Niall flanking her, they escorted Brenda out of the suite, her protests muffled by their firm grip. Once Brenda was removed, order began to reassert itself, but the echoes of what could have been hung heavy in the suite. Troy's chest heaved, the fight draining from him as he looked around at the shaken faces of friends and family.

Then without warning, a sharp gasp cut through the residual tension. Mia's hand flew to her stomach, her eyes wide with surprise and pain.

"Troy . . ." Her voice trembled, not with fear, but with the sudden onset of something momentous.

It took him only a second to understand. "Your water—" he started, but Mia was already nodding, her other hand clutching his.

"Hospital. Now."

EPILOGUE

Two years later...

"Can you believe it, Phil? The Las Vegas Raiders have done it! They are this year's Superbowl World Champions!" Chuck's voice boomed over the broadcast.

Phil bobbed his head, chiming in, "What a game it has been, Chuck! And let's talk about tonight's MVP, Troy Harris for a second! That man has played some exceptional football today. Look at that incredible catch in the third quarter, Chuck. Double coverage and yet, Troy just leaps into the air. It's like gravity's got no claim on him. He's a force of nature!"

"Phil, I gotta say, the man's got springs for legs, but it ain't just the jump. It's the focus, the control. You see how he keeps his eyes locked on the ball? Like it's the only thing in the world. How about that fourth quarter showdown?" Chuck pointed to the screen with animated gestures. "Troy outmaneuvered the Falcons' defense like they were standing still. He pulled a few of his old juke moves on them. That's gotta hurt."

"Absolutely," Phil agreed. He leaned in, speaking to the camera, "I mean, we're talking about a guy who's not just fast, he's cunning. Control is right, and when he lands—bam! Nothing can knock him down. And those hands! If there's a clutch moment, you bet Troy's snagging that ball from the air like it's his birthright."

"Look at him lift that championship trophy," Chuck pointed out, his voice tinged with a respect that bordered on reverence. "You can tell how much this means to him. And after the knee injury a couple of years ago putting him on the sidelines with his former team, the Falcons and getting to the playoffs back-to-back for losses with the Raiders. Who could deny him this moment?"

Phil nodded, sharing in the sentiment. "Nobody, Chuck. Not after today. Troy Harris played like every down was his last . . . like every catch could be the difference between redemption and regret."

Chuck dropped his voice to a conspiratorial whisper that nonetheless reached millions, "Speaking of big life changes, word on the street is Troy has signed a multi-million-dollar deal with another team, but we haven't heard who just yet."

"Talk about a plot twist," Phil replied. "But that's talk for tomorrow. Tonight, Troy Harris, and the Raiders own this town."

SoFi stadium was alive, a pulsing mass of energy that seemed to have a heart and mind of its own. The atmosphere was charged with excitement, the electricity spreading from person to person and creating a shared sense of euphoria. Neon lights danced across giant screens, casting vibrant hues over the thousands of supporters, their faces adorned with silver and black paint to show their allegiance to the team.

Troy's breath was ragged, visible in the cool California air. Every exhalation was a testament to the intense and heated battle that had just taken place. The scoreboard glowed with the final declaration of victory, casting a warm light over the sea of silver and black—the colors of triumph—that filled the stands. The atmosphere was alive with an electric symphony of whistles, cheers, and stomping feet, mirroring the pounding heartbeats of every Raiders fan who had experienced every play as if it were life or death. As his hands gripped the cold metal of the championship trophy, the weight of it felt right; it was an extension of himself, a symbol of the control and power he'd fought tooth and nail to attain.

The energy of the place was almost tangible, a frenzied crescendo that reached its peak when the championship trophy was brought onto the field. It glinted under the spotlight, a beacon of glory that beckoned the champions forth. Troy hoisted it high, his lips parting in a feral grin as he turned to face the thousands whose screams were now his name. A camera zoomed in on Troy, capturing the moment his hands wrapped around the coveted prize.

"Look at him," someone in the crowd shouted, their voice swallowed by the collective elation, "Troy! Troy! Troy! That's our boy!"

Shawn and Romeo converged on him, their own faces alight with victory's sweet glow. They slapped Troy's back, their muscular forms creating a fortress around their star receiver.

"This is it, Trouble T-Roy! All those nights, all that grind—it's paid off!" Shawn hollered.

Romeo chuckled, his smile infectious and wide. "Man, they ain't ready for us! Vegas can't handle this much heat!"

Their teammates formed a circle around them as the three friends stood tall and confident, portraying a sense of leadership and unwavering dedication. Troy's usual aura of arrogance and self-importance had been replaced by a genuine earnestness that touched the hearts of all who witnessed it. This was more than just a display of athletic ability; it was a triumphant statement, a quiet rebuttal to the doubters, the naysayers who had once deemed him unworthy.

As the jumbotron replayed highlights of the game, and Troy's exceptional performance, it was evident that his past wounds did not dictate his present. They were simply part of an ongoing story—a story of a man who fought for more than just recognition; he fought for family bonds, for love, and for a future beyond the glitz and glamour of Sin City.

The stadium echoed with the energetic beat of "APESHIT" by The Carters. Celebratory confetti still lingered in the air, creating a colorful display of triumph as Mia stood on the sidelines holding their daughter, Nova, close to her chest. The toddler's eyes were wide with wonder, tiny fingers pointing at the jumbotron where Troy's larger-than-life image beamed down at them. Nova's squeals of delight pierced through the cacophony of the roaring stadium in pure delight whenever she caught sight of her daddy.

"Look, baby! There's Daddy!" Mia shouted over the noise, a proud smile spreading across her face. She balanced Nova on her hip, her other hand clutching a designer bag that held snacks and toys meant to keep a two-year-old entertained during the chaos of the Superbowl.

"Daddy! Daddy!"

Nova clapped her hands and pointed with pudgy fingers. Her excitement was infectious, and Mia found herself bouncing Nova, joining in her daughter's joy.

Then he was there. Troy, larger than life, threading his way toward them with the grace of a panther that had just claimed its territory. Nova's excitement reached a peak as she let out a high-pitched shriek and leaped from Mia's arms into her father's open arms.

"Whoa, lil' superstar!" Troy hoisted Nova up in the air, stretching his lips into a grin that was mirrored by his daughter's elated expression. He spun her around, her giggles blending in with the faded cheers of the fans.

"Did you see Daddy out there, huh? Did you see me catch that ball?"

"Ball!" Nova repeated, mimicking a catching motion with her small hands.

"Yep, that's my girl," Troy said proudly, planting a kiss on her forehead.

Lowering Nova back into his arms, he looked over her head, noticing his brothers, Mikey and Dorian, along with his dad, and stepmom heading toward them. They all showered him with congratulatory embraces and kind words. His dad, Mike, was beaming with pride for Troy's greatest accomplishment.

"Congratulations, X-Man! I knew this day was coming! This is what I was talking about when I said keep showing up and putting your heart out there. So proud of you!"

"Thanks Dad."

"Anytime, son. I love you."

"But I wuv my Daddy more, Poppy!" Nova squealed, wrapping her arms tighter around Troy's neck.

Everyone chuckled at Nova's fierce possessiveness over her father. It was no surprise. She was a daddy's girl through and through. With a sandy complexion, smooth tawny skin, slanted eyes, and long jet-black pigtails that reached past her shoulders, she was a perfect combination of Troy and Mia. After the laughter died down, Mike reminded them that they needed to hurry and get to the other side of the field before Krystal missed out on a once-in-a-lifetime opportunity.

"Yeah, I was told by my cousins to get that prayer from Ciara. I couldn't come home without it. We'll see y'all up in the suite. Now come on, Mike," Krystal called out, tugging him in the opposite direction.

Mikey and Dorian had already left them and were standing over by Shawn and Romeo with the rest of the Raiders to get their pictures taken with the official Superbowl champions. Through the falling confetti, Troy caught Mia's gaze and shared a smile with her. It reflected their deep love and admiration for each other.

He moved closer to Mia, leaning in as he asked her, "Next year this time, what do you think about being back in Atlanta?"

Mia's eyes widened in surprise. "What are you saying, Troy?"

"I'm saying we could be sipping some sweet tea on the deck over-looking the pool of our new home in Peachtree Hills. And just maybe our family would have expanded by one with my boy. What do you think about that, Bonnie?" he murmured to Mia, the hint of a dream flickering in his eyes.

Mia nodded, her long black hair cascading over her shoulders as she leaned in to press a kiss to Troy's cheek. "Back in my hometown. A little brother for Nova . . . I think I would love that, Clyde. Can you make it happen?"

"I'll see what I can do." Troy angled his head and planted a kiss on her pouty lips.

Nova whined and pushed Mia away, demanding, "Mooove, Mommy! Daddy kiss me too!"

Troy nuzzled his face against Nova's neck, eliciting a chorus of giggles from her. He drew his two favorite girls into a tight embrace, feeling a wave of gratitude wash over him. Winning the championship was an incredible achievement, but it was also Mia's unwavering support that he was truly thankful for. She stood by him through the highs and lows of fame and fortune, serving as his rock and anchor amidst the whirlwind of success.

The challenges they'd faced—the injuries, the scandals, the whispers of doubt—none could tear asunder what they had forged together. Their love was a fortress, a stronghold against the world's chaos.

Just then, the jumbotron flashed to life once more, stealing the attention of the crowd. The announcer's voice broke through, heavy with the weight of news that would ripple through their lives.

"Breaking update, folks!" the voice boomed, Chuck's familiar tone was laced with excitement. "We've just confirmed that Troy Harris, tonight's MVP, will be taking his talents back to Atlanta. It's official—he's signed with the new franchise, the Atlanta Pioneers!"

A collective gasp swept over the crowd, the news dropping like a bombshell. This was a game-changer, a new playbook they'd have to write together.

"So, it's official?" Mia grinned.

Their story was far from over. It was evolving, adapting, much like the city that never stopped reinventing itself. Atlanta was their mecca, the place they could always return to and find new opportunities and experiences.

More confetti fell from above, a mix of silver and black, each piece reflecting the emotions of those about to embark on a new journey. Troy gazed into Mia's eyes, his face a blend of excitement and apprehension. Her silent question hung in the air between them, begging for an answer. His reply:

"Yeah, Sym, we're going home."

THE END

If you can't get enough of this couple, sign up for the VIP newsletter and receive this bonus epilogue: https://BookHip.com/RZXSACQ

Thank you for taking this journey with Troy and Mia. If this is your first time reading about this couple, start here where it all began: https://book s2read.com/u/4AA7JK

CONNECT WITH MO

Let's stay connected on social media.

Mo's Corner – https://bit.ly/MoFlamesCorner

Facebook – https:www.facebook.com/mo.flames

Instagram – https://www.instagram.com/moflames_author

TikTok – https://www.tiktok.com/@moflames_author

Threads – https://www.threads.net/@moflames_author

X – https://x.com/MoFlames

THANK YOU

Thank you so much for reading! I ask whether you enjoyed this story or not, to please consider leaving a review wherever you purchased this book and/or mark it as read on Goodreads. I also hate errors, but they do happen. If you catch any, please send them to the publisher directly at info@flamesenterain.com with **ERRORS** as the subject.

AFTERWORD

Welcome home, to our boy Troy! If you don't know about my campaign #TroyisBae or #TeamTroy, let me tell you. This was truly a labor of love. I fought for Troy's redemption through sweat and tears. No, seriously. There were some nights I walked out of the writing lab in tears over Troy's story, out of pure frustration. I told my writing crew I steer away from traumas for this very reason. It's not in my wheelhouse. But I wrote a flawed character who had a troubled past. With this came the challenge of telling his truth. So, who was Troy Harris? This man's story deserved to be treated with care considering the topics covered. I'm not a product of his circumstances. Nor am I a Black man. I would never know what it's like to go through what he endured growing up with a mother like Brenda, "but I hope that I've given my character the redemption he deserved. His work isn't done yet. But believe me when I say, he and Mia continued their therapy sessions—which I will encourage both men and women to do. There's nothing to be ashamed of. And it's nothing wrong with talking to a licensed professional about navigating life, especially when we are hurt from our childhood. Just know that I did the research and asked a LOT of questions to help navigate the development of Troy's character throughout these four books he's been a part of. So, if you've been riding along with me and can see the growth of this man from The Enough Series to his redeeming breakout, you tell me if I've done him justice. Either you're #TeamTroy or #ByeTroy. Now I'm gonna tell you like I've told my followers, I don't care, argue with yo' mammy, yo' pappy and er'body else. There will be ZERO Troy slander in these here streets. I'm #TeamTroy cause he is bae!

Alright, moving onto our girl Angela, Mia's best friend. Did y'all peep what's brewing with her and Jamal? Whew chye! When you talk about somebody who is " diabolical in the MoVerse, Jamal comes to mind. Now if y'all recall Jamal was gallivanting around town with his new lover, Christian while Angela was grieving the "loss of her brother, Tré. To make matters worse, unbeknownst to Angela, Jamal was responsible for Tré's death. Y'all know I'm over here weaving a helluva web of deception on that one. The players involved in Jamal's and Angela's entangled love triangle will have y'all going what the? Y'all know me, just pay attention in the MoVerse, you've seen these characters around before. They're close in proximity. Remember, six degrees of separation—any person on Earth can be connected to any other person through a chain of acquaintances with no more than five intermediaries. Basically, I'm always writing with the concept of "friend of a friend of a friend" for my characters. Somebody gon' know somebody. Just be on the lookout for their story.

"I'm sure there are other burning questions you have about what's happening in Atlanta. I'd love to hear them. 'Cause I got answers and they're coming in the form of mo' books!"

ACKNOWLEDGMENTS

To my editor, Krystal—my heartfelt thanks for your endless patience and unwavering support on this authorship journey. Your guidance, wisdom, and mentorship mean the world to me, and I'm incredibly grateful to have you in my corner and on my team. Because of you, our boy "Troy has finally getting the redemption he deserves, with his story beautifully crafted for readers to enjoy seamlessly and professionally. Thank you for another completed project!

To my amazing betas and proofreaders, Shannon, Shika, Tori, and P. Bancy—thank you endlessly for your invaluable feedback. You've helped ensure readers get a polished story free of any boring bits, filler scenes, or plot holes.

And to my readers who show up for me every single time, THANK YOU SO MUCH! There are never enough words to express how much it means to me you're a part of my world. Just know that I appreciate each and every one of you. My Flames, keep burning bright. I see you!

ALSO BY MO FLAMES

Series
Enough Series

One Ain't Enough – https://books2read.com/u/4AA7JK

One Still Ain't Enough - https://books2read.com/u/4jNLe5

One Is Enough - https://books2read.com/u/breAeE

Infinity Series

Make You Mine - https://books2read.com/u/4jNQok

Love in Minor Series

Love in A Minor - https://books2read.com/u/bMVvKB

Standalones

Reckless Desire - https://mybook.to/NBwmbDV

Falling for Jordyn - https://mybook.to/y8zVSy

Anthologies

Holiday Bliss (Christmas with The Carters) - https://books2read.com/u/496El8

Non-Fiction

Girl, He Don't Want Your Ass, The 10 Signs He's Not Interested - https://mybook.to/FI9iyAN

ABOUT THE AUTHOR

Mo Flames is an avid reader, writer, wine lover and a super fan of The Office. She pens contemporary romance stories with complex characters, controversial topics, and unpredictable plot twists. Mo's experiences and creativity fuel her written words. She's never been bashful about racy relationship topics. She's unashamed and unapologetically real. It echoes with her tagline, 'leaving that fire between the sheets...literally.'

When she's not writing, she enjoys playing the Sims, reading romance and suspense, binge watching The Office, Snapped, Criminal Minds or any crime television shows. She resides in Atlanta, GA with her husband and daughter.

For more books and updates:
www.moflames.com